From the Hotel Insiders

"The book spells out, in lurid detail, what goes on behind the scenes at a hotel..."
Kitty Bean Yancey in USA Today's
Hotel Hotsheet

"If you stay in hotels or work in the Travel Industry, you'll love this book. *Saving the Hotel St. George* captures the real world of guests and employees and the amusing, tragic, and happy human events that make the hotel business fascinating."
Joseph McInerney
President
American Hotel & Lodging Association

"The world of hotels and hospitality were accurately depicted in many of the scenes in Arthur Hailey's 1960s book HOTEL. Greg Plank combined real life background and experience as an excellent successor to HOTEL".

Dr. John Hogan CHA CHE

Saving the Hotel St. George

The real world of guests, employees,
and true hotel happenings.

A Novel

Greg Plank

This is a work of fiction. All of the characters, names, incidents, organizations,
and dialogue in this novel are either the products of the author's imagination or
are used fictitiously.

Dedication

This book is dedicated to some very special people. They work in hotels and in the travel business. They are also the frequent travelers who stay in hotels. The Hotel St. George is a place you remember because of the people.

In special memory of: my parents Marguerite and Saylor Jacoby, for their love, faith in God, and showing me how to live a loving life and laugh a lot. To my late wife Linda, for giving me 42 great years, three wonderful daughters and her encouragement. To Donna Lane Plank, she made us feel good and laugh, but left us too soon.

Acknowledgements

To my wife Linda and my children Jennifer, Melissa, and Laurie, I give my thanks for their support and patience, and for letting me share their lives and love. To my grandchildren Aaron, Emily, Lucas and Hannah, I give my thanks for their love and insight in how to enjoy life's simple wonders. To my sons-in-law: David, Steve, and Greg, for taking care of my greatest treasures, and to Barbara for adding laughs and affection.

To my mentors: Virgil LaPenta, Vic Grohmann, Howard Heinsius, John Gillespie, Bill Morton, Hal DeFord, Bob Baersch, Bob Walker, Irv Zeldman, Dan Mazzari, Bill Mangan, Don Leonard, Ted Laughner, Ben Smith, Art Moger, Seby Jones, Sam Apostle, Doug Collins, David Krischer, my professors and classmates at Cornell Hotel School, and my high school English teacher Ann Tompkins, I give my thanks for their guidance. To Joe McInerney who has helped me and my family through the years. He taught me honesty, fairness, and integrity in personal life and in business. To Jack Vaiden, Roger Solomon, Carlo Wolff, Glenn Crowe, and Craig Mullinax, who all supported me in this effort, I give my appreciation for their friendship and encouragement over the past four years. To my brother Lee Plank, I thank him for lovingly helping our mother and me in some very tough times, and for always being special to be with. To Dr. Eli Farri, a special friend, who taught me that with faith and caring you can overcome anything. Thanks to Robin Smith, a great editor, and to Tim Eaton, my consulting editor, who both helped make my story much better. To Dr. Terence Moraczewski, who has been a great inspiration in caring for and about people. To Rick and Lucy Harris who encouraged me. Their son Noah Harris was a talented and beloved young man who gave his life in Iraq for all free people and our country. I hope all who read this book remember his name and thank all those who have sacrificed for us. To Don Brown, a hotelier who became an exceptional preacher. Thanks to Glenn Jones, Kevin McCarthy, Dorothy Curcuru, Joe Ash, Keith Pierce, Scott Gold, Chetan Patel, John Buttolph, Jim Scott, Judi Traver, Cliff Barr, and Chuck Coscia, who are great friends and hotel people. To the teams I worked with at Sheraton, Hawthorn Suites, Ramada, Travelodge, Country Hearth, and Suburban Lodges, you are all tops and did great things.

chapter

ONE

At ten a.m. a phone in the executive offices of the Hotel St. George was used to call an office in Langley, Virginia.

A coarse, businesslike voice answered, "International Pipelines."

The caller said, "We have to get Edwin Christian out of South America ASAP. It's time."

The man on the other end replied, "He'll be out by tomorrow."

Two months later, Edwin Christian, the retired Marine special reconnaissance officer who had faced combat in the unreported terrorist wars around the world, was about to fight a civilized, non-violent war to save a hotel. The battles would be unique: scam artists, murder, rape, city officials, financial hardship, challenging guests, a cross dresser, muggers, a car thief, dysfunctional siblings, and exotic dancers. He stood on the front steps of the law firm of LaGrange, Harrelson, and Smith. He was there for the reading of his grandfather's will. In the next hour, he would become the owner of the Hotel St. George:

once the crown jewel of hospitality in the city, now a respectable but aging part of the city's history. It was one of a dying breed of independently owned upscale hotels battling the large chains. Edwin had no idea what challenges the aging hotel, with its hundreds of employees and 800 rooms in the middle of the city, were about to offer him.

Edwin's grandfather, Aaron David Christian, A.D. to most people, had been a successful hotel and construction company owner. When A.D.'s only son had been killed in Vietnam in 1972, A.D had taken over the duties of raising Edwin and his two siblings. Edwin was the youngest of the three by fifteen years and had spent much of his childhood with his grandfather. His mother was there, but she never quite came back emotionally after her husband died, and she had suffered a stroke a few years ago. While growing up, Edwin's weekends and summers had been spent at the Hotel St. George, following different department heads and employees around. He had not been in the hotel in ten years.

In college he studied civil engineering for two years, but the classroom and college atmosphere just didn't fit him. His soft eyes and handsome face brought him good times at social functions, and a good number of dates. He preferred the more physical life. With a five eleven well-muscled body, he did well in college sports, but that was not enough to satisfy him. He dropped out and enlisted in the Marines, eventually being picked for a special reconnaissance unit. He enjoyed the strenuous regimen and working in small teams in the field. He stayed for eight years, and worked his way up into the officers' ranks. When his assignments began limiting his time in the field, and the military politics started to frustrate him, he decided to find something more taxing and less political. Armed with his civil-engineering background and his special-ops training, he was recruited by International Pipelines. After three months of training, and a quick course in basic Spanish, he was assigned as a crew chief in the back country of South America. As part of his reason for being there, he would report his observations on any guerilla movements or drug trafficking in the area, calling daily via satellite phone to a contact. He had no idea where his calls were being answered. He could call at any hour and ask for Carlo the Wolf. The voice on the other end was electronically masked to be undistinguishable. Carlo the Wolf was Edwin's only link to the outside world. He always wondered who Carlo really was. He gave his information in code words, making it sound like a report on the pipeline progress.

Two months ago, a helicopter showed up in a clearing near the pipeline. A military advisor jumped out and shouted, "You've got exactly five minutes to gather your things and get on the bird."

Less than five minutes later he was in the chopper, hovering over the clearing. The military advisor told him he didn't know why they were pulling him out. All he knew was Edwin would be on a flight to the States by dark. It was clear to Edwin: his grandfather was reaching the end of his battle with heart failure.

He stood in front of the old blueblood law firm with the loss of his grandfather still dulling his thoughts. His grandfather had brought him here often in his youth. He would sit in the outer reception area while A.D. conferred with his old friend and legal advisor, Justin "Justy" LaGrange.

A.D. and Justy had met when A.D. worked on his first business venture. Justy was a private school rich kid who had graduated from an Ivy League law school. A.D. was a kid from Pittsburgh where his father worked in the steel mills. He dropped out of school in the seventh grade and worked the rest of his life to support an aging mother and, eventually, a family. A.D.'s first business venture was a small contracting company renovating historic homes in the upscale sections of the city. Christian Construction grew to be a very large and successful company.

As he stood on the steps, hesitating to open the large oak door, Edwin thought back over the last two months, since his return from South America. He had spent every moment with his grandfather. He and A.D. visited the places they had enjoyed together in Edwin's youth until A.D. was not able to travel. When A.D. had insisted he spend the time alone with Edwin, they set up a special room for A.D. in his mountain house. The two talked non-stop about the life they had shared. A.D. fought hard, but he went downhill quickly and had passed away in his sleep two weeks ago.

Edwin swallowed hard, straightened his tie, and entered the reception area of the law firm. He was surprised to see Ann Baxter sitting at the receptionist's desk. Ann was normally in her own office next to Justin LaGrange. She was the heart of the law firm. For thirty years she had kept everyone organized, and as secretary of the corporation, she ran the business side of the firm. Ann would often oversee Edwin when A.D and Justy LaGrange met. Like many young boys, his first crush was on an older woman, Ann Baxter. As Edwin got older, he noticed A.D. always took time to talk with Ann privately when they visited the law offices.

"I was so glad when you returned to be with him," Ann said. Her pale blue eyes went straight to his and a warm smile filled her face.

"I only wished we had had more time. He went so fast," Edwin replied.

"Most good things do go fast, Edwin. It's one of the frustrating things in life," Ann said. "How are you doing?"

"I'm still slightly numb but I'm full of memories, and I'm starting to be able to laugh again when I think of some of the things we did together."

"I know he's laughing with you. God, did that man love to laugh."

"What are you doing out here? Did Justy demote you?"

Ann smiled. "With the family gathering Justy thought it best if I greeted them and headed off any interruptions. Your brother and sister are here, but your mother is staying home with her new nurse."

"I wonder how this is going to go. I haven't seen any of them since I've been back. I wanted to spend every minute with A.D. After he died, I just needed time alone," Edwin said.

"I thought that must be the case when I didn't see you at the funeral," Ann replied.

"It was probably selfish of me, but I'd said my good-byes to him and needed some time to pull myself together. I've hated funerals since my first year in the Marines. I stayed in the mountain house until today. I'm sure I hurt some feelings," he said, still a little conflicted by his choices.

"They'll get over it," she replied reassuringly. "They're in Justy's study. You know where it is."

"Ann, I know you were, umm, close with A.D. When things calm down, we should have lunch or a drink. I think A.D. would enjoy being talked about."

"Don't men keep any secrets?" she asked.

"Not about things they're proud of," Edwin replied.

Ann blushed and looked at the ceiling to avoid Edwin's gaze. She looked back at him and caught the same smile she had seen on a small boy's face years ago.

"I better walk the family walk and go greet my loving siblings," he said.

"Don't be too charming. You'll remind them of A.D. and they'll resent you," Ann cautioned.

As Edwin's hand reached for the large brass lion's head door-knob on the carved oak doors of Justin LaGrange's study, he reflected on how little time he had ever spent with his older brother and sister. When A.D. had taken over the family duties, his brother was away at private school and his sister was engrossed in the social side of high school. They spent time together at holidays, but that was about it. His sister Daphne had become the town socialite. Every cause that could get her on the society page became her mission: Saving the seals; rescuing the historic Arkwright building; hosting the poochie parties for the animal shelters. Out of a sense of guilt or real concern, A.D. had funded the parties through the hotel. Daphne had been through two short marriages, with no resulting children. She lived in her own world of indulgence and personal image. The plastic surgeon had done well sculpting her body and face to deny the effects of time.

His brother Henry was a study in power and ego. He had taken over the construction company and hotel during A.D.'s illness. As a child, he had bullied Edwin, and one night, Henry grabbed Edwin by the neck and demanded that he do Henry's chore of taking out the trash. When Edwin refused, Henry grabbed harder and never saw the punch that flattened and bloodied his nose. Henry lied about the incident; Edwin kept quiet as A.D. and their mother questioned them, and Edwin was given added chores as punishment. The day he was to clean the garage, A.D. showed up in work clothes and helped him. Not a word was spoken as they worked.

When they were done, Edwin gave A.D. a puzzled look. A.D. put his arm around him, smiled, and said, "Good punch."

The incident was never mentioned again, and Henry never again tried to press his age advantage.

chapter

TWO

Edwin took a deep breath, opened the door and was immediately greeted by Justin LaGrange.

"It's been a long time, Edwin. I'm so sorry for your loss. He was a great man and a great friend. You look well for such an ordeal."

"You look well yourself, Justy. I know how good a friend you've lost," Edwin replied.

Out of the corner of his eye he caught the surprised look on the faces of his brother and sister when he used Justin LaGrange's nickname.

"Edwin, it has been a long time," Henry said. He was trying to smile, but wasn't very convincing.

"Edwin, my love. You're even growing into your thirties," his sister gushed.

She was sitting in a large leather chair by the fireplace with a glass of white wine in her hand. It didn't surprise Edwin, even though it was eleven a.m. Daphne was dressed in a long black dress with a string of pearls hanging down to the top of her well-engineered breasts. Edwin could only think "sorority rush" as he smiled. He shook hands with Henry, who was wearing the biggest watch Edwin had ever seen. His cuff links bore the Presidential seal, the coveted recognition of loyal campaign contributions and fund-raising.

"You look prosperous as ever," was all Edwin could think to say.

"It's good to see you back, Edwin. I'm sure A.D. enjoyed his last days with you. I'm sorry I couldn't be part of it, but the businesses had to be run. The economy is not cooperating with hotels or construction," Henry offered.

"A.D. appreciated you taking over. He mentioned it often in his last few weeks," Edwin said.

He bent to kiss Daphne on the cheek and remarked how good she looked. He was tempted to add "for an aging broad," but controlled himself.

"You've been back for two months and we've had no time together," Daphne said.

"As A.D. got worse, he wanted to be alone and talk about the outdoors and sports and the late nights we had. He didn't want to be seen in his condition by anyone, even family and friends."

"Men are so strange about certain things," Daphne said. She looked to Justy for another glass of wine. "No matter. We'll have to catch up at the hotel. You're invited to the Literacy Society's gala party. There will be a few of your old friends there who are dying to see someone who lived in the jungles of South America."

"Is there a theme or do I just come dressed as a book?" he quipped.

"You'll have to wear a tie, unless I come up with a fun theme," she replied.

"Your sister has amassed quite a track record in raising money for the causes," Henry said.

"From the looks of the cuff links, you haven't done badly yourself, Henry," Edwin said.

Henry accepted the compliment with a genuine smile and a nod in Edwin's direction.

Justin LaGrange took a copy of the will and started the formalities. They all agreed reading the entire will wasn't necessary. They had all read copies of it. LaGrange went through the major points.

Daphne asked that some of the personal comments be read. Henry objected but Daphne insisted, waving her hand at him as if to dismiss him.

Justin LaGrange spent the next twenty minutes going through the financial points of the will. Their mother, Marguerite "Mimi" Christian, received the large family home and a considerable amount of money allowing her to live in any style she wished. If she chose, she could live in the hotel with all expenses covered. Henry got control of Christian Construction and A.D.'s collection of vintage automobiles along with a large trust fund for his children's education. Daphne received a sizable trust fund for her charitable work and all her expenses. In each financial statement, A.D. took the time to point out personal weaknesses of the recipient and lend advice to each. Edwin was given control of the hotel along with a capital and operating account to help the hotel out. A.D.'s only advice to Edwin was to trust the hotel staff and treat them like the family they were.

A.D.'s final statement was, "To all of you I leave my love, and an honest wish that you all do well and live life fully, but not stupidly."

"A.D. always could criticize with the best of them. Even from the grave the old bastard got us all," Henry said. "Of course, he went easier on you, Edwin, but that was to be expected. You were always the son."

"It was a matter of timing, Henry. If Dad had died earlier, you would have been home and gotten the attention. As to old bastard, a man as passionate and giving as A.D. has the right to say whatever he pleases," Daphne said.

Justin brought up one more bequest in the will. It was a special fund for "Charitable Purposes" for some small groups and loyal individuals that was to be administered solely by Edwin.

"That's a fairly large sum for a few inconsequential charities," Henry shot in.

Edwin explained A.D. was concerned about his loyal employees and wanted to be able to help them as they aged.

The most deserving loyal individual, unbeknownst to the others, was sitting in the reception area in the person of Ann Baxter. Edwin thought she might know about the fund, but nothing was ever said. Ann and A.D. enjoyed a special relationship after the death of

A.D.'s wife Mary. The fact no one in the room knew was a tribute to A.D.'s total loyalty to friends and loved ones.

"Well, is that all of our official family duties for the day?" Henry asked.

"That's it," Justy replied. "We can fill out the paperwork at any time."

"Justin, are we having lunch?" Daphne chimed in.

"It will be up shortly. The hotel is providing it," he said.

"Delightful," she slurred as she wobbled to the bar for her fourth glass of wine.

"I'm not really hungry, and with a hotel to run, I better go make sure we charged you for everything, Justy," Edwin said.

"Leonard Chambers has been the manager at the hotel since A.D. first started to show his illness. He's a veteran and knows the business quite well. I know him since we're both on the board of The Patriot Society. I think you'll find him quite a help," Henry informed Edwin.

"I'm sure I'll spend time with him very soon," Edwin replied. "Does he know about the provisions of the will?"

"I took the liberty of telling him everything about the hotel. Perhaps you should have him introduce you to the staff," Henry offered.

"I think it would be better if I reintroduced myself. I've known many of them my entire life. It might be awkward with a third party interceding," Edwin said.

"Suit yourself, but I wouldn't undermine his authority too quickly, Edwin," Henry replied, slightly annoyed.

"Don't worry. I won't be barking anytime soon. God knows my knowledge of hotel operations is confined to busboy and dishwasher," Edwin smiled.

"Enjoy the luncheon. Justy, thank you for your help and the years of friendship and concern," Edwin said as he left.

Ann Baxter was showing a hotel employee with four large containers of food where the private dining area and kitchen were. She looked up as Edwin approached the desk.

"How did it go?"

"Actually, it went very well," Edwin replied. "I have no idea what you know about the will; although I don't think you miss much around here." He started to feel awkward and hesitated.

Ann smiled. "You think we should have lunch or a drink sooner rather than later?" she volunteered.

"Thank you, Ann, that's exactly what I was trying to say."

"Settle in at the hotel and give me a call. I'm not going anywhere soon," she replied. "A lot has changed since A.D. got sick, especially at the hotel. Take your time and don't make any big decisions or take too much advice too early."

"I'm sure I'll find out what you mean, and I'll call you for lunch. And, Ann," he hesitated, "thanks for what you did for A.D., professionally and personally. It was special to him."

Ann Baxter blushed again as Edwin walked through the large oak door to the street on his way to the hotel.

chapter

THREE

It was lunch hour, and people rushed by Edwin, pursuing their errands and trying for a quick bite to eat before returning to work. He stopped at the traffic light at Twenty First and Simpson. The hotel was five blocks south and east on Van diver Square. The small park honored one of the original settlers, whom most city dwellers had forgotten long ago. The only people who knew the significance of the name were the tourists on the sightseeing buses. He looked across the street at Jimmy's Tap and Talk in the corner of a fading four story brick building. Jimmy's was a local watering hole for a long list of characters: police, newspaper people, politicians and a variety of others who could fill a hundred Damon Runyon books had visited daily over the past forty years. Jimmy was a bit of a local celebrity who had once been the featured spokesperson, so to speak, in television commercials. Jimmy would greet every guest and to be recognized by name was something of a validation as a local character of note.

Edwin first visited Jimmy's when he was six years old. A.D. would take Edwin to the hotel on weekends and place him in the charge of one of the executive staff. It was Edwin's unique form of hotel school. On the days A.D. would pick Wallace James "Wally" Callahan, the hotel's director of security, Wally would take Edwin to Jimmy's at lunchtime. Wally had been a proud member of the city police department until he took a bullet during a failed grocery store hold up on the North Side. The bullet entered his left knee from behind when the teenage perp slipped while running out of the store and discharged his gun as he fell.

Cops often have a defensive way of making fun of adversity. It's not a mean thing. When you deal with the ugly under-belly and twisted minds of people as a profession, there has to be some form of psychological release. Wally never lived down the joke he was shot while fleeing from a pimple faced kid. The fact was the bullet had ricocheted off of a light pole and found Wally's knee. In a huge amount of pain, Wally had crawled the four feet to the fallen youth and put him out cold with one punch. The cops always reminded Wally it was good he had to crawl, because he couldn't have moved that fast on his size twelve feet. The knee would prevent him from going back into the field and Wally was not the type to take a desk job. The police chief at the time was an old friend and he called A.D. on Wally's behalf. Wally took his disability retirement, bought two suits, and became director of security for the hotel.

When Edwin accompanied Wally to Jimmy's, he was placed on a corner barstool with a soda and a large bowl of peanuts. As he watched and listened to the bar's inhabitants, Jimmy's became Edwin's favorite place. He didn't understand all of the adult jokes, but he would smile along with them, afraid to laugh out loud and call attention to himself. The stories of the cases and crimes the cops were working on were better than anything on television. Wally had never moved up to the rank of detective because he never took the exams. He loved patrol duties and the contact he had with his citizens. His street smarts, knowledge of human behavior, and his overabundance of Irish common sense gave him a simple insight: All crimes were a result of human choices. He had quietly helped solve some of the most complex crimes in the city by getting a stumped detective to think like the criminals.

Edwin walked the five blocks to the hotel and stopped at the edge of Van diver Square, across the street from the Hotel St. George. The fluted marquee and the twenty international flags gave it a royal appearance. The hotel was built just before the Great Depression by Barney Gregory. Having made a fortune in the insurance business, Gregory wanted a monument to himself and decided a grand hotel was just the thing. He imported much of the building material and all of the furniture from Europe. He also brought European craftsmen over to do the intricate decorative ceiling in the lobby and public spaces. He was the envy of the upper crust in town, but after a few years, he became bored with the hotel and decided to build a world-class golf course. The funds from the hotel financed it. When Gregory died, his family decided the golf course was a better tribute to his life and sold the hotel.

The Hotel St. George passed through several hands over the years. Thirty years ago, A.D. Christian bought it out of bankruptcy and restored it. The old hotels were often the product of successful men's dreams and ego. They survive or die, because strong people, like A.D. Christian, fall in love with them. They are the granite mistresses of a lifetime.

Edwin watched the front door of the hotel, guarded by "Slim" Johnson, the hotel doorman for the past twenty-five years. The name didn't fit him—Slim had not seen the ground directly under him for thirty years. The large round belly on his six-two frame showed proudly under the long royal blue doorman's coat with the brass buttons. The bill of his cap was adorned with the gold "scrambled eggs" of a ranking naval officer. It was a fitting adornment for Slim. His ship, and he captained it well, was the four hundred feet of curb in front of the hotel. As a doorman, he was paid well. As the keeper of the private VIP parking spaces in front of the hotel, he was paid handsomely in tips.

Slim also directed the valet parking attendants. The hotel had given him total control of parking the day that the stockbroker and his lunchtime wife had wheeled up to the front door in his Mercedes convertible. He got out and tossed his keys to the guy standing near the valet parking stand. "Keep it warm, I'll be back in an hour." The girlfriend giggled and they disappeared into the hotel.

Cedric "The Touch" Peoples was in the right place, but he was not employed by the hotel. When the stockbroker returned an hour later, his car was nowhere to be found. "The Touch" had borrowed it for his annual trip back home up North. It was found two weeks later, stripped of anything useful, two blocks from the bus terminal.

Wally Callahan was called on the situation as the stockbroker bellowed, "I'll own this hotel in a matter of days. I know very important people in this town."

Wally was aware that every guest with a complaint and the money to own a Mercedes thought they knew very important people. Wally walked him to the security office so he wouldn't disturb every guest in the hotel.

"This is indeed a very alarming and serious situation, sir," Wally said sympathetically. "I assume you have the claim check to show proof of our taking control of your vehicle. Don't you?" Wally asked.

The stockbroker's stammer sounded like a frightened animal's whimper. "No, I didn't get the claim check because the valet didn't offer one," he replied sheepishly. "He was a young-husky man."

"Did he have the hotel's blue uniform on?" Wally asked.

"I didn't notice, I was in a hurry," he mumbled.

Wally had seen the young lady with the gentleman as they had entered the hotel. *I'll bet you were, sport.*

While Wally was taking care of the stockbroker, John Vincent, the hotel's concierge, was entertaining the young lady at his desk in the lobby. During their conversation he had asked her the same questions he imagined Wally was asking the gentleman. John Vincent, better known by almost everyone in the city as Jack, worked well with every department in the hotel. As a concierge, he had to anticipate any request and fulfill it through the various hotel departments. Jack picked up the phone and called Wally. It was almost as if he knew Wally needed to talk to him.

"I'm here with a very pleasant young woman who would like to know when her gentleman will be ready to leave," Jack said.

"Did you happen to ask any questions about the incident?" Wally asked.

"Wally, my dear man, you know I did, and there is no valet claim ticket. As I'm sure you've already found out. The valet person was also not in the standard hotel uniform."

"Tell her I think it will be ten more minutes, Jack. And thanks," Wally said.

"So what are you going to do about my car?" the stockbroker growled.

"Well sir, without the claim check, I don't see how the hotel can be responsible," Wally answered in a stern voice. "What I can do is help you report it to the police as a stolen vehicle."

"That is simply not acceptable. I want to talk to your general manager, and you'll be hearing from my lawyer and a few other important people. This is a travesty and a total injustice," the stockbroker yelled as he turned to storm out of the office.

"What I could do is get you and your wife up in the lobby together with our insurance people and see what they say. Of course, they might have to visit you at home, and they'll need a copy of both of your driver's licenses," Wally advised in his best police voice.

The stockbroker eventually got an audience with everyone he asked for, but the car remained his problem to solve. Wally, feeling sorry for a man who could not tell his real wife the truth, helped the man put in a plausible insurance claim. The guy was an obvious idiot to lose an $80,000 car, but everyone makes mistakes.

After the dust settled the parking was taken away from the front office manager and given to Slim. Wally Callahan and his staff made occasional quiet trips through the garage to keep the inappropriate behavior at a tolerable level. A parked car in a quiet hotel garage is a great place to take a nap or pursue physical relations with a coworker. Jack and Wally wondered if there was something special about sex on imported leather seats.

Edwin stood in the square as he remembered the incident and watched Slim run his curbside ship, and his thoughts turned to the entire hotel staff. He knew them more as babysitters and teachers than employees. He wondered how they would take to their new owner in his grown-up form. He crossed the side street and walked to the back of the hotel. The alley behind the hotel was actually below grade from the front as the land began its slope toward the harbor eighteen blocks away. He entered the alley where all deliveries were made and headed for the large doors and loading dock in the center of the alley. He had decided he would gain little from a pompous entrance into the lobby. The Dumpster area was much dirtier than he had ever seen it.

It was obvious that someone was not "managing by walking around." There are two kinds of managers in the hotel business: the ones that sit in their office and manage by meetings and reports, and the ones who walk around the hotel at all hours. A hotel is a collection of people, both guests and employees. People have a strange way of altering their behavior when they think they aren't being watched. The good employees appreciate bosses who get involved. In most cases, if a hotel is clean, well kept and friendly to the guest, regardless of its age, the manager runs the hotel by walking around. Edwin made a mental note of the condition of the back entrance and the broken sheet rock on the walls just inside the door.

chapter

FOUR

Dennis Farrow was sitting in an office with glass windows on three sides, set up so everything and every person entering or leaving the hotel's rear entrance could be monitored. The person occupying the office, referred to as the cage, was part security and part receiving clerk. He would check employees in and out and inspect any bundles or bags an employee might have with them, as well as supervise all deliveries into the hotel. It's the first line of defense against in-house theft. Fifteen years before, the storeroom clerk had been caught with a full tenderloin taped to his leg under his pants. He was terminated on the spot. The fact that he had worked there for ten years left everyone wondering how many tenderloins had walked out the door.

When Dennis noticed Edwin, he walked out of the office and extended his hand.

"Edwin, err, I mean, Mr. Christian, I hear you're back for a while. It's been a long time."

Obviously Dennis, and everyone else in the hotel, had heard who the new owner was.

"It's still Edwin, unless we're in front of guests. How's your family?"

They talked about Dennis and his family and Edwin's travels for a few minutes.

Edwin wondered where the phrase "for a while," implying that he would not be here for long, had come from. He was not about to feed the rumor mill by asking Dennis about it. His comments would be around the hotel before he got to the second floor. In a hotel, there's a communication system the Pentagon would like to have for its speed. The accuracy of the information is sometimes not as good, but for an informal system with hundreds of employees acting as relay points, it's pretty close most of the time.

"I was sad to see A.D. pass away. He was one of a kind. I'm sorry for your loss," Dennis said.

"Thanks, Dennis."

"He would have been proud. I caught Premier Poultry stuffing extra ice in the delivery boxes again. They were ten pounds short. I've had to do a lot of that lately. With the fall off in business, Mr. Chambers cut out my assistant, and the back door has to be manned at all times," Dennis volunteered.

"How bad is the business?" Edwin asked.

"I don't see the financial statements anymore, but the deliveries are about two-thirds of what they used to be. There've been layoffs and cut backs in hours in every department under Mr. Chambers' regime," Dennis replied.

The word regime registered with Edwin.

"Is that why the back door looks like crap?" Edwin asked.

"Every expense in the place has been cut. The pressure washer broke two months ago and engineering can't get the approval for a new one."

A.D. Christian had been a tough businessman, but he rewarded loyalty and loved the hotel and the people who ran it for him. Letting a part of the hotel get run down to save a few hundred dollars in expense would have been out of the question.

"I guess I have a lot to catch up on," Edwin replied.

"No lie, Edwin, it's good to see you again. You look well, Boss."

"So do you, Dennis. I'm glad your kids are doing so well."

The word boss made Edwin smile as he turned left down a long corridor.

Hotel people refer to a hotel as two distinct parts. The front of the house consists of the areas the guests get to see: the guest rooms and the public spaces. The back of the house is the kitchen, storage areas, equipment and mechanical rooms, and all other areas the guests seldom get to see. Edwin walked deeper into the back of the house. To his right was the food storeroom where dry stores were kept, mostly items that were boxed, bagged or canned like pasta, canned vegetables, rice and the like. There was also a large walk-in cooler with fresh vegetables and dairy products. A large walk-in freezer was next to that, containing everything from ice cream to frozen vegetables and desserts. The meat was kept upstairs on the kitchen level behind a small butcher's cutting room. The liquor was held in a locked cage on the same level. The hotel's layout was an inefficient one. Things had to be taken up the freight elevator to the kitchen level. In downtown hotels, ground space is very expensive and the architects are forced to stack things to get maximum use out of the available land. Vertical designs are a real challenge to the operator.

Edwin could hear whirring sounds and voices in English and Spanish coming from two large doors. Four women and one man toiled with huge piles of towels and sheets in front of the large washers and dryers lined up against the back wall. Working hardest of all, in the middle of the fray, was a small woman in the black dress of the housekeeping department. She had coal black hair with a touch of gray beginning to show. It was Mary Rodriguez, the Executive Housekeeper. She controlled one of the largest departments in the hotel, and probably the most important. Without clean rooms and public spaces, all the smiles and good intentions meant little to the guest. Mary caught sight of the man standing in the doorway. A puzzled look turned to a huge smile.

"El Jefito!" she exclaimed and ran to put her arms around Edwin.

Edwin hugged her back. El Jefito was a term Mary had made up years before when A.D. would assign Edwin to work in the house-keeping department. It meant little boss. At the time Mary was the lead maid, but the term maid had not been used in the hotel business for several years. Everyone was now a housekeeper. Desk clerks were now guest service agents and waiters and waitresses were servers.

"We heard you would be coming. You have grown so well and so handsome," Mary said.

Edwin caught himself starting to blush as the others looked on. "You always charmed me, Miss Mary, but your cookies I fell in love with," he replied in perfect Spanish.

"Your Spanish is good, Edwin. A.D. told us you were in South America working on the pipelines. Did you meet a senorita?" she asked. The others in the room giggled at the question.

"I met a few, but none as special as you," he answered. "Why is the Executive Housekeeper doing laundry?"

"This is my team, Edwin. With the cuts in expenses, we have to run several loads a day. We don't have the amount of linen we used to. They tried to get me to save further on the chemicals by filling the washers to the top, but I refused. As I taught you, a full washer does not get the linen clean enough and it leaves hair in the load. There is nothing a guest hates more than someone else's hair in their bed. I told them I would quit first. I think they might be considering it."

Edwin had to smile. He thought they might think about firing Mary Rodriguez, but they wouldn't make it through the exit inter-view. Although Mary stood not an inch over five feet, she was prob-ably the toughest person on the staff pound for pound. A six-foot, two-hundred-pound male guest found that out the hard way twelve years before, when Mary was the lead housekeeper.

That morning, Mary was training a young housekeeper and had gone back to the housekeeping closet down the hall as the trainee had entered Room 1412. A drunken guest was hiding naked in the bathroom. As the trainee entered the room, he shut the door and began to undo her blouse from behind. She screamed loud enough for everyone on three floors to hear. Mary got to the door faster than an Olympic sprinter. Fortunately for the trainee, and not so for the attacking guest, he had forgotten to throw the deadbolt on the door.

Mary used her pass key and was in the room in seconds. She stabbed the man in the back of the head with her key. When he turned in pain and disbelief, his mouth gaping, she stuck a toilet bowl brush she had grabbed from the cart in his mouth. Before the man could get his hands to his mouth, Mary let fly with a punch directly from her shoulder, the way her brother Juan the boxer had showed her when she was a little girl in Mexico. Any heavyweight would have been envious. It caught the guest directly in the nose and knocked him backward. He tripped over his suitcase, and took out the TV and the table lamp on his way down. He was stunned, bleeding from the nose and frantically trying to spit the cleaner out of his mouth.

The screams and Mary's ear shattering yell of "You son-of-a-bitch" brought guests and employees running. When Wally Callahan got to the room, the man was still lying on the floor spitting and throwing up. An ambulance team and a cop showed up shortly after. The guest was taken to the emergency room to get his mouth and broken nose attended to. Wally took a picture of the room and the torn blouse and mark on the neck of the trainee. He knew there would be a lawsuit and he wanted to press charges. If he didn't, he was afraid Mary might come after him next. The guest was the vice president of a large paper company from the Midwest. He made bail the next day and the paper company's attorney called the hotel two days later. Wally faxed him a picture of the trainee with the bruise and the torn blouse. The lawyer called back two days later and, in a very conciliatory tone, offered five thousand dollars to the trainee for her "inconvenience." Mary and Wally really wanted to stick it to the pervert and press charges, but five thousand dollars would be far better for the newly immigrated trainee.

A.D. decreed, "It's twenty-five thousand or we'll see you and Romeo in court." Three hours later the lawyer called back and said the check was in the mail. A.D. gave the young trainee fifteen thousand, used twenty-five-hundred to repair the room and gave Mary seventy-five-hundred. The matter was closed, except for the new respect Mary enjoyed. The staff referred to her as Ali for the next two months.

"Do me a favor and don't quit. Your team would be lost without you," Edwin said.

"If El Jefito becomes El Jefe, maybe good things will start to happen again," she replied.

Edwin took a few minutes to talk to each of the employees as Mary watched and smiled at her former charge. When he finished, he said, "I'll be around, Mary."

He patted her on the shoulder and thanked the others in the room for their hard work. Edwin walked to the freight elevator and pushed the call-button.

chapter

FIVE

Edwin was puzzled. The first two people he had met talked about the tight expense controls being imposed on the entire staff. Even if business was down, A.D. had continuously put the profits back into the hotel and had paid off the mortgage years before. The hotel's cash flow should be more than able to pay for repairs and normal expenses. He wondered if Leonard Chambers, the general manager his brother had put in the hotel, was just one of the control freaks that were trained in the art of penny pinching for the sake of penny pinching. Controlling costs in a hotel is almost an art form. It's the balance of controlling cost while keeping the building up without sacrificing service and reputation.

As the elevator doors opened, the heat and humidity of the kitchen hit him like a warm blanket. The kitchen, with the ranges and ovens going all of the time, the dish machine, and the compressors from the coolers putting out heat, was like a July day in South Florida. In July it could beat a rain-forest heat index. Behind the main cooking line, two white-coated men stood face to face and appeared to be trying to control a fat white animal. Edwin recognized the ritual of pulling the white sauce. The sauce was made and then wrung through cheesecloth to make sure there were no lumps. The chef and his assistant would twist and pull the sauce to strain it into a large pot. Edwin recognized Chef Mazzari with his black chef's hat. The other man was Clarence Edmunds, the sous-chef.

The Chef looked up, and without a smile said, "Grab an end, and make yourself useful."

It was classic Chef Mazzari. When A.D. had assigned him to the kitchen Edwin quickly found out kitchen work in a busy hotel was hard work. At the end of a hard morning, the chef would invite Edwin to sit at the chef's table situated in the center of the kitchen. He got to eat creamed capon along with hard French bread. After lunch, the chef would spend fifteen minutes with Edwin, talking about his impression of the food, the kitchen, and the hotel. The chef would also talk about his large family and his experiences in Italy as a boy.

He had started cooking in Italy and had come to America in his early twenties. He got a job washing dishes until he could convince the French chef and crew at the hotel where he worked he could cook. They were hard on the young Italian, but Luigi Mazzari was tough. He worked extra hours and learned French so he could understand the intricacies of the menu and the recipes. After five years, he was accepted as an equal. When A.D. was looking for a chef, he got a call from a man with a heavy French accent who recommended Luigi Mazzari. Mazzari had now been at the hotel for twenty-four years, having started as one of the youngest chefs in the city.

The chef handed his end of the cheesecloth to the broiler cook and motioned Edwin to the chef's table.

"The times are sad without A.D. How are you, Edwin?" the chef asked.

"Things are lonely, but they get better with time, Chef. How's your family?" Edwin replied. "As I get older, I wonder where you found the time to have all those children."

"You forget. I'm Italian," the chef replied.

"I've been here for thirty minutes, and all I hear is cuts in expenses and poor business. Is the economy that bad?"

"Business drops for many reasons, not just the economy," the chef said, shaking his head. "The cuts have been steady from the beginning of Mr. Chambers' leadership. I tried to talk with A.D. when he visited the hotel, but Mr. Chambers was always with him. I couldn't get any private time with him."

"So if it's not the economy, what is it?" Edwin asked.

"I still have drinks with the other chefs in town. They thank me for the business we're pushing their way," Mazzari replied.

"Pushing their way?" Edwin asked.

"Edwin, with the cuts in expenses, quality has to suffer. Many of our upscale clients have moved to other facilities. There are three new hotels in town, and we are the aging queen. We haven't renovated the banquet and meeting rooms in five years. I've had to drop some of the niceties to meet the demands for cutting food cost. We almost lost the Business Council because of food quality. Chambers ordered that I use liverwurst in the Beef Wellington instead of pate."

Edwin looked puzzled.

The chef explained Beef Wellington is made with a whole-tenderloin of beef. It's coated with pate of goose livers and wrapped in pastry. An amateur wouldn't know the difference between pate and liverwurst, but the members of the Business Council ate in the finest places.

"There are a lot more good, past customers I could list, but you don't have the time," the chef ended. "Let's walk around while we talk," the chef said as he got up.

They walked past the main cooking line with the steam coming out of the steam table where the hot sauces were kept. They walked past the large steamers and the ovens that backed up the line into the banquet preparation area. The quarry tile floor was slippery, and Edwin had to watch his footing. The chef walked without noticing it. He had done it for years and his feet instinctively steadied him. The chef stopped in front of the silver cage. The hotel had a large assortment of silver serving pieces. Mazzari pointed at the burnishing machine which is a large drum filled with different-sized metal

Greg Plank

shot. It tumbles the silver with the shot and the silver is polished. To do it by hand would take several people several hours each day.

"We don't use that much anymore. We haven't done the money in eight months."

Some of the finer hotels send the coins to be used in giving guests change down to the burnishing machine to have them polished. Giving guests shiny coins and crisp bills is a nice touch. Originally, the coins were polished because women wore white gloves in public and the hotels did not want the coins to soil the gloves. The gloves are gone, but the tradition remains in some hotels.

They walked silently toward the butcher shop. Andy Scott, the butcher, was standing over a beef rib. Andy had played football in college and spent one year in the pros until his shoulder was blown out. He handled the heavy meat like it was a small toy.

"You sure you have the right end of that knife, Andy?" Edwin asked.

Andy looked up and smiled. "I'm sure the Chef would prefer I use the dull end. He likes a lot of fat on the ribs to make them roast tender."

"Andy would trim a meatball if you put it in front of him," Mazzari replied.

"Your meatballs need trimming with all the crap you put in them," Andy said with a smile.

"The recipe is from Italy, not Alabama," the chef retorted.

The two men had heckled each other for years. Their banter kept the kitchen staff loose on busy days.

"Edwin, we sure miss your grandfather. I think it was the chef's meatballs that must have got him. He was too strong for anything normal to slow him down." Andy cleaned his huge-muscled hands and offered one to Edwin. Edwin's hand disappeared in the butcher's large paw.

"How's the family?" Edwin asked.

"Morris turned out a little shorter than me. He's a running back at State. Doin' pretty well—could make all conference," Andy answered with pride. "Brittney is a senior in nursing school following in her mother's footsteps."

"Great," Edwin replied. "It's good to see you and the chef are still here."

"If the chef would buy some decent meat, I'd last a lot longer," Andy said, getting serious.

"I buy what they let me buy. Cost rules around here," the chef volunteered in defense.

"The cost cutting's killing us," Andy said as he picked up the knife and stuck it in the wooden block.

"You look pissed," Edwin said.

"I just hope we get someone around here who'll throw on third and long instead of making the quarterback over there eat the ball every time," Andy snorted, pointing to the chef.

"We'll see what we can do," Edwin replied. "Keep the sauce smooth, Chef."

He left the two men standing together. Over his shoulder he heard one man say, "I hope he means it."

"You got my vote," the other replied.

chapter

SIX

The comments about cost-cutting and low staff morale bothered him. He had learned in the Marines that fear and other things
that nag at you can be your best friends: if you learn to manage them
and put them in perspective, they keep you alert, aware, inquisitive
and sometimes even alive. He passed the back entrance to the restaurant, dodged a server with a full tray, and headed to the main lobby.
The carpet by the elevators was well past worn. Another bad sign.

The lobby was Grand Hotel style. Its forty-foot ceiling was
supported by ornate, hand-painted wooden beams. When the ceiling needed refreshing, A.D. had brought artisans over from Europe.
Thick oriental carpets were scattered strategically over the marble
floor. In the center was a large upholstered bench circling a ten-foot,
inlaid wood monument. Atop the monument was a large brass pine-
apple, the international symbol of hospitality. Edwin noticed the
flower arrangements that used to be fresh were now artificial. The
antique furniture was showing wear.

Across the lobby was a large desk with an elaborate brass lamp on it and two large Queen Anne chairs facing it. Behind the desk sat a familiar figure—Jack Vincent, the concierge for over twenty years. As Edwin approached, Jack was on the phone trying to get coveted tickets for the hit play *Dining at Roger's*.

From the conversation, Jack was not going through a normal ticket source. He didn't notice Edwin taking a seat.

Jack was saying in his comforting but official voice, "Melvin, I know you can get them for less. Gouge your other clients, but remember I'm the one who got you the Louis XIV suite when you wanted to boff your newest encounter." He emphasized boff. "Next time you get heated up, you know where not to call."

His voice was growing irritated, but Jack always kept his cool. Serving people who took themselves far too seriously had made him the ultimate diplomat. "That's a little better. Next time you get a regular guestroom over the Dumpster," Jack spat into the phone.

After a few seconds he said, "Now you're up to the front of the house, but still a regular room. Melvin, I know it's a very popular play even though it sucks, but I put myself out for you every time you get the itch," Jack said and paused.

"Finally, you're back in the suite. I need the tickets by noon tomorrow, compadre. Thanks, I look forward to seeing you then," Jack said, victoriously.

A regular person listening might have called the vice squad. Edwin knew a concierge had to keep lines open to a variety of resources to serve demanding guests. An unofficial barter system of favors enabled a good concierge to get things normal people couldn't.

Jack hung up, noted his transaction on an index card, and put it in his top drawer. When he looked up he was startled to see Edwin. "I'm sorry to keep you waiting."

"I'd like four of those tickets for tomorrow night," Edwin said.

Jack put on his glasses and looked directly at Edwin. "Oh my, God! You still enjoy scaring the crap out of me."

"A leftover from my youth. You still say it like it is, Jack. A.D. loved the way you could be down to earth one minute and aristocratic the next," Edwin said, returning Jack's smile.

"A.D. needed someone to tell him the truth instead of blowing smoke up his ass. You look a lot like him, Edwin. How are you?"

"I was getting better until I started to walk around this place."

"Welcome to the aging queen, and I'm not referring to myself," Jack quipped.

"How did things get this bad?" Edwin asked.

"It's a combination of economic downturn, A.D. being out of the picture for almost a year, and a general manager who sees his mission as breaking balls and cutting costs," Jack said. "I don't know, but I've often thought there has to be something else driving the situation."

"Is that your intuition or do you have an inkling of something else?"

"Just my intuition. I really don't have anything to base it on other than the fact A.D. was never left alone with the staff when he visited," Jack replied.

Edwin decided to change the subject.

"You and Wally still busting each other's balls?" he asked.

"Not as much since this has been happening. The old staff tends to stick together. I get the feeling it really aggravates Chambers," Jack said.

As Edwin stood to leave, he said, "Don't change, Jack, the world would go out of balance."

"Too late to change. I was born on a full moon. It's good to see you. I hope you're planning to stay a while."

There it is again. "Not to worry, Jack. Is Chambers in the executive offices?" Edwin asked. "I think it's time I met the gentleman."

"If he's in the hotel, he's either there or in the dining room."

"From the looks of this place, he sure as hell isn't walking around much," Edwin said over his shoulder.

"Bless you my son," Jack replied.

"And you, Jack."

Part way across the lobby, Edwin was brought to a halt by a commotion at the front desk. A businessman holding two bags, with a computer case over his shoulder, was in heated conversation with a small attractive guest service agent.

"This is a hotel, right?" he asked. "And hotels have rooms, right? Well I've had this reservation for a month and I want my room."

The young girl seemed on the verge of tears.

"Sir, as I have explained, our computer system is down and I cannot assign rooms at this time. We will be happy to check your luggage. You can enjoy a beverage or snack in the dining room at our expense until I can clear a room for you," she offered.

"I don't want a snack, I want a room. I have a very important meeting. I've been flying since six a.m. and I need to freshen up before the meeting. I'll ask you one more time, where is your manager?" he said loudly through clenched teeth.

The computer has been a miracle-advancement in operating hotels. The undeniable drawback, however, is that unless you can afford an often-pricey backup you're at the mercy of something that, like human beings, can occasionally fail.

When the businessman repeated his request for the general manager, Edwin wondered where the front office manager was. He should be out here protecting his employee.

"Look, missy, I want the damn room that I reserved a month ago. It says right here on the confirmation, 'early arrival requested.' If you can't find my room, at least find your gutless manager."

"Mr. Olson, my name is Susan, and I am trying to help you." Her lower lip was beginning to tremble. She apologized again and disappeared through the door in the center of the front office wall to find her supervisor and regain her composure.

Edwin was about to intervene. He felt sorry for the girl, but understood the man's frustration. The guy was a bully and couldn't control his temper, but he had a problem. Just as he began to step toward the man he felt a hand on his shoulder.

"Not on your first day, Boss. Things have changed in the past ten years. You might not be able to find the one thing this gentleman wants." It was Jack Vincent.

Jack approached the man from the side so that he would not startle him. Jack's uncanny sense of body language helped in tight guest-service situations. Jack introduced himself and asked to see the man's reservation. For an instant the man seemed appeased.

"Jack, was it? I'm having a really bad day. If you can't help me, don't stand here, and try to screw me over like everyone else."

As Jack read the confirmation, the young guest service agent and a youthful man with a nametag cautiously emerged from the front office.

"Ah. Mr. Olson, this is Robert Mason, our front office manager," Jack said. Help had arrived, Jack thought—until Mason opened his mouth.

"Sir, I'm sorry for your inconvenience and apologize on behalf of everyone in the hotel. As Susan explained, our computers are down, and we cannot assign rooms at this time," he said, almost patronizingly.

Jack could see the hair on Olson's neck start to bristle.

"Robert, Mr. Olson does not need the apology of the entire hotel. Mr. Olson needs a room," Jack said sternly.

Jack was instantly Olson's newest best friend. The man's shoulders sagged a bit as he started to relax.

"Robert, you did run the hourly occupancy report, did you not?" Jack asked pleasantly.

"We didn't run one at noon, but we did at eleven," Robert replied sheepishly. It was hotel policy to run the list of occupied, vacant and clean rooms each hour so they could operate manually should the computer system go down.

"We didn't have the full housekeeping input on clean rooms, so we're not sure how accurate it is."

"Why don't you get it anyway, and we'll have a look," Jack ordered.

Robert and Susan disappeared into the front office.

"Do you depend on computers in your business, Mr. Olson?" Jack asked.

"Yeah, they're just like women. You can't live with them, and you can't live without them. They're both complex."

"Interesting observation," Jack replied.

Edwin smiled. The whole staff knew Jack was gay. He didn't hide it, but he didn't advertise it either. Jack was probably as comfortable in his own skin as any person Edwin had ever known.

The two young front office people returned with four pages of paper. Jack looked at the pages and wrote down five room numbers on a piece of paper and handed it to Mason, saying, "Make keys for these rooms and go check them starting on the upper floor. Mr. Olson, you can wait here or you can accompany Mr. Mason. It appears that time is urgent for you right now."

The man looked at his watch. "Damn, it's getting late. I'll go with him."

"Splendid. I understand your inconvenience and frustration, Mr. Olson. I'll get a bellman. Front," he yelled.

A bellman appeared. Jack handed him a five-dollar bill and told him to take special care of Mr. Olson. As the front office manager, bellman, and Olson headed toward the elevators, Edwin walked over to Jack.

"Nice play, but what if none of those rooms is clean?" he asked. "He'll be twice as upset when he gets back."

"Odds are one of the rooms will be. I picked ones close together on the upper floors. Housekeeping cleans the better, upper floor rooms first. They bring more rate. At least now Mr. Olson is part of the solution. Besides, Robert has a passkey and hopefully is smart enough to put Mr. Olson in a suite parlor with linen to freshen up, if they don't find a clean room. He'll get to his meeting and I'll buy him a drink on his return," Jack said.

"What about your five bucks?" Edwin asked.

"I'll have plenty of chances to get that back," Jack replied. "This is a hotel."

"I guess it's still a hotel. I better go ask Mr. Chambers what he thinks it is. Nice save, Jack," Edwin said.

Jack smiled proudly as the boss turned into the elevator lobby.

chapter

SEVEN

Edwin's eyes caught the scratches and marks on the dark wood paneling of the elevator. They were from luggage and luggage carts as they bang against the wood. *Damn*. They should have been sanded, stained, and varnished each week. From the looks of the marks, they had been accumulating for some time. Edwin began considering how tough he should be in his first meeting with Chambers.

"If you can't control yourself, you can't control the situation," he reminded himself.

As he left the elevator he passed the glass door of the sales and catering offices and noticed the unattended receptionist's desk.

I hope she's out going to the ladies' room.

Leaving the reception desk in a sales office empty was akin to not having anyone at the front desk. He reached the end of the hallway and pushed open the glass door marked Executive Offices in gold letters. An attractive woman in her forties sat behind a desk. A picture of A.D. hung in a gold frame behind her. Donna Lane had been Executive Assistant at the hotel for 15 years, thanks to Wally

Callahan. Wally was having a beer at Jimmy's Tap one night. He was listening to one of his old police buddies talk about a domestic call he had that day.

"She was beat up worse than a fifth-rate boxer. The guy was twice her frickin' size," the cop said. "Her old man was working out on her and the two kids were in the one bedroom bawling their eyes out and pleading with him to stop. It took both of us to get the cuffs on him."

They took the abusive husband to jail and the woman and her kids to the hospital. Eventually, the judge issued a restraining order and put the husband on probation. It turned out the woman had a secretarial job, but with the beatings, she was ashamed to show her face at work. She also didn't want to leave the kids anywhere the husband could reach them. Wally mentioned the conversation to A.D. A week later, Donna Lane was sitting at the desk she now occupied. She looked up as Edwin entered the reception area.

"Well, the prodigal grandson returns," she said, walking around the desk to give Edwin a hug.

"If I knew what prodigal meant, would I be offended?" he asked.

"Not in the least, Edwin. You should go to church more often."

"Thanks for getting me back from South America," he said appreciatively.

"The timing was A.D.'s. I just called where he told me to."

"Somehow I think they recognized your voice," he said. "How are the kids doing?"

"They're both finishing high school and looking toward college," she said proudly.

"And your old man?" he asked.

"Their father hasn't been heard from in fifteen years," she said.

The conversation led to how A.D. had helped mentor her boys, and that it was obvious to Donna A.D. missed having Edwin around. The comments made Edwin feel a twinge of guilt.

"Is Mr. Chambers in?" Edwin asked.

"He's been expecting you. He thought he'd give you a tour and introduce you to the staff. He suggested a small reception with the department heads, but I discouraged it," she said.

"Thanks. I've already started my tour and I know them better than he does even though it's been a few years," he said tartly.

"I'll ring Mr. Chambers. I hope you stay long enough for us to reminisce," she said. She announced Edwin had arrived.

There it was again. Where was the short-timer stuff coming from?

"Mr. Chambers has a couple of things to finish up. He asked you to wait just a few minutes."

I made him wait. Now he makes me wait. The business version of pissing on bushes to mark your territory.

Edwin decided to keep his cool at all costs, and he and Donna talked about family as he waited.

Their conversation was interrupted when a tall man with graying hair, wearing what appeared to be a very expensive gray pinstriped suit and a red power tie emerged from the office. He extended his hand.

"Leonard Chambers, Edwin. I've been waiting to meet you," the man said.

Edwin noticed that Chambers could not resist the waiting jab as he took the man's hand. His handshake was limp and insincere. Edwin returned the shake with a bit more pressure than normal and looked directly into Chambers' eyes.

He smiled. "I've been waiting to meet you too."

"Come in to my, err, I guess your office. How long has it been since you've been in the hotel?" Chambers asked.

"Probably ten years or more," Edwin replied. He walked into the office and sat in the large chair across from the desk.

"No, sit over here on the couch. It will be more informal," Chambers offered. "Would you like coffee or some other beverage?"

Here we go with the let's-be-buddies routine. Edwin looked around the office. It was much like he remembered it, except for the I-Love-Me wall above the couch. There were pictures of Chambers at different ages with famous celebrities, athletes, and politicians. A benefit of running hotels is that you meet famous guests, which often ends in a photo opportunity. There is often a certain pride in hosting and getting to know celebrities and other important people.

"What hotels are these from? They're impressive," Edwin asked, pointing to the wall.

"They're from a variety of places. Possibly the fame or shame of my career," Chambers replied, trying to lighten the conversation.

Edwin noticed the same presidential cuff links on Chambers' shirt as those he had seen on his brother.

"Looks like an impressive career," Edwin responded, trying to figure out if the guy was just a blowhard.

"It's been comfortable and exciting at times. You've certainly taken a different route, according to your brother," Chambers offered.

"I grew up around the hotel, but I gravitated toward a more physical life. We'll have to see if I can adjust to a more genteel way of life," Edwin said, wondering how Chambers would take a comment that might mean Edwin would stick around.

"The Marines, working in the jungles—I'm not sure a hotel can provide enough excitement for a physical kind of guy," Chambers replied.

Don't over-read him. He could be encouraging a short stay or just making conversation. It was obvious Chambers and Henry had talked about Edwin.

"I was thinking we could have a meeting of the employees to introduce the new owner," Chambers offered.

"Thanks, but I'm not the formal type. If you don't mind, I'd enjoy meeting them as I walk around the hotel," Edwin replied. "I've already walked some of the back of the house."

He watched Chambers' face tighten. Edwin wondered if Chambers was curious about what Edwin thought of his informal hotel tour, or about how he got into the hotel without one of his sentries calling Chambers.

"That's fine, Edwin; after all, it's your hotel. Perhaps the next department-head meeting would be a good time. I'm sure you have a lot of questions. I'm at your disposal, as you get up to speed. If I may ask, have you any thoughts on the ongoing management here?" Chambers asked, smiling.

"I haven't run a hotel before. Your expertise will be valuable," Edwin replied.

Chambers leaned forward and cleared his throat. "My question comes from my concern for the hotel. Two people trying to run the same business usually results in disaster. Forgive me, but I have no idea how active you want to be in the hotel."

"I agree. People can't work for two bosses, especially if the bosses have two different theories of how to do things. It ends up looking like two guys trying to get into the same pair of pants. As the owner—granted, an inexperienced one—I think I should have input, but I'll rely on the expertise of someone with more experience. As we get to know one another, we can decide if we have the same objectives," Edwin said.

"My first objective is to get this place back on track financially. It's been a struggle. The St. George is no longer a crown jewel," Chambers replied.

"With the physical conditions I've observed, it's far from a crown jewel," Edwin said. "Why has the condition of the place gone so far downhill? It looks old and tired."

Chambers put down his coffee cup and folded his hands. He explained, rather quickly in a laundry list, "The economy has not been great, and the competition's facilities are newer. I've had to cut wherever I could to pay the mortgage. This hotel's very expensive to run. We need a certain amount of food and staff regardless of how many guests are in the house. The utility companies don't have a good sense of humor or much patience. Everything has to be paid on time, and the real problem is that the volume of business goes up and down, and the competition has been cutting rates to steal business for the past year."

"Can we back up just a little, what mortgage? A.D. had this place debt-free ten years ago," Edwin replied.

"There's a twenty-million dollar mortgage on the hotel with a fairly high interest rate. It takes two million a year to pay it," Chambers replied.

"When was this place mortgaged? A.D. would never put himself in that position. He hated long-term debt," Edwin asked.

"You'll have to ask your brother about that."

"I will. On another note, I can understand some wear and tear on the place in hard times, but there seems to be some plain cleaning up to do. Cleanliness is normally not an expensive virtue. The back of the house could use a little soap and water," Edwin replied.

"I don't know what you've observed, but I'll walk the house myself," Chambers said defensively. "I'd appreciate any observations you have, Edwin."

I hope you can find your way around. I don't think you walk the house very often.

Changing the subject, Chambers asked, "Will you be staying in the hotel? We've held a suite for you, and, eventually, your mother."

"I'll take an apartment in Old Town as soon as I find one. I appreciate your concern," Edwin replied.

"It's my pleasure to serve your family. After all, you do own the place," Chambers said.

"For now, I'd like to finish my informal touring. Would you please have the front office manager—Mason, I believe his name is—program a passkey for me?"

"Yes, it's Mason. A good young man. He has some things to learn, but he has a hotel degree and is eager to please. I'll call him right away," Chambers replied, extending his hand once more. This time he gripped Edwin's hand more firmly.

"Thank you. I look forward to us getting to know each other," Edwin offered.

He would bet Mason went to the same hotel school or was somehow related to Chambers. Mason had more than some things to learn; he also needed balls. Any department head who would let a young girl take a tongue-lashing from an irate guest while he stayed in the back office had a serious character flaw.

"Call me with anything I can do. I'd also appreciate your comments from your tour. In fact, I wouldn't mind going along with you," Chambers volunteered.

"Please don't bother. I know you have more important things to take care of. We'll have plenty of time to talk," Edwin said. *There is no way in hell I'm following you around this hotel. I want to hear what the staff really has to say.*

He asked Donna to call his brother and invite him to lunch at the hotel when he was available. Donna looked at him questioningly. Edwin knew she was dying to know how the meeting with Chambers had gone, but he was not going to pass judgment on Chambers yet. Chambers had closed the door to his office. Edwin could imagine him talking on the phone to his brother. He thanked Donna with a smile and went to pick up the passkey from the good young man with no backbone.

chapter

EIGHT

The petite guest-service agent was standing behind the desk. She smiled at Edwin. "Mr. Christian, I have the passkey you wanted, sir."

Edwin smiled and said, "You look a lot better than earlier. Is Mr. Mason around?"

"He's taking a late lunch," she replied.

"I'll catch up to him later. Thanks for the key," Edwin said.

As he started his tour, he was almost run over by Wally Callahan. "Nice to see you again, Edwin. I'd stop to reminisce but we have a problem on the fourth floor."

"What kind of problem?" Edwin asked.

"We have a dead body in Room 441, and it isn't pretty," he whispered. "The housekeeper found her, after a guest complained of a strong odor in the room."

"The guest was staying in a room with a dead body and complained about the odor?" Edwin asked.

Greg Plank

"It was hidden in the wooden bed frame under the bed. Nobody looked until the smell got bad. Housekeeping used the ozone machine and sprayed deodorizer around when they couldn't find the cause. It got worse so they looked under the bed thinking a guest might have left food under the bed for some strange reason."

Edwin knew some very interesting things are found under hotel beds: pieces of erotic clothing, food, drugs, sex toys and just about everything else.

"Are the police up there now?" Edwin asked.

"They're on their way. I want to get there before they arrive. I also want to keep it out of the press," Wally replied.

"I'll go with you," Edwin volunteered.

Tragic events are bad for any business. Trying to keep them out of the press, or at least not have the hotel name used, is important. A good relationship with the police and the press is critical. Most hotels, and any good business for that matter, have emergency and incident policies. It's imperative to have a designated spokesperson. A manager's worst nightmare is seeing a tearful employee, with the hotel sign directly behind his or her head on the evening news, saying, "It was horrible. The body and the room were covered in blood."

The police don't like it either. They prefer to keep some details of crimes quiet to aid in their investigation.

"It ain't pretty. You sure?" Wally asked.

"I'm sure I've seen worse, Wally. I've been around the world in the past few years," Edwin replied.

In the elevator, Edwin asked, "How are you going to keep this quiet in the press?"

"I called one of my old cop buddies, he's now a captain, on a land line to report it," Wally replied. "It didn't go out over the radio so it won't be picked up on the scanners the press use."

At the end of the fourth floor hallway, Jack Vincent and Mary Rodriguez were standing outside a room.

Jack spoke first. "I've moved the Sandlers, who were staying in the room, to a suite. I told them that until the police cleared the scene, their belongings must remain in the room. I also made it clear they should stay put until the police talk with them."

"Thanks, Jack. If you can keep them under control, it'll be a big help," Wally said. In his effort to get things organized, he didn't notice he had put his hand on Jack's shoulder in an appreciative gesture.

Jack looked at Edwin and winked.

Could the homophobe in Wally be shrinking? Edwin wondered.

Wally was in his control mode. He asked Mary how the employees who found the body were doing. She suggested counseling. They were shook up and fairly superstitious people. Wally agreed and told her to keep them in the other room until the police could question them. He asked Jack to get beverages and snacks brought up for the police and tech crew.

"Anything to serve my man Wally," Jack said, smiling.

Wally, suddenly queasy at the thought of being known as Jack's man, said "Yeah, whatever."

"By the way, where's Chambers? I thought I'd see him here for a serious event in his hotel," Edwin asked.

"You're freakin' kidding, right?" Wally asked. "Chambers won't show until all the mess is gone."

A man in a well-tailored suit, holding a cigar, came down the hall. Two uniformed police officers and a woman in a lab coat followed.

"Edwin, we are honored. The Captain of Detectives has arrived," Wally announced.

"I only came to see if you're still alive and ask why you did this heinous thing, you Irish bastard," the man replied.

"I'm not a bastard. You knew my mother, and this is a non-smoking floor," Wally parried.

"The bastard part was because I had to walk the beat with you for two years. Your mother was a lovely person, and the cigar is my deodorizer for looking at dead bodies."

The two officers and the lady seemed stunned to hear anyone talk to a captain as Wally had.

"This is Captain John 'Moose' LeRoy, my old partner," Wally explained.

LeRoy turned to the people with him and said, "This is the infamous Wallace Callahan. He still blames me for his getting shot by

45

a pimple-faced perp. It's too bad too. He was the best beat cop the city's ever had."

"What's that gonna cost me?" Wally asked.

"The truth is free, but not controlling your guests' homicidal tendencies isn't, and getting my personal attention is gonna cost you plenty," LeRoy replied.

"Look out, Edwin. You better open up the liquor room or the meat locker. Moose, this is Mary Rodriguez, our Executive House-keeper, and Edwin Christian. He's A.D.'s grandson. He just inherited the hotel."

"The kid at Jimmy's bar? You're a lot bigger than the last time I saw you," LeRoy said. "You still eating twenty pounds of peanuts every day at lunch?"

"No, now Wally keeps me occupied with more exciting things like dead bodies," said Edwin, shaking the captain's hand.

"Time to get to work, team. Talking with old friends is fun, but we're on the taxpayers' tab. Wally, we'll take control of the room for now," LeRoy said, lighting his cigar.

The scene was grisly. The girl looked to be in her early twen-ties. She was bound with tape at her ankles and wrists. A plastic bag was taped over her head. There was a good amount of bruising on her chest. The team put on masks to cut the odor. LeRoy puffed on his cigar for a minute before fully entering the room.

Over the next hour the fourth floor was a busy place. Jack Vin-cent himself delivered the room-service cart with coffee, beverages, ice, and sandwiches, knowing to involve as few people as possible. LeRoy and the female technician looked over the crime scene while the cops guarded the door and checked any guests coming off the elevator. Anyone with a room at that end of the hall was asked to wait in the lobby. The officers said there was a very sick guest in the room who would be leaving soon.

The captain interviewed Mary and her staff. Mary acted as the interpreter, but LeRoy had a pretty good understanding of Spanish. His conversation with the Sandlers was much more difficult. They could not understand how they could be given a room with a dead body in it. All they wanted was a copy of the police report to give to their lawyer. LeRoy wanted to tell them that when they checked in they looked like two really big pains in the ass and the hotel wanted to do something special for them. But he kept that to himself and fought to keep a civil tone. After telling them the police report would be confidential for a while, he went back to see if the technician was done with the Sandlers' personal things. Mary Rodriguez returned them to the couple. Jack Vincent told them all of their hotel charges would be complimentary. That seemed to calm them some. They decided to stay in the suite for two more nights.

After the coroner had removed the body Jack gave the captain copies of the registration material and hotel bills from the last four occupants of that room. LeRoy joined Edwin and Wally as they walked toward the elevator.

"This gives a new meaning to putting a bag over your date's head," Wally said.

"I've often wondered about your sense of humor, Wally. It does look like suffocation. The M.E. will do the full autopsy tomorrow," LeRoy told them.

He continued reviewing what they knew. "We can rule the Sandlers out. I'm done with them, but I have a feeling you guys aren't. They kept insisting I give them a police report for their lawyer. I'm not going to do that for a while. I think this is part of another murder we're investigating."

He explained that a month ago another young lady, in the same condition, was found at the Merrill Hotel. She was an exotic dancer. He asked Wally for the security tapes from every camera for the past two weeks.

"Not a problem," Wally replied. "They're not great quality; the system's old."

"We can probably enhance them at the lab. You know what I'm looking for," LeRoy said. "What have you gotten off the reading of the lock?"

Electronic guest room locks can be "read" to see what card key has been used to enter a room and when. The guests are safer and the hotel avoids cases of, "The housekeeper must have come back and taken my grandmother's priceless necklace."

"The stuff looks pretty normal—guest keys properly issued and housekeepers' passkeys. But there is one passkey we can't place," Wally said.

LeRoy's eyes grew noticeably brighter. "Just like the Merrill incident. There must be an inside connection somewhere," he said. "I want to keep this quiet. If the press comes around, send them to me."

Wally and LeRoy kibitzed for another few minutes, giving each other a hard time over the stupid things they had done as young cops.

Finally LeRoy said, "I'm sorry about A.D. He was a great guy and a good friend of the cops. He sponsored three teams in the Police Athletic League. Whenever a cop died, his out-of-town relatives stayed here free. But that all stopped as he got sicker."

"When I asked your brother he said he'd look into it," Wally said.

"I'm not my brother," Edwin replied, smiling.

"Sounds like there might be a little bit of the old man in the kid, Wally," LeRoy said. "Hey, kid, I mean Edwin, call me John or Moose. Forget the captain crap." He stepped into to the elevator and pushed the button as the door closed.

"Nice guy. Was he always a cop? He has a business-like way of handling things," Edwin asked.

Wally explained John LeRoy had joined the police department after a stint in the steel business. John wanted to help people and he liked a little action in his life. He was a couple of years older than Wally when they graduated from the academy and were teamed up on the street. LeRoy had lasted through six mayors and four different police commissioners. He was non-political and concentrated on building his team, had continuously gotten the top scores in the police exams, and ran a tight department with high morale. John LeRoy was a people person. His men had seen him cry shamelessly with widows and families, and he constantly reminded them, "We work hard for the victims and the innocent. They deserve our best." Every police commissioner John 'Moose' LeRoy had worked for loved to have their picture taken with him. He was a cop's cop and everyone in law enforcement knew it.

chapter

NINE

Edwin went to the executive offices and asked Donna if she knew a good real estate agent in the downtown area. Donna called a friend; the agent was free that afternoon, so she and Edwin spent three hours looking at apartments in the Old Town section. He put a deposit on a vacant loft twelve blocks from the hotel; he could occupy it immediately. He called Chambers and asked if the hotel had any excess furniture. It belonged to him anyway, but he wanted to keep peace in the family and not get any employees in trouble for helping him without consulting Chambers.

Chambers and his wife had brought some of their own things for the manager's apartment and they had stored the hotel's furniture in the basement. Chambers offered to have some staff move it the next morning. Edwin thanked him and gave him the address.

At ten the next morning, three hotel employees showed up with the furniture. Mary Rodriguez was with them, carrying a full supply of cleaning materials. Edwin knew not to argue with Mary, who was determined to clean the place; he bought coffee and pastry for the crew. When everything was done he handed each of them fifty dollars. They tried to refuse the money, but Edwin insisted.

By noon, Edwin was moved in. After a quick shower, he walked to the hotel to meet his brother Henry for the one p.m. luncheon Donna had set up.

As Edwin approached the hotel, he could see Slim Johnson, the doorman, welcoming guests and barking orders at the valet-parking attendants and bellmen. Slim made his large frame dance as he hurried to open the doors of cars and taxis for guests.

Not a small feat for someone with the abdominal proportions of Rhode Island.

"Good Morning, Mr. Johnson. How's your day going?" Edwin asked.

Slim looked at him, puzzled. He prided himself on remembering people who had stayed at the hotel.

"I'll be damned. The Christian young one returns. Top of the day, sir," Slim replied.

"I'm glad you're still here, Slim," Edwin replied. "Lose any cars lately?"

"You must have talked to Jack. He gets excited easily," Slim said. "I understand you been travelin' the world. A lot of water under this old bridge and a good amount of changes since I last saw you."

"From what I've seen, that's the truth," Edwin said, returning Slim's handshake.

"I assume you're here to have lunch with your brother. He just arrived," Slim replied.

"Was that a good guess or does everyone know I'm having lunch with my brother?"

"This is a hotel and not a convent with a vow of silence," Slim countered. "I'm also glad a young single man like yourself is smart enough not to live in the hotel."

He took Slim's comment as a friendly acknowledgement he'd made the right decision about living outside the hotel. He also decided to do his laundry outside the hotel. He wasn't going to have the staff checking his underwear to judge the quality of his social life or spend time reading his bed sheets like a romance novel.

"I also didn't want you, Jack and Wally voting on the quality of my dates each morning. No woman deserves that kind of scrutiny."

"You've made three old men sad, sir. But we can live with the disappointment," Slim said, putting his hand over his heart.

"I'm sure you could live with just about anything," Edwin replied, smiling.

As he entered the lobby he waved to Jack, who pointed to the restaurant and crossed himself. Edwin walked to the dining room.

"Good day, sir, my name is Patti. How may I help you?" the hostess asked.

"I'm having lunch with Henry Christian."

"You must be Edwin Christian. I'm sorry I didn't recognize you, sir. I'll take you to his table," she said nervously.

"No need for apology. We've never met," he replied. He knew she had apologized because many hotels place pictures of important guests or company executives on central bulletin boards so the staff will recognize them. It adds to the personal service, and no general manager wants an important guest or superior walking around the hotel unrecognized. Some managers have a standing order that whenever one of the people posted enters the hotel, they be notified immediately.

Henry was sitting at the corner table by the windows. It was a quiet observation post where no one went unnoticed and no employee could approach unseen to overhear something said in private.

"Thanks for coming, Henry. We have a lot to catch up on," Edwin offered.

"I'm sorry we haven't had time since you've been back. A.D. surely dominated your time. I must admit Daphne and I were a bit offended. We've been here over the years carrying the load, so to speak, and we get shut out at the end," Henry replied.

Edwin knew Henry was trying hard to maintain control. His need to dominate made him start a conversation by putting the other party on the defensive.

"I'm sorry if you and Daphne felt slighted. A.D. talked of you both often and appreciated your efforts. At the end, he just wanted to die quietly and not burden you. He thought you had done more than enough," Edwin said, offering an olive branch. He knew Henry's ego wouldn't allow him to pass on an apparent surrender.

"Well, A.D. always had his own way of doing things," Henry replied.

You egotistical stuffed shirt. You're wearing a $600 sport coat and you live in a 5,000-square-foot-house, all thanks to A.D. The man's dead, and all you can think about is yourself.

"He certainly offered his thanks in compensation," Edwin replied, struggling to keep his composure.

"I dedicated my life to Christian Construction. I'm not sure he really appreciated some of the messes I cleaned up so he wouldn't have to get involved," Henry replied.

I wonder who caused those messes? Edwin noticed Patti approaching the table and sat back.

"Gentlemen, may I get you a beverage or would you like to order now?"

Henry ordered a martini, Edwin an iced tea. Patti took the order and went on to explain the specials. Henry asked that she return later to take the order.

"So, how's the construction business?" Edwin asked.

Henry folded his hands under his chin with his elbows on the table. He measured his words. "It's a struggle, but we're making progress. The bidding is the tough part. With construction down, the competition is cutting prices to the bone. The government jobs are even tougher — the paperwork in the bidding process would strip every tree in Wisconsin," Henry said. "The airport project has been a nightmare. They keep changing the specs and expect you to re-bid immediately to keep the project going. It's put us behind a bit on other projects too."

Patti placed the drinks in front of them. "Would you care to order now?"

Henry ordered the mixed grill and Edwin asked for the creamed capon. As Patti left the table, Henry called, "Better bring another." Three-quarters of his martini was already gone.

"From the looks of the hotel, this business isn't all roses either," Edwin offered.

"What do you mean by looks?"

"It's looking tired and worn," Edwin replied.

"Well, my boy, there are three new hotels in town, and the competition and the economy have made it tough to put much capital back into the old broad. I'm afraid it might be time to sell it unless you're sentimental enough to make a go of it for A.D.'s memory."

"I haven't seen enough to make a judgment yet, and I haven't gotten the chance to look at the financial side," Edwin said.

"Let me save you some time," Henry replied. "The hotel has had a full year of losses. The cash reserves are depleted and the credit lines are about exhausted. If I hadn't brought Chambers in to cut the fat, we'd be down the tubes."

Patti returned with the second martini.

"Where did you find him?"

"Leonard was between assignments and had come back to town to spend time with relatives. I was a guest at a luncheon of the Skal Club here at the hotel. Skal is a society of hotel and travel executives. He wanted to stay in the area and he liked the hotel. I couldn't find anyone with his background in town, and I needed help with the hotel. We talked a few times, and I put him on contract," Henry said and took another gulp. "He's done a great job controlling expenses."

Edwin decided Henry had consumed enough to loosen up.

"Chambers indicated there was a large mortgage on the hotel. I don't recall A.D. ever putting debt on the property," Edwin offered guilelessly.

Henry cleared his throat, stalling for his answer. "As I just said, the construction business has been challenging, to say the least. It was better to pull some money from the hotel. A lot of companies look at balance sheets when they consider bidders on future jobs. They don't look fondly on companies with too much debt. A.D. signed the note himself. The long-range potential of the construction company is far greater than the hotel," he said, his arrogance starting to show again.

"It just seems odd that A.D. would encumber the hotel. It was his first love. How bad is the construction situation?"

"Really, Edwin, don't bother yourself with that. If you'll take some brotherly advice, the best thing to do is sell the hotel. It's seen its best days, and is consistently losing money. You can pay off the mortgage, get a good piece of money and get on with your life of adventure."

"I want to look at the whole situation. When can I get a copy of the hotel financial statements? Chambers told me that I must see you for those. Besides, I'm looking forward to relearning the hotel business," Edwin replied. His enthusiasm was clearly disturbing Henry.

"I'll have my girl get them to you by the end of the week," Henry replied.

"I'd really like them by tomorrow."

"I'll do what I can," Henry snapped.

"I can come to your office or I can pick them up at the accountant's office. I'm sure they're part of the estate settlement," Edwin said, his tone strenuously pleasant.

Henry assumed the look of a wounded elephant ready to run over the hunter. Just as Edwin leaned forward to emphasize his point, the food arrived. Henry ordered his third martini. Edwin wondered how a very successful construction company could get into financial trouble.

"Mother has been difficult since A.D.'s death. Her nurse, Mrs. Chang, has a hard time controlling her," Henry said, changing the subject.

"What happened to Mrs. Martinez? She never had any problems with mother," Edwin asked.

"She just seemed to be getting too old to handle mother physically," Henry replied. "Mrs. Chang came highly recommended."

"What did mother have to say about that?"

"Mother doesn't really have much to say about anything. Not to be cruel, but she hasn't spoken much since the stroke."

"She can communicate, though," Edwin retorted.

"Actually, Edwin, Mother is more into acceptance these days. She knows Daphne and I have her best interest at heart. We've been taking care of her for all the years you've been away," Henry replied.

He couldn't let that jab go. Edwin wanted to get the lunch over with; Henry seemed ready to order his fourth martini.

"I appreciate you taking time out of your busy schedule, Henry. I'm sure the financial statements will bring up some questions that only you can answer. I look forward to getting them," Edwin said. He signaled for the check. "Stay well, Henry, and thanks for the time. Excuse my leaving, but I have a lot to catch up on."

"And you too, brother. I know you'll come to the only conclusion, which is to sell the hotel. But I guess it's better if you get there yourself," Henry smiled as he finished.

Mr. Ego is sitting on the money from the mortgage on the hotel and he's acting cavalier. He got up from the table and extended his hand.

Edwin walked to the hostess stand. He thanked Patti, signed the check, and left the restaurant. As he entered the lobby, he saw Donna Lane and waved to catch her attention. He told her he was going home to finish up the loft. He didn't want the staff to suffer from the effects on his mood Henry and his pompous performance had left.

chapter

TEN

For the rest of the weekend, Edwin ran some personal errands, shopped for light food items, and added some decorative items to the loft. He walked around the city visiting the competitive hotels. In the late afternoon on Sunday, he decided it was time to visit his mother at the family home. She looked well, and, without a lot of confusion in the room, she communicated well. Because of the stroke, she would know what she wanted to say, but often could not get the whole sentence out. When she would have to pause, she used a trigger word. Hers was crap. As a young woman, she had always had a good sense of humor. By five o'clock, he had gotten her to try a scotch and water and play a game of gin rummy. She protested that with her disabled hand and trouble with numbers she couldn't play. She won two out of the three hands. He could tell by the look in her eyes, she was proud of the accomplishment. In her halting way, she asked about the hotel. He told her of some of the happenings, but made light of them so she wouldn't be concerned.

Throughout the visit, he could see his mother was perturbed by the constant attention her attendant, Mrs. Chang, paid to her. He could sense the lack of a relationship between the two women and it bothered him.

"What happened to Mrs. Martinez?" Edwin asked.

She raised her hands palms up, a sign of I don't know.

"Who hired Mrs. Chang, you?" he asked.

She shook her head no and said, "Enry."

Once again, Henry's actions puzzled Edwin. Mrs. Martinez and his mother were almost like sisters. She gave his mother respect and let her try things on her own. There were broken glasses and spilled things, but she got to try to live her life. Mrs. Martinez would clean things up, and they'd laugh about it.

At nine o'clock, Edwin realized she was getting tired. He hugged his mother, kissed her, and promised he would see her soon.

She shook her head yes and said, "Love you."

The ride back to his loft was filled with a mix of emotions as he thought about his mother's contented demeanor as they played cards together, and the frustrated look she had when Mrs. Chang was around.

Monday morning he woke at five as usual. He took his run by the harbor. When he got to the hotel, he went to see Donna.

"Do you still have the phone number for Mrs. Martinez, the lady who used to care for Mother?"

"Yes, I do," she answered.

"Can you see if you can get her on the phone?" Edwin asked.

Five minutes later he looked up from the daily report he was reading.

"Mrs. Martinez is on line one," Donna said. He thanked her and picked up the phone. Edwin and Mrs. Martinez talked for twenty minutes. Finally, he asked her to come back to help his mother. She accepted immediately.

"The hotel limo will pick you up at seven-thirty. Donna will give the driver the address," he said.

"What about your brother? I don't think he'll be happy," she replied.

"I'll take care of Henry. Thanks for coming back. I'll see you soon. I miss your carne asada," he said and hung up.

He went into Donna's office and asked who paid Mrs. Chang. When Donna responded that the hotel did, he asked her to get a check for three months of Mrs. Chang's salary. She had it back to him in half an hour.

Edwin went to the lobby and asked Jack if the limo was available.

"Can I help with anything?" Jack asked.

"No, just taking my mother a present," Edwin said.

In the limo he asked Mo the driver to take him by his loft. He went up and packed a suit and clothes for the next day and some casual clothes for the evening. An hour later, he was standing in front of the family house. He asked Mo to wait for a passenger, went to the door, and rang the bell. Mrs. Chang answered with a surprised look on her face.

"Is there a problem, Mr. Christian?" the woman asked.

"There's no easy way to do this, so I'll just tell you straight out. I have a check here for three months salary for you. I've decided that you and mother just aren't the right fit. I'm replacing you immediately. If you have no place to stay, I've reserved a room for you at the St. George. We'll pick up the charges for your room and meals until you find a place. I'm sorry. I just don't think you and Mother work."

The woman looked at him with hard eyes and a bit of shock. She knew there was no point in arguing and left to pack. She called Henry from her room to complain as she gathered her things. Edwin went to the porch to check on his mother.

Marguerite Christian was surprised to see her son. He sat down next to her and said, "Mrs. Chang has decided she has other obligations, so I'll stay with you for a while. I have a woman coming for an interview in the morning. Until we get someone else, Daphne and I will have to do."

She still looked surprised, but accepted his announcement. He was fairly sure she didn't mind Mrs. Chang was leaving. They spent the afternoon in the garden, Edwin supporting her as she walked. For dinner, he cooked steaks on the grill and made a large salad and heated some French bread he found in the freezer. Their conversation was mostly about him. At nine o'clock she looked tired. He took her to her room, nervously unbuttoned her blouse and skirt, laid out the nightgown she pointed to and left the room while she changed. When she called him back, he put her in bed, checked that her paging device was in place, kissed her good night and left the room. Daphne had arrived and was waiting downstairs.

"Henry called me. You had the gall to fire Mrs. Chang?" she asked in a rage, her slur pronounced. Edwin wondered how she'd been able to drive home.

"More like good sense. They just didn't fit together. Mother didn't seem happy," he said, fighting not to tell his sister to stuff it up her butt.

"How can you tell she's not happy? She's a stroke patient. She can't tell you what she really feels," Daphne argued. "She's Henry's and my mother too. You didn't have the courtesy to consult us."

That was all he could take.

"How the hell would you two know what she can communicate? You're running around town protecting your social status, and Henry's busy puffing himself up to run for governor or something. If either of you would take the time to pay attention to your beloved mother, you'd know she's not happy—she communicates just fine."

"Well, little boy blue comes home and has all the answers. We're the ones who've had to endure her illness all these years," she spat back.

"Well, all the enduring you have to do now is being pleasant to your mother, and help her shower in the morning. After that, you're off the hook. I've made plans for her care," he replied.

Daphne was smart enough and self-centered enough to know she didn't want him mad enough to upset her next social extravaganza at the hotel. She settled into a quiet pout. Edwin poured himself a bourbon on the rocks and took a walk in the garden. The stars were bright and the moon was full. He wanted to cool down after his bout with Daphne.

What a control freak. The whole world is all about her, and she uses guilt as her main weapon, he thought as he headed back into the house and to bed.

chapter

ELEVEN

The next morning, Edwin heard a car pull up out front. He opened the front door and Mrs. Martinez was standing there with two suitcases and a large smile. She and Edwin hugged and Edwin took the suitcases up to the housekeeper's quarters. As he walked past his mother's bedroom on the way back down, Mrs. Martinez was already helping her dress and the two women were laughing like sisters. Twenty minutes later, Mrs. Martinez brought her into the breakfast room before going into the kitchen to cook breakfast.

His mother smiled at him through her tears. "Ank you. A nice gift," she said in her halting language.

Mrs. Martinez brought juice for both of them. "He's the good son, Mimi," Mrs. Martinez said and hugged Edwin again.

"I'm sure you girls have some catching up to do. I'll take the limo back to the hotel. Mart, don't get Mother into too much trouble, and you have my permission to throw Daphne out if she gives you any problems. If she's not all sweetness and light, my cell-phone number is on the phone pad," he said. He kissed them both, picked up his things and left. He could hear them talking excitedly as he went. The limo driver stopped to let him drop his stuff off at the loft before taking him to the hotel.

It was mid afternoon as he entered the lobby. Donna Lane waved urgently at him.

"You waving to say hello or do you need me?" Edwin asked.

"Mr. Chambers sent me down to ask if you can come to his office," Donna replied.

"He wants the furniture back?" Edwin asked, smirking.

"No. He had a call from the lawyers for the Sandlers, the people staying in the room with the dead girl. They haven't gotten much cooperation out of the police getting a report, and they're threatening to sue the police department and us. He wants to talk to you about it."

Edwin thought it strange Chambers would want his opinion on the matter, but he remembered Chambers had not dealt with the situation when it happened.

"Just tell Leonard I was there and I'll handle it for him. So, you want to know how lunch with Henry went?"

"It's none of my business. He's your brother, I'm just an employee," she replied shyly.

"B.S.! You have a future at stake, and I need someone to trust as I try to figure things out. A.D. trusted you. That's good enough for me. The lunch went pretty much as I expected. Henry's still full of himself. Based on his answers to some of my questions, I think he's lying. I can't figure out if he has something to hide."

"My sense is he plays it very close to the vest. He did that more and more as A.D. got sicker. If you asked him about money or finances, I'm positive you didn't get the whole story. I don't even think Mr. Chambers knows a great deal about the finances except for the daily numbers."

"That's what I asked, and it seemed to spoil Henry's appetite. I cut out before the fourth martini. Did he always drink that much at lunch?"

"Lately, he always meets Mr. Chambers in the bar in the late afternoon. I see the complimentary bar checks and they're big," she said.

Edwin went to his office in the sales area. Bill Smith, the sales director, was standing at the reception desk. Bill was a throwback to the old days of hotel sales. He could drink with the best of them and not show it until he got the order. Comfortable with any personality type, he was ruthless as a salesman. He hated the competition and loved to take bookings from them.

Ten years ago, Bill learned the head of a group he was trying to book was staying at the competition. Somehow, probably thanks to a good bottle of scotch or a fifty-dollar bill, he got a room service uniform from the competition. At seven the next morning, he wheeled a full deluxe breakfast on a covered room-service table into the competing hotel, went up the service elevator and delivered the breakfast to the prospective client. That night the client moved to the St. George, and Bill got the group's business. The competition's sales director threatened everything from lawsuits to bodily harm until Bill took his ex-pro football butcher to one of the sales association luncheons and introduced him as his assistant-in-training.

"It's been a long time, Bill and you're just the man I wanted to see. It doesn't look like we're setting any records in occupancy," Edwin said.

"Things have changed in this town. The competition will cut rates at the drop of a hat, and the customer knows it. The city is overbuilt, and most of these kids who call themselves sales directors would rather cut prices than sell," Bill replied.

"I'd like to understand the market, but right now I have something to take care of," Edwin said as he shook Bill's hand.

A few minutes later, Donna entered Edwin's office and explained, "The Sandlers' attorney claims his clients have suffered great mental anguish and nobody seems to care. He said the city's failure to respond is causing additional stress."

"What do you normally do in a case like this?"

"In the past, I've contacted our insurance company and also our attorneys," Donna replied.

"Captain LeRoy seemed to have a pretty good reason for not releasing the report. It might be best to contact our lawyers and leave the insurance company out of it until we can speak to the captain. Why don't we get Wally Callahan up here?" Edwin asked.

A few minutes later, there was a knock on the door and Wally Callahan entered and greeted them in his normal matter-of-fact manner. "What's up?"

Edwin explained the situation. Wally thought it best to talk with the captain and pushed some numbers on his cell phone. The captain was at lunch. Wally told him what was happening and that they didn't want to interfere with the investigation. He handed the phone to Edwin.

"Thanks for letting me know. You can give your lawyers the basics. They can start to think about their reply," Captain LeRoy said.

Edwin asked Donna to get Justy LaGrange on the phone. Two minutes later she handed him the line.

"Thanks for taking the call, Justy. We have a bit of a situation here and need your help," Edwin started.

"Not at all. That's why we get our obscene fees. What can we do to help?"

Edwin went over the situation with the Sandlers.

"It appears to be a bit dicey, but not too large a problem. If I may suggest, we have a new associate in our office. Rather than charging for a partner's time at this point, I suggest I have her get involved. She's young, but she worked at the Department of Justice for a couple of years, and has a good head for dealing with people. Of course, I'll oversee it," Justy suggested.

"You wouldn't be giving your old client a rookie, would you?" Edwin asked.

"She's my niece. I wouldn't subject her to anything she couldn't handle. She also played a key role in those multiple murders on the West Coast for the FBI. She's seen much worse than this," Justy said.

"You haven't under-represented us yet. Let's go with it," Edwin said. "What's her name and when will we hear from her?"

"She's right here. Jennifer Lee Brown—she prefers Lee—meet Edwin Christian," Justy said.

Edwin flushed. The girl had heard his rookie comment.

"Hello. I look forward to working with you. Thanks for taking a chance on me," a soft voice said.

Edwin recognized a zinger when he heard one, even if delivered by someone who sounded like a college freshman. His embarrassment turned to curiosity. Her comment was strong, but came wrapped in an almost-innocent voice.

"I look forward to meeting you, Lee. When can we get together?"

"I can stop by the hotel after work. Would five-thirty be convenient?"

"That's fine. Just stop at the concierge desk. Our concierge, Jack Vincent, will find me," Edwin said.

"See you then, Mr. Christian."

Edwin thanked Justy and hung up, trying to picture the person with the young soft voice. He thought it had a sensuous touch.

He went outside to follow up with Bill Smith. Vinnie DeTesta, the banquet manager, and Bill were in a heated discussion.

"Come on, Bill. I know we need the money, but naked girls in the ballroom for lunch?" Vinnie asked. "Let me guess — they want specially decorated chicken breasts and rump roast on the menu."

"That's not a bad suggestion. I think they'd like that," Bill replied.

Vinnie rolled his eyes. Bill saw the inquisitive look on Edwin's face and explained the situation. The Bar Owners and Operators Brotherhood, affectionately known as BOOBs, was not an official association, but it elected officers and had an outside executive run the annual meeting, where they shared information and talked about new entertainment trends. They were serious and successful business people, but many liked to let their hair down. They took over the entire hotel and drove the staff to exhaustion. Parties in the hospitality suites went on around the clock. The hotel didn't make much money on the booze because the association paid a small corkage fee per bottle and the liquor distributors supplied the booze. They did fill the hotel and, counting the food revenue, it was a lucrative booking. Wally Callahan would move into the hotel and hire off-duty police to bulk up the security force and handle any bizarre situations without calling in regular police. Putting conventioneers in jail was not good for repeat business.

"What's with the naked women in the ballroom?" Edwin asked.

"The BOOBs have a special session of exotic dancer previews. More of them are getting into the gentlemen's club business, and they invite the top exotic dancers who tour the country to come and show their stuff, so to speak. It's a three-hour lunch with a stage and interview area so the girls and the owners can get together and talk about bookings," Bill explained.

"Are we hiring for the lounge?" Edwin asked.

"I don't think we could afford the brass pole right now," Bill replied.

For the next hour, they discussed the sales situation for the hotel and for the city. The larger chains had system-wide loyalty programs giving repeat guests points for goods, vacations and those coveted airline frequent-flyer miles. It was becoming increasingly hard for an independent hotel to compete. The growth of the Internet was also cutting into business. Internet shoppers provided an increase in rented rooms, but the rates were often drastically reduced. The age of the hotel and the lack of upkeep had also put it behind its shiny new competitors in the traveling public's perception of its quality.

Edwin was starting to get depressed over his new inheritance. He was curious about the failing financial situation of the hotel. He started to ask questions about changes in the past year. Vinnie and Bill had approached Henry with their concerns about the noncompetitive condition of the hotel only to get a pep talk and a lecture on economic austerity. Chambers cited the fact that the hotel had a large mortgage to pay and said he was helpless in getting anyone to invest capital to improve the hotel's condition. He left the impression that if they didn't like it, they could leave. Both thought Chambers was Henry's puppet. They agreed that while Chambers was powerless and not the least bit helpful to the staff, his wife Victoria had brass balls bigger than basketballs. She was demanding and treated the staff like they were hand servants, especially housekeeping. She had put housekeepers, with the exception of the impervious Mary Rodriguez, in tears with insults. Half of them didn't speak enough English to understand all she said, but the delivery left little in doubt.

She also tried to make Jack Vincent's life miserable. Her daily calls demanding he get her tickets to entertainment events that had been sold out for months always finished with, "Jack, my darling, that's why you're the concierge." Jack was not a complainer, but he was totally frustrated by the situation.

Donna entered the office to remind Edwin he had a meeting with the attorney soon.

"Thanks for your time, guys. When I get the financial statements, I'll go over them with you. And I can't wait to meet the Queen of Darkness," he said with a smile.

chapter

TWELVE

The lobby was busy. The loud and laughing Bar Owners and Operators Brotherhood were checking in. Edwin looked into the bar. It would be a good, informal place for him and Lee to talk if it wasn't filled with BOOBs. It was empty with the exception of Marty Rosenbloom, the bartender, who was wiping glasses.

"You ever wear any of those glasses out, Marty?" Edwin asked.

Marty broke into a broad smile. "At six dollars a drink, who wants to see spots?"

"I should have come by earlier, Marty. I haven't forgotten old friends," Edwin said as an apology.

"Not to worry, kid. I know ya love me."

Edwin had a special affection for the seventy-eight-year-old bartender. Marty Rosenbloom had taught Edwin a lot about life and about people. Marty had joined the hotel staff at the age of forty-eight, just after his wife died. Marty wanted a place with people around him to lessen the loneliness. Marty's life had been one of hard times and good times. At nineteen, he was drafted into the Second World War and assigned to an infantry battalion. He landed in France just after the Normandy invasion and fought on to Germany. He faced the frozen forests of Belgium in the middle of the Battle of the Bulge. Edwin asked Marty if the freezing cold was the worst thing about the battle. To Marty, the worst part had been to shoot the young teenagers Hitler had forced into service in this last-ditch effort.

Marty's unit liberated a concentration camp. Marty was proud and sad about it. What he witnessed would be with him for a lifetime. Marty only talked about his war experiences once. Edwin always thought Marty's love for people and his patience as he listened to the most nonsensical personal problems of the patrons was Marty's way of making up for what he saw that day in the concentration camp.

Edwin told Marty about his meeting with the young female lawyer. Marty asked if she was good-looking.

"I've only talked to her on the phone. She's Justy LaGrange's niece. We have a hotel matter to discuss," Edwin said, a little defensively.

"Must have been a pretty interesting voice," the old bartender replied.

"Just don't stare or hover over us when I bring her in," Edwin said.

"Can I smile if she's ugly? Justy LaGrange ain't the best looking guy at the dance," Marty asked.

"Just behave yourself. I'm going to get her now."

The lobby was getting more congested. The exotic dancers were checking in and they were obviously proud of their well-sculpted breasts. *Boobs for the BOOBS.* A few well-muscled men in suits were standing in the corners of the lobby. He remembered the off-duty police for extra security. They were focused on the crowd and obviously enjoying the sight of the ladies.

Jack Vincent was sitting in his chair in animated conversation with someone sitting across from him. As Edwin approached, Jack stood up.

"Mr. Christian, this is Lee Brown," Jack said in a gracious tone.

The person in the chair stood up and offered her hand. She was just over five feet tall with her hair in a French twist. She wore a blue business suit with a skirt and a starched white shirt. Edwin noticed her athletic legs and sparkling eyes. He was concentrating on her girl next-door looks, when he noticed her grip was very firm. He realized that he was staring as she said, "Mr. Christian, it's a pleasure to meet you. My uncle speaks highly of your family."

Her voice still intrigued him.

"I thought we could talk in the bar instead of my office. It will be quiet and we won't be interrupted. Do you mind?" he asked.

"It's been a long day in the legal world. A casual place would be nice," she replied.

"Thanks for meeting Ms. Brown, Jack," Edwin said for lack of anything else to say.

"Jack was enlightening me on your present guests. An interesting group," she said.

"Jack is a very enlightening fellow. I hope he didn't give away any hotel secrets," he said, with a sweep of his hand, "The bar is this way."

Without thinking, he offered his arm to escort her. She looked at him for a second, but politely took his arm and thanked him.

What a dork I am. Why did I offer my arm? I'm acting like I'm in high school. He looked back at Jack in bewilderment. Jack was smiling like a Cheshire cat in a fish factory.

As they entered the bar, Marty was just hanging up the phone. He wore the same smile Jack had

Jack called Marty. The joke's on me. I'm fighting terminal embarrassment and these two old farts are having the time of their life.

Lee chose a seat in the corner and sat down. Edwin stood there with a smile on his face, not knowing what to say.

"By the way, please call me Lee and I like a person who can laugh at himself," she said.

The eyes and the smile were captivating. He was impressed with her quick uptake on the situation and the straightforward way she handled it.

"I'm sorry. I've been in the jungles for the past year. My social graces are a bit rusty," he offered. "Can Marty get you something to drink?"

"If you don't mind, even though this is business, an Absolut martini would hit the spot. It's been one of those days," she replied.

"Would the lady like some veggies in that?" Marty asked.

"Lee, this is Marty Rosenbloom. He's kind of a fixture around here and a wise man who is sometimes a smart ass," Edwin interrupted.

"And I'm sure the customers love him," she said with a smile toward Marty.

The old bartender beamed. Lee asked for olives and the drink straight up. Edwin ordered an ale.

They began trying to get to know each other. She had graduated with honors in psychology and then went into law. The psychology and her uncle's contacts had gotten her into the Justice Department. Her superiors had steered her into some pretty tough cases; fanatics who hated the government, drug dealers and more than one grisly murder. They liked the fact she had a psychology background. They especially liked her calm manner and her soft young voice. Some of the hardest criminals found it easy to talk to her and spilled more than they would to an FBI agent.

She worked out to relieve the pressure. She liked staying in shape, and had been a gymnast and played soccer in high school and college. The discipline had stuck.

Edwin sat quietly and let her talk. She was very casual and open about herself.

She asked him about his background. Her questions led from one to another in a natural rhythm. Edwin realized she thought every one of them out before she asked them. *She paid attention in interrogation classes.* She was interested in his athletics, travels, and his time in South America. She questioned him about his grandfather and how Edwin saw the future of the hotel. They had talked for forty-five minutes without mentioning the matter she had come to discuss.

"I think I'm taking too much of your time on non-legal matters. I know you're busy," he offered.

"Don't be silly. I get enough law all day long. Don't worry, this was not a billable hour," she replied.

I'd be willing to pay if you asked.

"You're the client. What do you need?" she asked. She opened her purse and took out a small pad of paper and a pencil.

"That pad's pretty small for a lawyer," he offered.

"In the government, we had to move fast. Carrying a briefcase most of the time was out of the question. I learned to use this size pad from the cops I worked with."

Edwin imagined this petite woman spending time with police officers like Wally Callahan. It seemed incongruous, but with her personality, she could handle it. He could only guess how many cops had told her, "My wife just doesn't understand me."

"So, why don't you fill me in?" she asked.

"I'm not completely sure how much I can tell you. The captain wants to keep this very quiet for now," Edwin replied.

"We're under client / lawyer privilege here. I can't repeat anything you say. Besides, in my business, you don't want to be on the wrong side of the good guys."

For the next ten minutes Edwin explained the details of the situation. Lee listened carefully and took notes with an almost shorthand character to them. She didn't interrupt until he was done.

After sitting for a minute and looking back over her notes, "It would seem the best thing to do is stretch this out for a while. Or we could offer a small settlement, but the type of attorney they've retained will be looking for the big bucks. They also might take our offer as an admission of guilt. If Captain LeRoy doesn't want to give up a copy of the report, going to your insurance company is out. The last option is for me to find a professional, but direct way to tell them to bug off," she concluded.

I guess she has played with the big boys.

She gave him a few moments to digest what she had offered.

"I kind of like the "Bug Off" letter," he replied thoughtfully.

She smiled, "It will buy us some time, and we can coordinate with Captain LeRoy. I think he'll appreciate the cooperation."

She took the last sip of her drink and gently took the olive from the glass and ate it. He thought the gesture exciting. Not as bawdy as the eating scene in *Tom Jones*, but sensuous. He asked if she wanted another. He didn't want the conversation to end. She declined and thanked him for the drink and got up slowly to leave.

"I'll get the letter drafted tomorrow and get you a copy to approve."

She hesitated for a moment and pulled out the pencil and small pad again. She wrote on it and handed him one of the small pages. "If you need to talk to me after hours, this is my cell phone and home phone."

He could feel the smile beginning to crease his mouth and fought to hide it. The look in her eyes and the return smile told him he hadn't done a very good job.

"Thanks for your time and interest. I enjoyed our conversation," he replied, almost sheepishly. He was trying to judge her level of interest but she wasn't going to give everything away. As he was shaking her hand, Bill Smith, the director of sales, entered the bar and motioned to Edwin. He walked Lee to the door where Bill was standing and said goodbye as she left. He didn't take the time to introduce her. Why start rumors?

Jack and Marty would take care of that.

In many hotels an old superstition still exists. There are no 13th floors. In keeping with that tradition, there will be no chapter 13. Of course, if you are staying on the 14th floor, you are actually on the 13th, but hotels are places designed and decorated to make you feel comfortable.

chapter

FOURTEEN

Edwin and Bill Smith watched as Lee walked through the lobby. "Cute. Nice gams and an athletic ass," Bill said.

"That's Lee Brown, one of our attorneys," Edwin replied. "What can I do for you?"

"We've got a room problem and Chambers is off property," Smith replied. "I need someone in authority to get Mason to do the right thing. He's the one who screwed up in the first place."

"Like what and how?" Edwin inquired.

Smith explained there had been a double booking Mason hadn't caught. The Bar Owners and Operators had all rooms reserved starting that night. Mason had booked in a young girl's soccer group for ten rooms and didn't check the departure date carefully. They were staying over tonight which meant ten rooms of BOOBs had to be "walked," or displaced for a night to another hotel. He explained Mason was not cooperating with his request to move the girls. Based on the fact that they may never be back and the Bar Owners might, Bill thought the best thing was to move the soccer team. Mason had stood behind the local law that if a guest was paid up, they could not be forced out unless they were a disturbance or damaged property. Bill explained any guest walked received a night's rent, transportation to the other hotel and a phone call home to tell their loved ones where they were. The policy was similar in all national chain hotels to be competitive. It would apply to the BOOBs or the girl's group.

"Does he really think the girls' coach wants her girls in a hotel with the Bar Owners and their guests?" Edwin asked incredulously.

"Who the hell knows? He likes policies. They protect some pretty crappy decisions," Smith replied.

"O.K., let's go see Mr. Mason. Gams mean legs, right?" Edwin asked.

"Yeah, legs. I forgot how young you are."

Robert Mason was nowhere to be seen. They walked a short distance beyond the front desk and entered the back door to the front office. Mason was on the phone. It didn't sound like a business call. When he saw the two enter he made a quiet apology and hung up.

"I guess this is about the soccer team. We can't put paid guests out. I explained that to Mr. Smith," he offered in defense.

"Robert, I really don't give a damn how this happened or what your interpretation of the law is. I want to resolve it," Edwin said in a stern voice.

"Have you secured the ten rooms for the guests to be walked?" Smith asked.

"Of course. They're at the Hudson," Mason replied in an annoyed voice.

"Why not move the girls?" Edwin asked

"I already told Mr. Smith that it's the law. Besides, they're out around town and I can't reach them," Mason replied.

"They're flying out tomorrow afternoon, right?" Smith asked.

Mason nodded his head.

"The new Merrill at the airport has an indoor pool and a good restaurant. Maybe the coach would welcome a kid-friendly place," Smith replied.

"They're out of the hotel. I don't know how to reach them," he replied.

Smith went to the computer and asked Mason for the coach's name and entered it. The registration for the woman came up. He picked up a pencil and wrote down a phone number.

"She left her cell number in case of an emergency at home. I think we can reach her," Smith said to Edwin.

Edwin asked Bill, "Who do you know at the Merrill who can do you a favor?"

"The general manager used to work here. I'll call him," Smith replied. He dialed a number from a small black book in his pocket. After a short conversation he hung up.

"Done deal, if we can get the coach to agree. We can take them in the stretch limos we're using for the VIPs. That might sweeten the pot," he said to Edwin.

"Thanks, Bill. Why don't you have Jack Vincent make the call to the girls' coach? He has that nice soft manner. He won't talk about the boobs in the lobby and the booze running in the halls to get the point across," Edwin suggested.

Smith left the office with a smile. Edwin turned to Mason. "We can talk about this and your observations about the hotel when the Bar Owners are gone. Don't you think your team could use some help out there?" he asked in a voice, with no emotion at all.

Mason got the point and headed to the front desk.

The commotion caused by the BOOB's check-in was increasing. Across the lobby, Jack Vincent on the phone, motioned to Edwin and pointed discreetly across the lobby at one of the off-duty cops who was moving through the lobby and shook his head. Edwin looked where Jack was pointing. A dancer was lifting her tee shirt. Her large breasts had jeweled hoops hanging from each pierced nipple. The men around her were clapping and hooting. Edwin moved forward and intercepted the off-duty cop. He introduced himself as the hotel owner. The cop stopped and shook his hand. Edwin motioned him aside.

"There's going to be a lot of that going on for the next two days. As long as there's no public sex, I'd just as soon let it go — unless a guy exposes himself. Then I might ask him to put it away. I especially don't want to do anything now. It might start things off on the wrong foot," Edwin explained.

The cop smiled.

"You make the rules. This'll make it an interesting job. I'll pass it on to the other guys. I'm the senior officer," the cop replied.

"Thanks, I'll make sure Wally Callahan gets the message too," Edwin replied.

"Wally's going to love this," the cop said.

"Obviously, you know Wally," Edwin replied.

"He's a legend. There's a lot of Wally Callahan stories used at the Academy in training," the cop answered.

"Are they the how-to-do-it, or the how-not-to-do-it type?" Edwin asked.

"Actually, they're the how-to-do-it type."

"God bless the city," Edwin said.

Edwin saw Jack had hung up the phone and went over to his desk.

"The soccer girls are taken care of. They'll be back in an hour and we'll whisk them off to the Merrill at the airport. The leader was hesitant at first, but with the noise in the lobby and some of the language, she agreed pretty fast," Jack told him.

"I'm glad you made the call from the lobby for effect."

"I did take drama classes in college. You have to set the scene to be credible," Jack said with a grin.

"How do we get them in and out without a lawsuit? I don't think the soccer league gives trophies for the stuff going on around here," Edwin asked.

"Slim Johnson will have two bellmen and they, along with Wally, can escort them through the lobby. Wally's people can quietly let the people in the lobby know they have to behave for a few minutes, and we can shut off an elevator for their use only while they pack and leave. I'll stick around too, just in case," Jack replied.

In ten minutes Bill Smith and Jack had solved a problem that Mason was happy to ignore. Edwin thought about Mason. *There's more there than meets the eye.*

"You look tired, Boss. Why don't you take off? Everything is covered here," Jack offered.

"I think I might just do that. A walk and a quiet dinner sound good right now."

"How did it go with Ms. Brown? She seemed very nice," Jack asked.

"She did seem nice. Very professional in an informal way. Her experience and directness aren't what you'd expect from her voice and looks," Edwin replied.

"And that fascinates you," Jack said with his Cheshire cat smile.

"Don't read too much into that, Jack."

"Reading people is my business. You're not that hard to read on personal issues. You're good at hiding emotions in business things like with Mason, but not around Ms. Brown," Jack replied.

"Great, she probably thinks I'm a total jerk just out of the jungles."

"I don't think so. She seemed very interested and she had a smile on her face for no apparent reason when she left the hotel. Now go home and get that quiet dinner," Jack instructed.

Edwin thanked Jack and gave him his cell number and asked to make sure Wally Callahan and the manager on duty for the evening had it. He started toward the back door.

chapter

FIFTEEN

Edwin decided to check on the kitchen. Chef Mazzari and his team were working on massive trays of hors d'oeuvres. The cook's beer sat in an iced bus pan on the stainless steel table. It had always been a policy of the hotel, like the old European ones, to give beer to the kitchen staff. In fact, in some union hotels it is written into the union contract. It was hot work and the beer was one small pleasure during a long hard day.

"I'd tell you to grab an apron, but you look like hell. Why don't you go home or go see that little girl you had in the lounge?" the chef said.

"I understand she wasn't old enough to drink, but Marty didn't want to card her and embarrass you," Andy Scott said in a friendly, heckling tone.

"How does this stuff get around so fast? Never mind, I don't think I want to know. That was purely business. She's from our law firm," Edwin replied.

"Yeah. Bill Smith said she was pretty firm, all right," the big butcher said.

"I'm getting out of here before this degenerates any further. Have a good night." Edwin was smiling as he left.

As he passed the cage at the back door, the security monitor that shows the views of all fifty-six cameras around the hotel was paused on the camera on the hospitality-suite floor. The security guard noticed Edwin's eyes on the monitor. On the screen, two bare-breasted dancers were walking down the hall with two well-oiled conventioneers.

"Not your ordinary evening I guess. You are looking at the other cameras once in a while, aren't you?" Edwin asked.

The young man reached for the button to put the monitor back into the rotating mode. Edwin reached out and stopped him. The guard looked puzzled until he turned and looked at the screen. Mr. and Mrs. Chambers had just come onto the floor, heading for their apartment. They were trying not to look at the topless dancers and their escorts. While Mr. Chambers' look was one of amusement, Mrs. Chambers looked like she had just consumed an entire case of lemons. She strutted with the head-up gait of a British palace guard. Mr. Chambers walked just far enough behind her so she couldn't see his roving eyes. She turned around abruptly and startled him. There were words exchanged, and she continued on her way holding onto his arm. The young security guard was fighting to keep from laughing out loud.

Edwin smiled at him, "You married?"

"Not to anyone like that. My wife would think it was funny," he answered.

"I don't think we want to be part of the Chambers' next conversation," Edwin offered. "Anyway, make sure you look at all the cameras tonight. With this gang in the hotel, who knows what could happen?"

"Yes, sir, I will. Have a good night."

"I'm sure you will," Edwin chuckled.

Outside the night was cool. He decided to take a walk before he headed home. As he rounded the corner of the hotel, he saw a gleeful bunch of young girls being hustled into a long limo by a red-faced coach. It was 7:30 and the city was quiet. He kept walking. He didn't relish the idea of cooking at home. He saw Jimmy's bright red sign and remembered the corned-beef sandwiches. As he entered, he felt like he was stepping back in time. Memories of his childhood visits flooded his mind. The times he had come here with Wally Callahan and the patrons and their stories that had entertained him. He slowly approached the bar and sat down on the nearest barstool. A familiar face appeared in front of him. It was Betty Sloan. She had been bartending at Jimmy's for over twenty-five years. Edwin remembered her long brown hair and sharp tongue. She had been quite the thing in the old days. She was now twenty pounds heavier, which didn't sit well on her small five-foot-three frame, but the smile was still warm and she had the same glint in her eyes.

"What'll you have, hon?" she asked.

"Hello, Betty. I'll have a draft ale and a corned-beef sandwich with fries."

"Sure, hon. You been in here before?"

"A long time ago," he answered.

She yelled his order into the window at the end of the bar and pulled the draft. As she walked back toward him, she reached under the bar and pulled out a bowl. She set the draft down and placed the bowl full of peanuts in front of him.

"Sorry about your grandfather, kid. Now there was a man with a good soul," she said, reaching out and patting his hand.

"You don't forget much do you?" he asked.

"Bartenders have good memories for drinks and faces. You've changed a bit, but not that much. I guess you heard Jimmy passed too, about a year ago," she said.

"That's two good souls gone," he replied.

"Yeah, but the corned beef lives on in his memory," she said.

Edwin felt a large hand on his shoulder and turned to see who it was.

"I thought I was supposed to buy your first Jimmy's corned beef," Captain John Moose LeRoy said and sat down next to Edwin.

"Jimmy never let you buy anything in here before," Betty said. She reached for a glass and drew a draft Budweiser for the cop.

"There's a first time for everything, love," the captain said.

"No way. Jimmy would turn over in his grave. You want one too?" she asked.

"Why not? Can't have the kid eating alone."

Betty looked Edwin up and down. She grabbed his chin in a motherly gesture and said, "I don't think this boy will be eating alone for long."

Edwin tried not to blush. Betty moved down the bar to order another corned beef. Edwin took another sip of ale and began bringing the captain up to date on the session with the lawyer. He told him about the letter to the guests' attorney to buy time for the investigation. Edwin told him Lee Brown had thought of it.

"If Lee writes it, it'll be a doozie," LeRoy said.

"You know her?" Edwin asked. "I didn't think she had been in town for very long."

"She's been here before when she was on assignment for the Feds. I worked with her on a couple of murders connected to a drug cartel. Pretty grisly stuff," the Captain replied.

The victims had been federal informers and were tied into a drug cartel. LeRoy's squad had made an arrest on another matter, and the guy tied in. The FBI and DEA got involved, and Lee Brown showed up to interrogate the suspect.

"Did the guy talk?" Edwin asked.

"Damndest thing I ever saw — this little girl in a room with a real thug who's handcuffed to a chair. Not exactly your perfect atmosphere for conversation," the cop said. "After three hours in a hundred-degree room, we had the guy's life story and enough to go on to help crack the cartel. Lee had sweated through her blouse, but she's tough and doesn't mind discomfort if it gets results. She was the one who told us to turn the air conditioning off. She never raised her voice for the whole three hours. Every cop in the office wanted to hit on her. One of my guys tried. In three sentences, she had destroyed the guy's macho image, and he didn't even know it. Lee Brown is one sharp broad, and when you get to know her, she's a very nice person," the captain finished.

Betty delivered the sandwiches. As they ate, the captain explained a meeting he had with Wally late in the afternoon. He had taken an enhanced picture from the hotel's security camera over to the hotel. Wally identified one of the people in it as Robert Mason. It showed Mason and the front office manager of the Merrill entering the St. George together on the night of the murder. He and Wally were convinced both murders had someone inside each hotel involved. They had decided to wait to approach the young men until they had more evidence. On his way out of the hotel, the captain had shown the picture to Jack. When he asked Jack if he had ever seen the two together before, Jack said he had seen them in the Tiger's Tail a couple of times on Thursday nights when it was Have It Your Way night. Those nights were attended by gay and straight people of both sexes and there were both male and female dancers.

When he asked if Jack saw the two with anyone else, he replied that on two occasions they were with an older seedy-looking man. Jack didn't know who the guy was. The captain asked if he thought the two were gay. Jack told him his gaydar didn't make him think so. When Edwin asked what gaydar was, the captain explained many gay people have an almost sixth sense about other gay people. They can just pick them out. He also thought that some gays are very intuitive and have a special feeling for others. The captain had used the help of some of his gay friends in solving crimes. The whole idea used to drive Wally Callahan nuts, but he had to admit that some had a special gift.

"You think Jack would go along with my guys for a Have It Your Way night? We might be able to get a photo of Mason and his Merrill friend with the older guy he mentioned," the captain asked.

"I think Jack would be glad to, but Mason knows him," Edwin responded.

"Jack said Mason didn't recognize him before when he was out of his concierge monkey suit," LeRoy replied.

Edwin agreed to talk to Jack and put him in touch with the captain. They finished their sandwiches as they talked about A.D. and his relationship with LeRoy. There was a lot about A.D. Edwin had not known. Betty came up to ask if they wanted another beer. Edwin apologized, saying he was too tired. He asked for the check.

"Like I told you, if I gave the captain a check, Jimmy would roll over in his grave or knock this place down," she said.

Edwin reached in his pocket and threw a twenty on the bar.

"You didn't say anything about tipping."

"A.D. taught you well. This old broad appreciates it," Betty replied. She leaned across the bar and kissed each of the men on the cheek.

LeRoy offered Edwin a ride home, and as they pulled up to Edwin's place, the captain said, "If you're thinking of going any further with Lee, I'd let her make the first move. She's pretty definite about what she does and doesn't like. I think men especially fall into that category."

"What makes you think I'm interested in a short lawyer?" Edwin asked.

"How stupid do you think I am? I knew your grandfather, remember? The fruit doesn't fall far from the tree," the cop answered.

"Understood, and thanks," Edwin said as he closed the door of the car.

He noticed LeRoy was writing down his address. The cop wanted to make sure he took care of an old friend's grandson. Edwin climbed the front steps and turned and waved to the captain. His mind was filled with Lee Brown. His last thought was of her before he finally fell asleep: *I wonder what I do next about the woman with the soft voice that obviously has her act totally together?*

chapter

SIXTEEN

Edwin rolled over and looked at the clock. It was five-thirty a.m. He didn't remember when he had finally fallen asleep. He skipped his run and went to the hotel. Slim Johnson, the doorman and one of the off-duty cops were standing inside the lobby.

"I thought you worked outside," Edwin said to Slim.

"Slow day in my department, Boss. I just thought I'd take in the view of this beautiful lobby."

"Especially since it was redecorated with large-breasted live statuary," Edwin responded.

"I thought that was an especially nice touch. I'm glad Bill Smith thought of it and booked them in," Slim said.

The young cop was smiling and involuntarily nodding his head.

"I didn't know you were an art lover. Just don't let the limo drivers in on your show. We don't need a crowd," Edwin offered.

"Yes, sir. I became an avid art lover yesterday; and, no, I won't let the drivers in," Slim replied with a salute.

"Your dedication to duty is astounding," Edwin said.

When he got to his office he called the hotel operator and asked her to page Wally Callahan to his office. He called room service and ordered a small breakfast. On his desk were two large manila envelopes with a courier service bill on them. Inside were the financial statements for the hotel. There was a note attached from his brother offering any help he needed in reading them. *I bet he'd love to guide me through them.*

He called the office number for Chambers. He left a message he would like to see him and Chuck Castillano, the hotel controller, at 10 a.m. While he waited for Wally, he sorted through the financial statements. The hotel had been profitable until a year ago. He noted the questions he wanted to ask about the statements in the margins. There was a knock on the door and he called for the person to come in. An attractive college-aged young woman entered with a tray. Her nametag read EMILY.

"Good morning, Mr. Christian, your breakfast is here. Shall I put it on your conference table?"

When he looked up he noticed she was wearing black trousers, a starched formal shirt with a bow tie and a cummerbund.

"Emily, is that our normal room-service uniform?" he asked.

"No, sir. Mr. Callahan thought we should dress as differently from some of the convention attendees as possible," she replied. "I took the liberty of bringing coffee too, just in case you had forgotten to order it."

"Thanks, Emily. By the way, are all the room-service people wearing that formal attire?" he asked.

"No, just the female staff."

"Does that make you feel strange?" Edwin continued.

She hesitated for a moment. "It did when he first gave us the order, but after being up on the guest room floors, I'm glad I look business like."

"Are your trips up there educational?" he asked.

"I'm taking sociology at the university. I've had two courses in deviant behavior, but some of the stuff I saw yesterday wasn't covered in the courses," she replied with a grin.

"I'd always heard a room-service staff sees a lot of unusual things on their rounds," Edwin replied.

"I've seen every body type in the world and every weird thing you can find in a guestroom, and I've been propositioned a few times," she answered.

"Why do you work room service? Why not work in a bar or night club?" he asked.

"The money's good and the hours fit my schedule. In a bar it's mostly night hours. That's when I prefer to study. I also don't like the subculture and some of the people you meet in some bars. It works out better for me this way. I can take the occasional gross-out from a stranger, but I don't have to work with them every day."

Her pager went off so she put the check in front of him to sign. Even though the food was complimentary, everyone had to sign a check for cost control and accounting reasons. He signed it and laid a five-dollar bill on top.

"Thanks, but you really don't have to do that," she said.

"Emily, I only finished two years of college. Count it toward tuition," he replied. "And, thanks for the coffee."

She laughed, thanked him, and left to answer the page. He started to go back over the financial statements just as Wally appeared.

"Hot off the presses," Wally said.

"The security report?" Edwin asked.

"It's more like a script for *Animal House IV*. Those folks know how to party."

Edwin looked the two pages over as Wally sat humming an old striptease song. The report was written in brief sentences like a police report.

"So, we had one John Barnard relieving himself in the large palm tree in the lobby. Wanda Lot, I presume that's a female, naked with an unidentified male in the elevator as the doors opened to the lobby. A noise complaint about Room 812, where security found twelve men and ten women in a single room in various states of undress. One Fred Unger passed out in the freight elevator with an empty six-pack and a bottle of vodka. Ten other noise complaints for various rooms. One room-service server forcibly undressed and fondled by two females. A lot of guys I know would have gone along. They dream of that kind of thing," Edwin said.

"That's Rudy," Wally offered. "He's the most married-for-life guy you'll ever meet. He told me to let the incident go, but I think it's etched in his mind someplace."

"One obscene, but fairly unintelligible, phone call to the front desk from Room 314. Candi Lane, that can't be her real name, calling multiple rooms at four a.m. trying to find her boss, Fred Unger. Finally, four reports of public nudity that were discreetly handled by our off-duty police friends," Edwin paused. "I thought it would be worse."

"You're right, but that's only the stuff we know about. Twenty bucks says housekeeping will find at least five headboards down. Luckily, I think we got credit cards and maxed out the credit approval amount on each of them. These folks are really very professional and most are businesslike. There are always a few who go over the edge. It happens in a lot of groups, and you can't tell what to look out for by the name of the group," Wally replied.

"You mean our little front office manager did something right?" Edwin asked.

"Only after Jack told him to do it. He argued at first, but Jack can be very convincing. You've never seen him when he does his Rasputin imitation," Wally snickered.

"What's next?" Edwin asked.

"Today is the big show luncheon in the ballroom with the dancers stripping all the way. My guys and the off-duty cops will seal it off starting in an hour. The chef and sous-chef Edmunds will be the only service personnel allowed in. The chef even bought a new madras chef's hat. He wants to look good for our special guests. After that it's back to the same coverage we had last night. Oh, and I'm leaving men on every entrance from the outside. We don't want the press or any other notables in the hotel," Wally explained.

"Where will you be? Serving the buffet?"

"I might stick my head into the control room in the back balcony of the ballroom just to make sure things are O.K. I can get you a reserved seat up there if you like."

"Thanks, but I think I'll keep my dirty-old-man side to myself. You better get going. You're going to have a very eye-opening day. By the way, have you heard from Chambers or his wife this morning?" Edwin asked.

"No, but you should see the surveillance camera scenes from the corridor last night," Wally replied.

"I saw them on my way out. Mrs. Chambers looked pretty mad. We can't show them at the Christmas party, but it would be funny," Edwin replied.

"She was only upset because the girls obviously had a better plastic surgeon than she did. She's pretty proud of her set," Wally offered with a smile.

"I was going to invite Chambers and her to dinner. Now I won't be able to maintain eye contact all night," Edwin replied.

"They're not that great, but she'll show them off for you."

"I'll take a pass for now," Edwin said.

Wally Callahan left, humming the same striptease song as he shut the door behind him.

While Edwin waited, he found Lee Brown's business card and called the law firm. Lee answered.

"Counselor, this is Edwin Christian. How are you?" he asked, trying hard to sound anything but anxious.

"I'm great," she replied.

"I wanted to ask you about the letter. There's not a rush, but do you sign it or do I?" he asked.

"I think it best if I sign it as your attorney. That way we get lawyer to lawyer, and he has to communicate with me. I'll bring it over this afternoon for your approval."

Edwin thought for a minute. He wasn't sure if he wanted her in the hotel with the present guests around.

"Why don't we meet somewhere for dinner? That's if you don't have plans. I'd like to get out of the hotel and try a local restaurant," he said awkwardly.

"How about Italian? There's a great little restaurant two blocks south of Van diver Square on the corner of Eighteenth. Let's make it at seven-thirty so I can get back to my place and change into something casual. The name of the place is Café Tuscany," she said.

"I'll see you at seven-thirty. You want me to make the reservation?" he asked.

"I'll take care of it. Leo Rappoli is an old client of the firm."

She hung up before he did. He wondered if there was any meaning in that and decided he was getting paranoid.

There was a knock at his door, and Chambers and Chuck Castillano entered.

"Good morning, Mr. Christian," Castillano replied. "It's been a long time. You may not remember me."

"How could I forget my mornings behind the front desk?" Edwin replied. "You used to let me do the filing when I got bored. I hope you were able to find those cards I filed."

"We never lost a one. For a twelve-year-old, you did very well."

"And you made it to comptroller. That's great," Edwin said.

"I brought as many reports as I thought might be helpful," he started. "I'm prepared to go over the entire financial situation. I brought reports going back two years to show you the trends. But let's start with your specific questions first," Castillano offered.

Edwin looked at Chambers. He appeared aloof and far away.

"O.K. with you, Leonard?" he asked.

Chambers looked slightly startled and agreed.

For the next hour he asked questions about the occupancy steadily going down and what appeared to be heavy-handed cuts in expenses and salaries. He admitted that he was not a hotel financial person, but he continued to pursue his opinion that cutting staff might affect service and accelerate the decline in occupancy by upsetting guests. Chambers let Chuck answer the questions. When he finally spoke, he said, "When I got here, the mortgage was putting a strain on the cash position of the hotel. Your brother informed me your grandfather was upset about it and wanted anything possible to be done." Chambers' answer was delivered sternly.

"Did you talk to A.D. about it?" Edwin challenged.

"I never really had a conversation with A.D. Your brother handled the communications. He hired me and I reported to him in view of your grandfather's condition," Chambers answered.

The staff told me you were with A.D. on every visit. So you never talked to the man?

Edwin's phone rang. He listened and put his hand over the phone and asked Chambers, "Have you had any dealings with the Health Department inspectors since you've been here?"

Chambers shook his head no.

"I'll be down in just a minute," he said.

"What about the Health Department?" Chambers asked.

"We might have a small problem in the kitchen. I'll go down. Thank you for your honest answers, gentlemen," Edwin said. He noticed a stifled yawn from Chambers.

"By the way, how's Mrs. Chambers taking living on the same floor as our special bar owner guests?" Edwin asked.

Chambers replied, "Don't ask.Years of living in hotels didn't prepare her for this."

"I'm sorry for the inconvenience, but it will pay some of the bills. Thanks for coming," Edwin offered.

The two men acknowledged his thanks and left. Edwin headed to the kitchen.

chapter

SEVENTEEN

Edwin leaned his head into Donna's office and told her he would "be on property" and his cell was on. "On property" is a universal term hotel people use when they're out of their office and in the hotel. Of course, some use it liberally, like having their assistant use it whether they're on the property or out playing golf.

On his way to the kitchen, he thought about the conversation with Castillano and Chambers. *Why would they cut service and lose good employees just before a major new competitor opened? Had they over-reacted to the new competition by cutting rates as the occupancy declined? Who in their right mind would cut sales staff and advertising with a new competitor entering the market? If I wanted to kill the hotel, I couldn't have come up with a better plan.*

Chef Mazzari was waiting for him. He was pacing back and forth.

"You look very bent out of shape," Edwin said.

"I don't know why this guy is here, but he's killing us. We've never had problems with the Health Department, and this guy has a pad full of supposed violations and he hasn't left the storerooms and walk-in freezer yet," the chef replied. His slight Italian accent was stronger than ever and his words came at machine-gun speed.

Edwin let him finish. You don't interrupt a troubled man. When the chef was done Edwin asked, "From the sound of it, he's on a mission. Who is this guy?"

"His name is Simon Bailey. He's the number-two person in the department. I don't think he's done an inspection in ten years."

"We don't want him anywhere near the ballroom when the girls are there dancing at lunch. Can you get him in the ballroom now?" Edwin asked.

"I can try, but this guy is a real dictator. He's walking around like he owns the place and keeps mentioning closing violators down," the chef answered.

In one hour, the Bar Owners and Operators would be filing into the ballroom. "Go back in and give it a shot, Chef. I'm going to try to get more information on this guy and his visit. If you can't get him into the ballroom in the next half hour call me on my cell. We'll have to go to plan B," Edwin instructed.

"What's plan B?" the chef asked.

"I don't have the first friggin' idea, but we'll come up with something," Edwin replied.

Edwin thought about who would have some idea of the workings of the Health Department. Jimmy's staff came to mind. The restaurant and bar had been there for years and every city official went there. He stepped into the chef's office and found an old stained phone book. He called Jimmy's.

"Jimmy's," a familiar voice answered.

"Betty, it's Edwin Christian. I need a favor," he said.

"What kind of favor, kid? I'm not young anymore, love," she replied with a laugh.

"Actually, I need information on a city official," he replied.

"Who?" she asked.

Edwin explained the situation and asked how the Health Department worked inspections and if she knew anything about Simon Bailey.

Betty told him Simon Bailey, better known as BB Bailey for ball buster, was an authority freak. When he was turned down by the FBI and local police, he used his family connections to get into a position of authority in the city. He prided himself on busting restaurants and had cost a lot of operators a fortune by demanding unnecessary upgrades and improvements. He kept his job because he looked the other way for friends of certain politicians, including the mayor.

"Who can call him off?" Edwin asked.

Betty thought for a minute. "It might be more important to find out who threw him at you. It's not normal for BB Bailey to be doing inspections. Somebody doesn't like you, your grandfather, or the hotel. Whoever it is didn't have the guts to do it when A.D. was alive."

"While I'm figuring that out, can he close us down without notice?" Edwin asked.

"He can try, but unless there's some evidence of public sickness, you have two weeks to remedy his violations. Your attorney can appeal the report and notices immediately, unless you have something else to hide."

"Thanks, Betty," Edwin said and hung up.

Something else to hide? I've got a ballroom full of naked dancing women. That's what I've got to hide.

As he sat thinking, Wally Callahan called. Edwin told him of his conversation with Betty Sloan.

"He probably can't shut us down immediately, but he can leak a bad inspection report to the media. That would hurt big time, and it could get the Bar Owners and Operators in the news. We could lose a lot of customers," Wally said.

"You know anybody who can keep it out of the press in case that's his game?" Edwin asked.

"I know the city editor. I've done him a few favors over the years. His son had a nose-candy habit. I kept it quiet and let him get the kid into rehab instead of jail. The kid's a doctor now and doing well," Wally answered.

"Keep his phone number handy, we might need it today," Edwin responded.

"No sweat, Boss. You gonna let him in the ballroom?" Wally asked.

"I don't think we have a choice. I'll work on that. Can you talk to some of your contacts and find out who unleashed him on us?"

"Yeah, I'll nose around," Wally said and hung up.

The chef entered the small office, still fuming.

"Did Bailey leave? I hope," Edwin started.

"No such luck. I tried to get him into the meeting space, but he refused. He said he wanted to see it when it was set up with the buffet out. He saw the luncheon listed on the function sheet on the bulletin board. He's up on the floors with Mary Rodriguez now looking at guest rooms," the chef replied. "I called Bill Smith and he talked the BOOBs into holding the girls off until a little later. They'll start the lunch and bring the girls in after Bailey leaves. They understand health inspections more than we do."

"I'm worried about what he's going to see on the floors with the interesting guests we have in house," Edwin offered.

"I wouldn't worry about that. Mary showed up with a rooming list and the first housekeeping report on what rooms have been cleaned. She knows what rooms to show the bastard," the chef said.

As they sat and waited, the chef related what BB Bailey had noted so far. It was all made up or nitpicking stuff. He had written down every small detail from a paper towel dispenser to the stains on the chef's apron.

As they waited in the chef's office, a five-foot-eight man with a pudgy build and blotchy complexion, entered the kitchen followed by Mary Rodriguez. She was behind him sticking out her tongue. Edwin vowed he was not going to laugh. He stepped out of the office and offered his hand.

"Mr. Bailey, I presume. I'm Edwin Christian, the new owner of the hotel," he said.

"Well, the off-spring of A.D. Christian. He certainly left you with a few serious violations in this old place," Bailey replied without offering his hand. Edwin's hatred for BB Bailey was instantaneous.

"Actually, I wasn't aware of any. I hope your report will be helpful," Edwin answered.

"It might be more harmful than helpful if I have to shut you down. We're talking the health of the public here," Bailey said in a condescending voice.

Bull! Edwin wondered why Bailey was going to so much trouble to bluff and pressure him and the staff.

While Edwin was trying to maintain his cool with BB Bailey, Candi Lane, the exotic dancer, was up in one of the hospitality suites chugging her fifth Bloody Mary. She looked at her watch and remembered something about dancing in the ballroom at noon. She was convinced the flower tattoos on her breasts and the swooping multi-colored parrot just below her navel were her best costume. She left her clothes behind, put on a bathrobe, and proceeded in search of the ballroom.

Edwin just wanted to get BB Bailey into the ballroom and out. Billy Caponi, president of the BOOBs, had agreed with Bill Smith to hold the dancers off until twelve-thirty. When Bailey said he wanted to see the ballroom, Edwin was relieved. They might get this over with fast.

Candi Lane had made her way to the control room above the ballroom and instructed the two audio-visual guys her music started with "When A Man Loves A Woman" and went to "Flash Dance." She also wanted to be sure the big spotlight was on the center platform and they would be sure it followed her because she moved a lot and her tattoos were a big part of her show. She opened the bathrobe for emphasis.

Edwin, Chef Mazzari, and BB Bailey were entering the ballroom. On the backside of the ballroom, Danny Everett, another off-duty cop, had succumbed to the gallon of Colombian coffee he drank and had left his post at the ballroom service door. Candi Lane walked in unseen.

The lighting was only high enough to eat by and it was hard to make out the faces of the men who were well into the buffet and even further into the free bar and imported draft beer. Bailey walked to the first table and picked up a fork next to one of the participants. He looked at it with the help of a small penlight he took from his breast pocket.

"Look, butthead, if you're not going to clean it, put my things down," the bar operator said.

"Sorry, sir, I'm just here to protect the health of all your friends. And yours, of course," Bailey replied, putting the fork down gently.

Bailey retreated to the buffet and was pulling his meat thermometer out to check the temperature of the food. Edwin froze when "When a Man Loves a Woman" came blasting over the sound system. He was almost blinded by the huge spotlight. He saw two large breasts with flowers moving and a parrot tattoo being thrust at the audience. BB Bailey looked up and stared. He didn't breathe for a full twenty seconds. Bailey finally caught his breath and summoned Edwin by waving his finger at him.

"This is the icing on the cake. Nudity and food service do not go together. This is a serious violation. Consider your hotel closed for food service," Bailey shouted with glee in his voice.

Edwin was ready to panic when a loud voice came from behind them. The music stopped. Candi Lane gave a few more pelvic thrusts before grinding to a stop.

Edwin and Bailey turned around to see a very tall man dressed in Johnny Cash black standing behind them giving the cut signal by moving his extended finger across his throat. Bailey froze. Billy Caponi stood behind them. Caponi had played professional football for the local team, saved his money, and opened the Tiger's Tail Lounge ten years ago. Billy was distantly related to the mayor and had strong contacts in the city. Owning a popular club and doing favors brought privileges.

"Why is Ball-Buster Bailey slinking around my meeting and causing trouble?" his gruff voiced asked.

"I had a report of health violations. I was trying to protect your group from any problems," Bailey responded nervously.

"Well, BB, while we appreciate your concern, we're fully aware of the health codes, and we're sure you don't see any violations here. Besides, you haven't shut the Tiger's Tail down when we have luncheon buffets or Happy Hour snacks. I kinda thought you enjoyed your visits," Caponi said.

"Well, I've looked at the whole place and I haven't analyzed my notes yet," Bailey uttered.

"The only violations we might have in my friend's place here are the violations that happen when Candi up there gets to your table. Sit with me. We have a lot of catching up to do," Caponi said.

Bailey followed Billy to his table. Edwin looked at the chef and returned his smile. Caponi raised his big arm and moved it in a forward motion pointing at Candi Lane. The music started again and Candi started gyrating. The audience cheered and whistled.

Edwin caught Billy's eye and mouthed the words thank you. Caponi gave him the thumb-up sign and put his hand on BB Bailey's shoulder, pointed to the flowers on Candi Lane's swinging breasts and said something into Bailey's ear. Bailey was smiling as Billy got up and joined Edwin and the chef as Wally Callahan showed up.

"How's your ass, Wally? It's nice that these folks keep a cripple employed," Caponi said.

"For a booze and boobs seller, you're a very considerate human being," Wally replied.

"Thanks for your help. I can't figure why the number-two guy showed up," Edwin said.

"Maybe super snoop here can find something out," Caponi said.

"I'm already on it, but not hearing much," Wally offered.

"Anyway, thanks for the rescue. I didn't know where that was going with Bailey," Edwin said.

"I've been hassled by some of those folks in the past. It was my pleasure to help you out," Caponi answered. "I better get back in there and keep BB and the rest of the animals in check. Nice to meet you, Edwin. Stop by the club when you have a free night. I think the girls would enjoy meeting a stand-up guy. Of course, if you hang around with Wally too long, that might change too," Caponi said putting his big arm around Wally.

"The pot just insulted the kettle," Wally replied.

"Birds of a feather and all that crap, Wally," Caponi said, heading back into the ballroom.

"Interesting guy," Edwin said.

"You don't know the half of it, Boss." Wally said.

chapter

EIGHTEEN

In late afternoon, Edwin went home to dress for dinner with Lee. He walked to his apartment to decompress and think about the day's happenings. He kept coming back to the question of why the number-two person in the Health Department would do a lowly inspection.

For two hours that afternoon, Jack Vincent, the ever-steady concierge, had been with Captain LeRoy and two of his detectives in a small restaurant on the north side of town. They met to plan an undercover night at the Tiger's Tail to see if Jack could spot the older man who had been with Robert Mason and the front office manager from the Merrill Hotel.

The two detectives with LeRoy were quiet at first, sizing up the gay concierge. Jack considered adding a little "flaming queen" tone to his speech pattern for fun, but decided it might be lost on these two guys and played it straight. The captain introduced Jack to Bruce "Bubba" Hall and Frank Wright. As the conversation and lunch proceeded the two loosened up. The detectives were fascinated by Jack's hotel stories. When they discussed the operation at the Tiger's Tail, it was agreed it should take place the week after on the same night of the week Jack had seen the three men together.

"You think your guy Mason will recognize you in the bar?" Bubba asked.

"When I dress casually, I look a lot different than I do as a concierge. They didn't spot me before. If I'm with you guys, no offense, I don't think they'll ever make the hotel connection," Jack responded.

"No offense taken. We'll be dressed in our non-cop stuff which might make you look a hell of a lot straighter than us," Frank said.

They finished the planning and agreed to meet the next week at the Tiger's Tail.

After his head-clearing walk to his loft, Edwin was ready for his dinner with Lee. By now he felt relatively comfortable around her, but he was still nervous about their first date. An hour later, he was in front of a small Italian restaurant. He was fifteen minutes early and wondered if that would make him look too anxious. He was surprised when the door to the restaurant opened and Lee invited him in.

"I hope you haven't been waiting too long," he said.

"I always get here early to talk to the Rappoli family. Papa Leo gives me the greatest cooking tips," she answered.

Adele, the oldest Rappoli daughter, escorted them to a round booth, handed them menus and explained the specials.

"Should we have a drink before dinner or wait for the wine list when we order?" Lee asked.

"After this morning, I think I could use a bourbon first, if you don't mind," he sighed.

"That's fine with me. I'll have a martini."

"Woodford Reserve on the rocks for you, Edwin?" Adele asked.

"How did you know that?"

"Your grandfather ate here often," Adele replied.

"Do I look that much like A.D.?" Edwin asked.

"Not only look, but sound like him," Adele responded. She suggested they allow Papa to prepare A.D.'s favorite dishes. He would enjoy doing something special for Lee and the grandson of a valued customer.

They sat and sipped their drinks. Edwin began to talk about the appearance of the Health Department at the hotel, and how he found it curious that a person high up in the department would be the one to inspect. He told her he had Wally looking into it. She wanted to know how the whole thing turned out. He thought she seemed honestly interested. The antipasto arrived at the table. As they ate, Edwin began with the whole story of the Bar Owners and Operators Brotherhood. He went through some of the points that BB Bailey had noted on the hotel as violations. He related the chef's anger and belief that each point was trumped up. Lee got a good laugh out of the irreverence that Mary Rodriguez had shown to BB Bailey. Later, she got a bigger kick out of the story of how Mary had almost killed the pervert who grabbed one of her staff. Edwin could see the a-woman-after-my-own-heart look in her eyes. It made him like her even more.

As they talked, the staff served a variety of small portions of veal, chicken, beef, and some unbelievable pasta. A mild Chianti and a crisp Pinot Grigio accompanied the various courses. As the conversation continued, they got back to personal subjects. Lee seemed genuinely concerned that Edwin had done nothing since his return from South America to start a life. He asked her what she did other than law.

"My hours are long, but I get my exercise every day. I read at night. I like adventure and romantic history — an odd combination, according to my mother. I work on weekends at the SPCA to adopt pets out. I'm a sucker for cats and dogs. On Sundays, I go to early church and spend some time with my parents. My father has always wanted me to take up golf, but I haven't found the time or commitment — and I don't like to do things half way. And on occasion, I'll go out for dinner with old friends. Not very exciting, but I like it."

"No love in your life?" he asked before he could stop himself. "I take that back. I shouldn't ask."

"I told you, I don't stand on ceremony. Ask whatever you like. If I don't want to answer, I'll call you off," she replied. "The answer is no. I have no love in my life at the moment. I think I might intimidate the type of men I like."

"Your smarts and looks might intimidate, but that voice and your eyes should overcome a lot," he said.

"You don't seem intimidated, just occasionally nervous," she replied.

"I'm not intimidated, probably too stupid for that. I guess I seem nervous because it's important I don't make a total fool of myself."

"Is that a general statement or does it just apply to me?" she asked.

"Not a lot intimidates me. I was trained not to let that happen. But the nervous part about making a fool out of myself applies to you."

"I like that, Edwin. I'm flattered."

"I guess all the warts are coming out," he said.

When the server came back to the table, Edwin asked for the check. He was told he'd have to see Papa about that. They were escorted into the kitchen. Papa put his arms around Edwin and gave him a strong hug.

"That was for your grandfather," he said. "A very special man."

"Thank you, Mr. Rappoli. That was the best meal I've had in years. The kind thoughts are even better. But I don't feel right about not paying," Edwin said.

"Perhaps some time you can do something for us at the hotel," Papa replied.

"Anytime, sir. It would be my pleasure," Edwin said.

"Watch what you say, young man. I have two unmarried daughters. Italian wedding receptions are very large," he said with a laugh.

They said their good-byes and promised to come back soon, but only if Edwin could pay.

"We'll talk about it," Papa Rappoli said.

They walked back. As they turned the corner, a car pulled up to park beside them. Out of the corner of his eye Edwin noticed someone get out in a hurry. Before he could turn around, a gun was pointed at them. The young man with a bandana on his head looked nervous. Edwin pulled Lee behind him.

"O.K. big man. I want your wallet and the lady's purse. Be quick and no sudden moves," the young man said.

Edwin reached slowly for his wallet. He took it out of his front pocket and handed it to the thief.

"Now the lady's purse," he replied.

"The lady doesn't have a purse," Edwin replied.

"I'll just have to check that out for myself," the young man said, motioning with the gun for Edwin to step out of the way.

Edwin moved to his left and a step forward toward the thief. The young man reached for Lee's breast with his free hand.

"Bug off, scumbag," Lee said batting the young man's hand away.

The thief was startled for an instant by her reply. *This little broad has guts,* he thought.

"A tough lady, huh?" the thief said.

In that instant, Edwin moved another step closer to the thief and grabbed his arm, pulling the gun down and away from Lee. He stepped into the man, wrapped his arm around his, and pushed as hard as he could on the assailant's wrist. All three of them heard the thief's forearm break. He dropped the gun and backed up in pain.

The driver's side door opened and another young man stepped out. Edwin picked up the gun and pointed it at the driver's head.

"One move and your right eye and brain will be across the street," he growled.

The driver started to get back in the car and Edwin shot the right front tire out.

"What don't you understand about one more move?" he asked as he leveled the gun again.

The young man froze and raised his arms. "It was his idea, man."

The other guy was on his knees, holding his arm and crying.

"So much for friendship. Are you O.K., Lee?" he asked.

She was as steady as a rock and looked as angry as he had ever seen anyone. "I'm fine, thanks," she answered.

A police car rocketed around the corner and came to a stop. Two young cops got out with their guns drawn.

"Drop the gun, buddy," the first one said.

Edwin put the gun down gently so it wouldn't discharge. The other cop had thrown the driver up against the car and was patting him down.

"Is he shot?" the cop asked, pointing to the one on his knees. "We heard a shot fired. We were just around the corner."

"No, but I think his arm's broken," Lee replied.

They called an ambulance and continued questioning Lee and Edwin. "You got any proof they were trying to rob you?"

"He's got Edwin's wallet in his pocket," Lee answered.

"Actually, it's just a leather case with business cards. He thought it was my wallet," Edwin replied.

Lee looked at him, a smile breaking out on her face. The cop retrieved the leather case and frisked the thief. He found a watch and another wallet in his pockets.

"You boys been busy tonight, unless your name is David Silberstein," the cop said to the thief.

The thief said nothing. The cop asked Edwin and Lee to come downtown to fill out a report. Lee pushed a number on her cell phone and after a brief conversation handed it to the cop.

"Yes, sir, I guess they can do it in the morning. We can book these guys. We have enough on them. I'm sure we'll find they have priors," the cop said.

The cop handed the phone back to Lee. She thanked the person on the other end and hung up. The cop handed them his card and asked them to be at the precinct by nine a.m. They agreed and continued their walk home as the ambulance arrived and the two young men were taken away.

"How'd you get us out of the report thing tonight?" Edwin asked.

"That was Captain LeRoy. I used to liaison with him when I did federal work."

"I kind of liked the 'Bug off, scumbag' part myself. And the 'tough lady' had an interesting ring to it too. You sure you're all right?"

She put her arm around his waist. He returned the gesture. They walked in silence for the last few blocks before Lee looked at him and asked, "Why did you give him your business card case? He might have gotten mad and who knows what he would have done?"

"I was watching his eyes. He was nervous, but he couldn't take his eyes off of you. He wanted your purse, and probably more. I was buying time so I could think. All that military stuff sticks with you," he replied. "I'm sorry he reached for you like that."

"He's not the first. I'm a big girl," she replied.

When they reached the large brownstone where she lived, he wanted to come inside in the worst way, but decided it wasn't the right time. She turned around and looked at him. She realized he was hesitating.

"We've had enough excitement for one night," she said in her soft voice. She stood on her tiptoes and placed her lips softly on his.

They stayed that way for a full minute. He didn't want to stop and she didn't seem to want to either. He had never been kissed that softly before. He promised to call the next day and reminded her if she woke up scared or concerned, he could be there in a matter of minutes.

As she turned to go inside, she said, "Likewise, big guy."

chapter

NINETEEN

When Edwin woke, the attempted mugging was on his mind, but more than that, Lee was on his mind. She was a mixture of contradictions. She seemed soft and young, but had the toughness of a well-trained Marine. She was sophisticated and well educated, but talked in everyday terms.

He got dressed and walked to the hotel. Slim Johnson was outside with the off-duty cop and four bellmen. It seemed like a lot of staff. Slim Johnson saw him coming and said something to the others. They almost snapped to attention.

"Top of the morning, sir. A sad morning, but we'll manage to have a good day," the large doorman said.

"Morning, gentlemen. What's so sad about it?" Edwin asked.

"It'd be our special guests are leaving today. We now sink back into normality," Slim answered.

"It's just one of those things you have to live with, Slim. You can always read the security reports with Wally when things get boring," Edwin replied with a smile.

"It won't be the same, sir, but me and the boys will survive," Slim said wiping a pretend tear from his cheek.

"Somehow, I think you'll make it. By the way, is Wally around this morning?"

"He was here early. Probably in his office going over last night's security report," Slim responded.

"Have a good day, gentlemen, and remember to carry the bags down and not the women," Edwin offered, shaking his head.

Edwin went to the front desk and asked for the papers in his mailbox.

"And could you please page Mr. Callahan to my office?" he asked.

As he opened the door to his office, Wally Callahan appeared behind him.

"You rang, Boss?" Wally asked. He sat down at the conference table and started to recap the events of the previous evening. Two reporters turned away by the rent-a-cops, four calls to the hospitality suite floor to quiet things down after three a.m., and one disturbance in the lobby. The vice chairman of the BOOBs had tried to jump over the desk when the night auditor refused to open the liquor room after hours. One of the off-duty cops grabbed the drunken guest by the belt and pulled him back. The vice chairman claimed police brutality. After a ten-minute shouting match, the night auditor called a very upset Mr. Chambers who came down and issued some additional booze.

"You've got to serve the guest, but I'm surprised Mrs. Chambers didn't come down and beat the guy to death," Wally volunteered.

"She's not guest-oriented late at night?" Edwin asked, with an amused smile.

"She's not guest-oriented at noon. If the service ain't for her, it doesn't count," Wally responded.

"Strange, a woman like that living in a hotel," Edwin mused.

"Damn, that's easy. She has a hotel full of servants," Wally said.

Edwin continued to be confused about the whole Chambers situation. Most hotel managers and their families are gracious, kind and patient with the staff and guests. They understood the staff served the guest who pays the bills. But there are those who do it for the power and the perks.

"You heard anything from your contacts on the health inspection?" Edwin asked Wally.

"It's funny. I'm not getting anything specific, but everyone I talk to agrees it's strange for BB Bailey to be out doing inspections. All anyone can think of is it must have come from above. I'll keep asking around," the big ex-cop replied.

"I don't mean to be paranoid, but I keep waiting for the other shoe to drop," Edwin said.

"That ain't paranoid, Boss. Something stinks. On another subject, I understand you and the lawyer ran into some of our local greeters last night down the street. You and the lady O.K.?"

"We're fine. It was just a couple of punks. News does travel in the police world. They call you at home to tell you?" Edwin asked.

"No, Moose LeRoy called this morning and wanted to know if you'd like a cop car to pick you up this morning. He's sending one for Ms. Brown."

"I'll take a cab, the cops got enough to do," Edwin replied.

"I'd reconsider. That was a pretty bold move last night," Wally replied. "Cops like to take care of people who help get the scum off the street."

"You're kidding me, right?" Edwin asked.

"Nope. They'll be downstairs in fifteen minutes," Wally replied.

"I'll take the ride."

"Good decision, Boss. I wouldn't mislead you."

"Yes, you would, just not about anything important," Edwin said.

"I'm hurt, Boss. And me having to work in the laundry today for the good of your hotel," the big man answered.

"You in the laundry?" Edwin asked.

"Big check-out and a half-a-house check-in. We don't have the linen stock we used to, so Mary Rodriguez and her staff will be washing their butts off all day," Wally responded.

Having the right amount of linen is really an important issue. Many guests pay little attention to the printed policy of check out time at eleven a.m. and check in after three p.m. They want their room when they get to a hotel and they want to stay as long as they want. To encourage timely departures to free the rooms up for house-keeping, hotels often charge a half-day rate if a guest stays past the stated check-out time. That's guaranteed to annoy guests, but the guests waiting in the lobby, for a room, are annoyed too — Take your pick who you want to argue with.

"That's nice, Wally," Edwin said. "Stop by the front office and tell Mason I think he ought to help out too. The boy could benefit from a mother like Mary in housekeeping."

"Outstanding idea," Wally replied. "I think your police escort is probably waiting on you about now."

Edwin followed Wally downstairs. He waited in the lobby to watch as Wally escorted Robert Mason to the laundry. Mason gave him a glance. The young man was not smiling. As Edwin passed the concierge desk, Jack Vincent looked up.

"That young man does not look happy, sir."

"I just sent him down to the laundry with Wally to help out," Edwin replied.

"Wonderful idea. I love redemption," the concierge said with a laugh.

"Have a good day, Jack."

"It's getting better every minute," Jack responded.

Outside, Slim Johnson was leaning against a patrol car with a young officer. As Edwin approached the two straightened up.

"Morning, Officer Stankowski. Thanks for the ride," Edwin greeted the young officer, reading the officer's nametag and extend-ing his hand.

The young cop shook Edwin's hand. "It's our pleasure to escort you, sir. The department appreciates your help."

On the short ride to the police station they talked about Edwin's time in the military. Inside, Edwin was escorted to the second floor. Two detectives were waiting for him. Edwin completed his statement in a few minutes and then began to answer the detectives' questions. They too were interested in why he took the chance in overpowering the perp. He explained his military training and background. The cops' respect for him seemed to grow as he talked. They didn't interrupt until he was done.

Detective Wagner said, "My brother was in special-ops for a while. I can see him doing the same thing."

"I guess it's instinct mixed with training," Edwin offered.

"Well, the good news is the public defender will probably talk them into copping a plea. That'll mean no trial," Detective Winston offered.

"The bad news is that some bureaucrat will want to investigate you for violating the law against discharging firearms inside of city limits. That was obviously self-defense. I think we'll get that swept away with no problem."

"There's always something, must drive you guys nuts," Edwin replied.

"Yeah, sometimes the suits are a bigger pain in the ass than the criminals," Wagner offered, referring to the bureaucrats.

The tape recorder had been turned off a few minutes before, and they talked. Captain LeRoy entered the room. The captain spoke briefly with the two detectives, asking how the statements had gone. The two cops told him everything looked good for a plea bargain. LeRoy thanked them and asked to be alone with Edwin. He brought him up to speed on the special surveillance with Jack at The Tiger's Tail. The captain was concerned that if things got out of hand and Jack was hurt, it could fall back on the hotel and maybe Edwin should consult his lawyer. Edwin replied that if Jack wanted to do it, he'd take the chance.

"Jack's a very unique person. Not exactly what your average homophobe pictures when he talks about the gay plague," Edwin replied. "Speaking of lawyers, have you talked to Lee?"

"Yeah, she's fine. In fact, I'd say from the tone of her voice and her comments, you gained a few points last night. Not that you care about your attorney liking you," LeRoy replied.

"You deciding to play the matchmaker?" Edwin asked.

"Hey, I got a lot of respect for both of you. She'll need someone tough or she'll run over them," LeRoy replied.

"I'm not as tough with women as I am with scumbags," Edwin replied.

Greg Plank

"I have a feeling you're a quick learner."

"God, I hope so," Edwin answered.

He was glad someone understood his dilemma with the tough little lawyer. They spoke for a few more minutes and left.

Edwin arrived at the hotel just as the Bar Owners and Operators check-out was getting into high gear. Slim Johnson was playing the role of admiral as he helped the bell staff load luggage and ushered the departing guests into the limos. It was obvious this could be a record day in tips for the entire staff. Slim was in his glory.

As Edwin entered the lobby, Candi, the exotic dancer from the day before, exited the elevator. She was dressed in a see-through white sheath. The bellman behind her was wheeling a luggage cart full of bags. The smile on his face was ear to ear as he peered around the luggage cart to watch her well-rounded ass vibrate across the lobby. Edwin hoped, as he headed to his office, the bellman didn't wipe anyone out with the overloaded cart. When he entered the reception area of the offices, a smiling dark-haired girl greeted him.

"How may I help you, sir?" she asked.

"I seem to be lost. Don't two crazy older men work here?" he asked.

A large smile replaced her confused look as she answered in Spanish, "I don't know their ages, but they said a new gringo from South America might show up sooner or later."

"The gringo is here," Edwin replied.

"I guess the gringo is actually El Jefe. I'm Maryann Gonzalez. My aunt Mary referred me. I'm here to help in sales," she answered.

"Welcome. Those two older gentlemen I referred to and the Hotel St. George can use your help. I think we can use your sense of humor too," he said.

"Is there anything I can get for you?" she asked.

"Some more business would be on top of the list," he said.

"We're already working on that, but it would help if I could get my business cards a little earlier than two weeks. They send away for them to save a few dollars," she replied.

Edwin picked up the phone and called Donna Lane. He explained the situation and asked her to get Maryann some cards ASAP.

"Damn, save a few bucks and lose the potential of a few thousand in business because you can't make calls. Some things defy logic. They're kind of ..." he hesitated.

"Insane?" she volunteered.

"Totally," he replied. He liked her directness.

"A Ms. Brown called. The only message was thank you," Maryann said.

"My attorney," Edwin replied.

"Si, El Jefe," she responded with a smile.

I wonder what she knows? He thanked her and went into his office.

chapter

TWENTY

Edwin picked up the ringing phone. "Edwin Christian, how may I help you?"

"Very good, Edwin. You remembered the proper greeting. Just calling to let you know that your sister Daphne has appeared on the radar screen. She called to have me send a limo to pick her up. She wants to meet with Vinnie and the chef about her upcoming party at the hotel," Jack said.

"Warn the troops. I'd like to skip it if I can," Edwin replied.

"None of my business, Boss, but you might want to be there. Without you, she'll try to run them over."

Edwin thought for a moment. "Why don't we try management in absentia?"

"Sir?" Jack asked.

Edwin explained he would put out a memo that no one could spend more than $1,000 without his signature. That way Daphne, or anyone else, would have to come to him. He could be the bad guy and save the staff from Daphne. Jack liked the idea, but suggested Edwin have Chambers sign it too so he didn't lose face with the staff. Edwin agreed and thanked him.

He told Jack he had spoken with LeRoy about the assignment at the Tiger's Tail and told him to be careful. The lobby would lack a certain amount of class without him. Jack thanked him and said he had to get back to work. The teachers were checking in as the BOOBs were checking out. The looks on the teachers' faces were something to behold as the dancers walked by.

Edwin walked over to Donna Lane's office. He asked her to put a memo together limiting expenditures of over $1,000 without his and Chambers' approval and asked her to have Chambers sign it. She said Chambers was out and she'd sign it for him and fill him in. He thanked her and went back to his office. He called the chef and told him to hold his ground firmly but carefully on anything preposterous that his sister requested. He walked into Vinnie DeTesta's office and repeated the message.

"I appreciate that, Edwin, but hell hath no fury like Daphne Christian when told no," Vinnie replied.

"She can't fire you. Besides, that's her act. After five minutes, she'll turn on the charm and try to woo you. She used to do it with A.D. all the time," Edwin said.

"How'd it work with A.D.?" Vinnie asked.

"Put it this way: She got the first horse and the riding lessons. She didn't get the second one," Edwin replied.

"This could be a long afternoon," Vinnie said.

"Have faith, Vinnie. She couldn't handle two wimpy husbands. How's she going to handle two experienced Italian men?" Edwin asked.

"If that's the case, I hope the chef has Mafia connections," Vinnie replied.

"Wear a jock strap, you'll be fine," Edwin said and left.

Edwin wanted to go over more of the hotel financial statements with Chuck Castillano the hotel comptroller. Without Chambers there, he might be more open. Castillano's office was small and cluttered. There were daily night-audit packs stacked on every flat surface. Each night a hotel closes its books and balances all charges, revenues, and receivables. All of the back up for the charges are kept by day in a packet. This information is stored for years for audit purposes or for guest disputes.

"Looks like a Boy Scout paper drive in here," Edwin said.

"Sorry. I'm usually pretty neat. With the cut-backs here, no one has time to help me store them in the attic storage area," the comptroller replied.

"You got time to go over some more of the operating statements?"

"No problem. I was going to see you later anyway. The hotel keeps a cash reserve account. Payroll is due this week and the account's getting low. The conventions this week will help, but we won't get all the receipts until next week," Castillano informed Edwin. "We have enough for the actual payroll, but we also have to deposit the payroll taxes in the bank at the same time. It's the law and the IRS has a challenged sense of humor."

Edwin asked to go over all the numbers first and then they'd see where they could get the money. For the next forty-five minutes, the comptroller guided Edwin through the statements. The hotel had cut expenses in every department, but the sales had continued to drop even more. The result was that the amount of cash the hotel had in the bank went up and down with the business levels. The mortgage payment against the note that had been taken out to help the construction company was often higher than the amount of house profit. Castillano showed his irritation that the proceeds from the loan had gone to the construction company with no benefit to the hotel. And the hotel and the staff had to do without for the good of Edwin's brother. Chuck was obviously guarding his opinions of Henry because he didn't know what kind of relationship Edwin had with his brother.

That ended when Edwin said, "So, my brother screws up and all of you have to pay the price? I agree it sucks."

It was the first time Castillano broke a smile. He explained it was actually a little worse than that. As part of the cost savings, they laid off most of the engineering and maintenance department. When they needed repairs, they bought the time and people from the construction company. So, Christian Construction got that money too.

"That why this place is getting to look like a dump?" Edwin asked.

"It shouldn't be looking that way. We pay Christian Construction plenty," Chuck replied.

"We'll look into that later. What about the revenues of the hotel? Why are the room rates going down?" Edwin asked.

Chuck reminded him that with all the empty rooms, the hotel was dumping inventory on the Internet. They got some bookings, but the rates were much lower there and customers knew it.

"An educated consumer," Castillano continued, "is often a business's worst enemy."

Edwin suggested Chuck should look into how the hotel was controlling inventory on the Internet. He said they were going to get control of things with Chuck as the organizer, starting with the memo limiting expenditures of over $1,000. He told Chuck about the reserve account that had been left for the hotel in his grandfather's will and asked him to figure out how much money they needed right away. Finally, he asked him to check the bank about the status of the mortgage.

"Thank you, Mr. Christian, that's a big help," Castillano said.

"Call me Edwin. I have a feeling we're going to have a very close relationship."

As Edwin left, Chuck Castillano raised a closed fist in the international victory sign.

On his way to his office, Edwin stuck his head in Bill Smith's office.

"Where's our new sales assistant?" he asked.

"Out reading function boards at the competition. That girl shows signs of unbounded energy. I wonder how she is in bed," Bill replied.

"Forget the bed stuff. The laws and politically acceptable standards have changed. You can pay big time for that these days. What's with the function boards?" Edwin asked.

Smith reminded Edwin every hotel posts the day's functions, like meetings and banquets, on function boards around the hotel to help their guests find out where to be and when. Hotel sales people had been visiting the competitive hotels for years to look at the boards and note the meetings and functions taking place. They go back to their office, wait a few days, and call the organization that had meetings at that hotel. A good salesperson might beat a price or offer a service that piques the meeting planner's interest. At the St. George, Slim and Jack were very good at spotting the competition and politely asking them to leave. If they refused, Wally was good at convincing them. Some used cameras or recorders so they wouldn't be seen taking notes. Jack and Slim had become good at zeroing in on that too.

chapter

TWENTY ONE

Edwin had not seen Daphne in the sales and catering offices. He called Donna to see if she knew what Daphne was up to. Donna told him Daphne had pursued her penchant for feeling important and a meeting was going on at the chef's table in the middle of the kitchen. Daphne had on the lowest-cut blouse Donna had ever seen her in and was enjoying entertaining the men in the kitchen.

Donna had gotten the memo out on the $1,000 limit. When it was shown to Daphne, she was not a happy camper and made it known, along with some observations about getting her little brother to loosen up. Edwin told her he'd go down to rescue the guys as soon as he made a call. As he got ready to call Justin LaGrange, Chuck Castillano called and informed him the last two months' mortgage payments had not been received by the bank. He didn't know anything else yet.

Edwin worried as he dialed the private phone number for Justin LaGrange's office. Justy was out of the office and Ann Baxter asked if she could help. He explained the special account in his grandfather's will and the tight money situation at the hotel. Ann remembered the account and said she'd look into it. When she asked how urgent it was, Edwin told her the hotel needed a moderate amount of cash this week and possibly more next week to catch up on the mortgage. She promised she or Justy would get back to him within the next twenty-four hours. He thanked her and asked if he could have a word with Lee.

"Edwin, I'm sorry I missed you at the police station," Lee said in greeting.

"I was concerned about you with the mugging and all," he answered.

"You forget — I've been around tougher guys than that. Besides, you moved so fast, I hardly remember any of it."

"I was worried you might think I put you in jeopardy," he offered sheepishly.

"If the kiss didn't show my admiration, what's a girl to do?" she replied.

"I guess I just didn't associate something that nice with crime," he replied.

"What a nice thing to say, and thanks for checking on me," she said.

Might as well move ahead.

"Thursday night is Jack Vincent's night with the police at the Tiger's Tail. I was thinking it might be helpful if you were around if something happened. Would you be available for dinner?"

"You want me to have dinner at the Tiger's Tail?" she asked.

"No, I thought maybe we could eat at the hotel," he said.

"I was kidding. I've been to the Tiger's Tail, but the hotel would be much better. You still have the creamed capon?" she asked.

"Absolutely. What about seven-thirty? I can send a limo for you," he replied.

"You don't have to impress me. I can walk. It's only a few blocks," she answered.

"No, just treating you like a VIP. The limo will be there, and Marty will have his blender ready."

"Edwin, the only other thing I need is for you to be relaxed. I'm looking forward to it."

"I'll be the most relaxed person you've ever met," he replied.

"I'll hold you to that. See you then," she said and hung up.

Remembering Daphne was in the kitchen entertaining the staff and torturing two Italian gentlemen, Edwin felt an urgent need to perform a rescue.

As he passed through the lobby, he noticed an older woman at the concierge desk pointing her finger in Jack's face. Edwin crossed to the floral arrangement in the center of the lobby and pretended to be rearranging flowers. From what he could hear, the lady was irate because she had not gotten a suite. As past president of the Teachers' Association, she thought she had a right to a suite. Jack was trying to explain all the suites were taken by the textbook and school supply companies that were exhibiting, and they were paying the association for the privilege, but her mind was made up and her ego obviously bruised.

"Either you don't understand, Mr. Vincent, or are incapable of comprehending this hotel may never see this meeting again. I am the only four-term president of the organization, and I hold a permanent seat on the board. I not only deserve a suite, I demand one. If you're incapable of doing that, get your boss down here and I'll explain it again to him or her," the lady demanded.

Jack was doing his best. He even offered a gourmet meal on the hotel.

"I don't need your charity, I need a suite," she countered.

Edwin walked over to the front desk and asked for Robert Mason. When he appeared he looked haggard and unfriendly.

"Mr. Mason, are they still holding the suite for my mother open?" he asked.

"Yes, sir. It's clean and ready for her with a few minor repairs," Mason answered.

"Is it in condition to rent?" Edwin asked.

"Yes, sir. The repairs are very minor."

"Good. Let's move the lady talking with Mr. Vincent into that suite. What's her name?" Edwin asked.

"That would be Mrs. Abigail Lovejoy, which is a complete oxymoron," the young man replied, exasperated.

Edwin smiled at him. It was the first hint of humor from Mason.

"I take it she only got to Jack after she worked out on you," Edwin said.

"It was twenty minutes of holding my temper while being verbally flogged."

"Thanks for the effort. I'll inform Jack and Mrs. Lovejoy of the change. Cut the card-keys for the suite," Edwin said.

Edwin headed across the lobby to save Jack. He introduced himself and said he understood there was a suite problem. Having the owner's ear, she went on to tell the entire story of her past presidencies and how important she was to the Teachers' Association and the hotel. Edwin got the impression she felt the entire education system of the country would be in jeopardy if it weren't for her forty years of public service and sacrifice.

"I'm sorry for any inconvenience, Mrs. Lovejoy. Actually, the staff has been working hard to remedy your situation. A suite was taken out of service for repairs. They've rushed the engineering department to get it ready for you. It's the largest suite in the hotel. Mr. Vincent will have a bell person assist you. Thank you for your patience."

Mrs. Lovejoy was speechless. Jack looked at him with eyes as wide as basketballs.

"I'm only sorry this could not have happened sooner. I dislike getting upset with people," she offered.

I bet you do, you old buzzard. Edwin smiled warmly at her.

"I'll get your key immediately," Jack said as he stood and offered his hand.

Ignoring Jack completely, Mrs. Lovejoy shook Edwin's hand and followed Jack to the front desk. She strutted with a look of triumph on her overly made-up face.

"Now I know why I'm so happy to be gay. Can you imagine living with a person like that?" Jack asked when he returned.

"Kind of gives witch a whole new edge," Edwin offered.

"I probably shouldn't be so harsh. She's aging and maybe getting that feeling of losing contact and influence. I don't know how I'll feel when I get there," Jack said.

"Is that how you get through the day, Jack? Giving everyone the benefit of the doubt?"

"No, it's how I sleep at night. I appreciate the rescue," Jack offered.

"Hell, Jack. This was nothing. There are two Italian guys in the kitchen getting beat to death by Daphne," Edwin said. "If I'm not out of the kitchen in thirty minutes, call 911."

The kitchen was its usual eighty-plus degrees. Sitting in the middle of all the commotion at the chef's table was Vinnie DeTesta, who had taken off his coat and was sweating through his shirt. The chef was behind the range cooking something, with Daphne bent over looking into the pan showing a full view of her breasts. Two young room-service servers were enjoying the show. The chef was having a hard time keeping his eyes on the pan. When Daphne saw Edwin, she came around the cooking line and gave her brother a hug. Then, in a lightning change of mood, her tirade began. She thought he was making a big mistake by nickel and diming the most important people in town. The hotel had always contributed generously to her affairs and gotten a good amount of publicity and repeat business out of it. He was being mean and making her, and especially the hotel, look cheap. Edwin listened patiently so he wouldn't become another part of her problem.

"I don't intend to nickel and dime anyone. I just see the need to control expenses for every department in the hotel," he replied. "Where do we stand now on the arrangements?"

Vinnie explained that Daphne had suggested a Greek theme because the event was sponsoring literacy and Ancient Greece has been recognized for its learning for thousands of years. The chef was trying some Greek dishes right now to decide on an entrée.

Edwin decided he had to put Vinnie in a tight spot to get some leverage. He asked him how many of the attendees at previous affairs had brought business to the hotel. Vinnie looked like he didn't want to and almost choked, but answered they had gotten a couple of weddings over the years.

"So, basically we're into charity with not a lot of return," Edwin said.

"You've become a mean-spirited prig," Daphne said.

"You probably considered a few other names, but there's nothing wrong with charity," he answered. "Anyone have any suggestions?"

The chef thought for a minute and suggested they go to some of the hotel's food and beverage suppliers to get some things for cost or as donations. Daphne could give them some publicity in return. He could call in some favors.

"Do we really want to share our spotlight with some grocers?" Daphne asked indignantly.

"In the true spirit of charity, why not let others feel good about themselves?" Edwin asked.

Daphne's expression hardened. Her little brother had thrown altruism into the argument.

"If they contribute, do they have to sit at the head table?" she asked, returning to her innocent tone.

"We'll have to give them some free tickets, but I doubt if any of them will even attend," the chef offered.

"Well, in that case, I guess we could let others share in our good efforts," she said. "But everyone will have to dress in the Greek toga tradition."

"Ah, the return to rowdy college days. We better get Wally to have extra security in case it gets out of hand," Edwin replied.

"This is the cream of society. I don't think they do that sort of childish thing," Daphne said.

"It might depend more on the flow of alcohol than on breeding," he retorted.

He kissed his sister on the cheek and made his exit, leaving them to discuss the details. He narrowly averted disaster at the door from the dining room, barely missing a busboy with a full tray of dishes. He helped right the tray and apologized.

"With those breasts hanging out in there, who could pay attention? No problem, man," the busboy replied.

Edwin didn't have the heart to tell him the breasts belonged to his sister.

chapter

TWENTY TWO

Edwin had seldom lost sleep in his adult life. He'd even slept in mud holes and on piles of rocks in the military, but now he was losing sleep over a certain attorney and the tight cash situation at the hotel. At five a.m. he decided trying to sleep was useless. He got up, splashed cold water on his face, put on his running gear, and started to run toward the river. *I've got to move fast on the money issue. I'll start with Justy LaGrange as soon as I get to the office. He might be able to help with the bank too.* He arrived at the hotel at eight a.m. Slim Johnson was at his post on the front door. He was arguing with a limousine driver. The conversation was getting heated.

"Look, sport, with no city permit, you ain't carrying any of our guests. So move it before I call a cop," Slim was saying.

"This is a free country. I am free to work my business," the driver replied.

"The front of this hotel may be in a free country, but I freakin' own it and I decide who parks here. Now move before I have you towed," Slim responded.

"This is a free country. I will never bring a guest here again, and I will tell my countrymen to do the same," the driver protested.

"You can take an ad out in the freakin' *New York Times* for all I care. Now move your freedom-loving butt," Slim growled.

The driver finally began to move the limousine away from the curb, as he gave Slim the international one-finger salute.

"Morning, Slim. Got a traffic problem?" Edwin asked.

"Morning, Boss. Just a rogue problem," Slim replied.

"Rogue? How could you tell?" Edwin asked.

"He's a rogue driver. These guys haunt the airports and drive the cops nuts. They won't pay for a permit or carry the required insurance. We don't want any of our guests getting into one of those cars."

"Don't the cops control them?" Edwin asked.

"They try, but you can't tell by just looking at the car. The cops are busy. It would be easier if they had to display medallions or stickers on the licensed cars, but the city council members are very aware of the ethnic varieties. They won't pass any regulations that will upset a potential voter," Slim said, frustrated.

"Thanks for looking out for the hotel," Edwin responded.

"That's just part of the job, Boss," Slim said.

Edwin went up to his office and dialed Justy LaGrange's office number. Ann Baxter answered.

"I'm afraid I don't have any good news. Mr. LaGrange said there is really nothing we can do to speed the process. He said he'd call the accountants and the bank to see if you can get a loan against the future funds from the account. But he said he wasn't hopeful," she replied. "Can I have him call you later? He's in a closed meeting now."

"That's fine, but time is of the essence," Edwin responded. "Thanks for your help."

Edwin was confused by Justy's apparent lack of concern for an old friend's grandson. He had been working with A.D. for years and he had known Edwin from childhood. Edwin began feeling that, for some unknown reason, he was getting the run around and his temper was rising at Justin LaGrange's lack of concern. He looked in his directory and called Lee's cell phone number.

"You're not calling to cancel our dinner, are you? I've been thinking about creamed capon for the last twenty-four hours," she said.

"Never. I have a problem and I don't know where else to go. Do you deal with probate?"

"No, my uncle handles that. What's your problem?" she responded.

He chose his words carefully as he described the money situation at the hotel, and his quandary as to why Justy LaGrange couldn't move the release of the special account in the will ahead faster or why it was screwed up in the first place. He decided to be honest and told her the whole story.

"I wish I knew someone influential at the bank. It would seem that with all the banking your grandfather did there, they would work something out. Of course, I understand that the president, Nathan Forrest, is relatively new. He probably didn't know A.D.," she said.

"Chambers supposedly knows him fairly well, and he's calling Forrest this morning. He didn't sound too hopeful last night when I asked him though," Edwin replied.

"Let me think for a minute. The bank is CC&A," she said.

There was a long silence on the line. After several moments she said she might know someone who could help. When she was with the government, she met a gentleman named Irving Kertzner. Years before he was on the board of CC&A. He was retired from the hotel business. His international contacts were very strong, and he had helped with a few cases where they were tracking money in the international markets. She thought he moved to Florida to be near his grandchildren. She asked him if Edwin still had someone he could contact at the company he worked for in South America. If they did that much international work, they might know Kertzner and where he was. He replied he still might be able to get in touch with his former contact at International Pipelines. She encouraged him to reach out to him.

"Stop worrying, and just make sure the chef puts his special stuff in the creamed capon. Things will work out," she said softly.

Every day for a year, he had called a number from his satellite phone in South America. The number was one thing he'd never forget. He dialed it. The electronically altered voice he remembered answered, "Carlo the Wolf. How's the hotel business?"

"How did you know it was me?" Edwin asked.

"Just a special form of caller ID, and a good guess, based on the area code."

"The hotel business is a bit more complicated than pipelines, and quite frankly, I have a problem," Edwin answered.

"Why call me? I only stay in them, and that's the extent of my hotel knowledge."

Edwin explained the situation and told him of Lee's suggestion about Irv Kertzner. He asked if Carlo might know of him and where to find him.

"Haven't talked with Irv in years. Great financial mind. In fact, he might still be involved with the bank. Got a pen? Here's his number. Just use Lee's name and not mine if you get hold of him," Carlo responded.

Edwin wrote the number down and thanked Carlo. The phone went dead on the other end.

It was too early for Chambers to have an answer from the bank. He decided to walk the property. As he left the office, Bill Smith was coming off the elevator.

"Morning, Bill. You look dapper today," Edwin greeted him.

"So nice of you to meet me and wish me luck. It's an important day," he replied.

"Wish you luck with what?" Edwin asked.

"Today I'm meeting with an old acquaintance to see if we can book some airline crew business in the hotel. Twenty rooms a night for a year," Smith said proudly.

"You really think we can get it?" Edwin asked.

"It might depend on the rate they're willing to pay. And we have to provide transportation to and from the airport. I just hope Chambers will approve the rate if I have to go really low," Smith offered.

"What's really low?" Edwin asked.

"Probably sixty percent of our normal rate, plus we have to pay the transportation costs," Smith replied.

"Not to show my ignorance, but what are the pluses at that low a rate?" Edwin asked.

Smith explained that the twenty rooms would be occupied three-hundred-sixty-five days a year. In light of the discounting on the Internet reservations, the crew is not such a bad deal for guaranteed business.

"If the rate becomes a problem, come to me," Edwin offered.

"I was hoping you'd say that. Thanks, Boss," Smith replied. Edwin turned to leave and Smith stopped him. "One more thing, Boss. I was thinking that if the negotiations get really tough, could we take one suite parlor out of service and make it into a lounge for the crews? They like to have a place to get together. It might give us a competitive advantage. And would you be available to meet them? My contact would like meeting the hotel owner," Smith requested.

"No problem. Pick out the parlor you think would work and talk to food and beverage about refreshment requirements. Better run it past Chambers and give him a chance to be positive. Have Donna page me when you need me," Edwin replied.

He was intent on finding Wally Callahan to get a report on his inquiries the previous evening. Edwin had called Chambers in his suite and asked him to join him in his office to talk about getting a short-term bank loan. It had taken Chambers thirty minutes to get there; it should have taken five. He had asked Wally to see if he could get anything on the phone activity from Chambers' suite between the time of his phone call and Chambers' arrival in his office. It was a private line, but Wally knew some people from the phone company from the old days. While they were talking, Wally mentioned that Mary Rodriguez in housekeeping had asked for his help. A room had been denying housekeeping services. That's a red flag in the hotel business. The hotel is in a hard place because it has to honor a guest's wishes, but it also has to look out for a guest. If someone was sick in the room, the hotel might be held liable. It was also a tip-off that something funny might be going on in the room. Wally was going to wait until Mason was gone and check on the room so he didn't raise suspicion.

As Edwin entered the service corridor behind the meeting rooms, he saw Vinnie DeTesta, the banquet manager, and Pas Medvier, the food and beverage manager, talking.

"Mr. Medvier, I haven't seen you since I've been at the hotel. I wondered what had happened to you," Edwin said.

"I didn't want to be here to see you cry when you saw how this place has gone to hell," the man replied in his French accent.

"After yesterday, I'll let Vinnie do all the crying. Did he recount his meeting with my sister?" Edwin asked.

Vinnie wasn't smiling.

"It's too early in the morning for tales of woe," Medvier replied.

"You're tan. They told me you were on an extended vacation. I didn't think you would miss the BOOB convention and the scenery," Edwin offered.

"I didn't miss much. I went to South Beach in Miami. My brother runs a restaurant there. The scenery is excellent year round," he replied.

"Glad you're back. How bad was yesterday, Vinnie?" Edwin asked.

"Not as bad as last year. I think she's either afraid of you or can't figure out what to expect from you. Thanks for the back-up," Vinnie said.

"You guys have a good day. Has anyone seen our illustrious head of security this morning?" he inquired.

Pas looked at his watch.

"At this hour, he's sitting at the chef's table having his fourth cup of coffee. Sorry about your grandfather. He was a prince," the Frenchman called after him.

"Yeah, he sure was. Thanks for the thought," he replied.

chapter

TWENTY THREE

Wally Callahan was sitting at the chef's table with a mug of coffee in front of him. He was reading the security report from the night before.

"You get out of here at a decent hour last night?" Edwin asked.

"Yeah, our little front office manager never stays late when the boss ain't looking," Wally replied.

"Find out anything interesting?" Edwin asked.

The big ex cop looked around the kitchen to make sure nobody was in earshot.

"I'm not sure what I found out. I left Chamber's phone number from his apartment for my contact. A call was placed to Christian Construction and lasted for fifteen minutes," Wally replied.

"What about the room you were looking into?" Edwin continued.

"It's strange. There's a credit card on it and one person registered. I ran the credit card for credit approval and it seems legit. But,

I remember housekeeping telling me there were two men in the room and they used a lot of towels. Something's fishy," Wally answered.

"What do we do next?" Edwin asked.

"That's what I've been thinking about. We have a right to inspect the room and if there are two guys staying in there, they owe us money for the second person. I can print up a bill for a second person and take it up there. I'll have Chuck do it. I don't trust Mason," Wally replied. "I'll also call Moose LeRoy. We haven't been on assignment together in a long time. He might enjoy this and I might need the back-up."

"Just keep me informed," Edwin said.

Chef Mazzari approached the table. "I'll take care of it today," Wally replied.

"I didn't think you could do anything in a day," the chef said to Wally.

"At least us micks are faster than you dagos," Wally replied.

"At stealing hubcaps maybe," the chef said.

"You two do this every day?" Edwin asked.

"Mostly. Just to show our true affection," the chef answered.

"Yeah, it's brotherly love and professional respect," Wally added.

"Chef, I have a visitor tomorrow night for dinner in the dining room. They're particularly fond of your creamed capon. Can you do a special version tomorrow and choose a wine to go with it?" Edwin asked.

"Of course I can. I'll make everything special," the chef responded. "Would you have intimate knowledge of this special guest to know what kind of wine he or she likes?"

"No, I don't," Edwin answered.

"Freakin' shame," Wally said.

"You two are unbelievable. You ought to do a comedy routine. Martin and Lewis aren't around anymore. You'd probably be more like Abbott and Costello," Edwin said as he left.

"You want to be Abbott or Costello?" the chef asked Wally.

"You're the Italian. I don't want no vowel on the end of my name. I got a reputation to keep," Wally answered.

Edwin headed back to the offices to check on Chambers. He greeted Donna and asked if Chambers was in. She looked over at the phone console.

"He's on the phone. He's been on the call for the last thirty minutes. Do you want me to interrupt him?" she asked.

"No, I'll wait." He picked up the hotel trade magazine to browse. In a few seconds, the door to Chambers' office opened and the general manager invited Edwin in.

"Morning, Leonard. I hope you have some good news," Edwin said.

"I wish I had. That was Nathan Forrest on the line. He was understanding, but he doesn't see how he could arrange a loan in that short a time. He can't just advance the money as an unsecured loan. To do the paperwork to secure it will take a couple of days," Chambers said.

Edwin thought for a minute. "What you're telling me is all the years of financial dealings and the millions my grandfather put through that bank have no bearing on the situation in Mr. Forrest's opinion?" Edwin said.

"No, Edwin. I'm saying he wants to cooperate, but it will take time," Chambers answered.

"We don't have time. Do you want to tell the staff they won't get paid on Friday?" Edwin asked.

"I guess we can go to Henry. The construction company may have some funds to advance on a short-term basis. In fact, he's coming over tonight at five-thirty for cocktails. It's probably the fastest way to solve the problem," Chambers offered.

"That's not on the top of my list. Henry's probably busy, but if he's coming over anyway, why not? I'll see you then," Edwin replied. "Thanks for your efforts."

He left Chambers' office and stopped at Donna Lane's desk. "If Bill Smith calls, I told him to have you page me if he needs me," he said.

"Not a problem, Edwin. Try to relax."

As he entered his office, his cell phone rang. Lee wanted to know if he had found Irv Kertzner through the contact information he had mentioned from his old company. She had found out that he was still on the board of the bank. Edwin told her he had gotten Kertzner's number, but that his contact asked that he use Lee's name when he contacted him.

"Hmmm. Interesting," Lee said. "Use my name then. Irv should remember me."

"Thanks. Oh, the chef said the creamed capon will be special."

"That's all the thanks I need," she replied.

He hung up and went to his private line and dialed the number for Kertzner in Miami.

"This is Irv," the voice said.

"Mr. Kertzner, this is Edwin Christian. Lee Brown said you might be able to help me. Thanks for taking my call," Edwin started.

"If you're a friend of Lee's, how can I help you?"

Edwin didn't know how much to tell him, but he figured if Lee trusted Kertzner he might as well go with everything. "How much time do you have?"

"I've got until four-thirty. My grandson has a basketball game today. So give me all the highlights and I'll ask questions as we go," Kertzner replied.

For the next twenty minutes, Edwin told the entire story of his grandfather's death, the inheritance, the need for a loan, the probate hold-up on the will, the bank's hesitance, and his problem with going to his brother for help. Kertzner interrupted with questions about the legal issues and about his grandfather's past dealings with the bank. He also asked if Henry had dealings with the same bank.

When Edwin was done, Irv said, "You would think, with all that family money going through the bank over the years, they could give you some special service. I don't know what the hell's wrong these days, service is talked about, but hard to find when you need it. The banking regulations and the mergers of the mega-banks often leave service behind. They recognize it and advertise it, but the delivery remains the problem. I'm not their favorite member of the board. I have a habit of telling them service sucks."

"Some people don't like honesty," Edwin replied.

"Especially if they think it will affect their bonus. The new guy Forrest was a merger guy. He's not your old fashioned, local banker,"

Irv said. "Service costs a little more money. Give me a little time and someone will get back to you."

"We're kind of tight on time. I hate to ask for favors, and you don't even know me," Edwin said.

"They'll get back to you today. If Lee will vouch for you, that's good enough for me. I'll be in town soon for a board meeting. We can meet then. She owes me a dinner. She can bring a client along and she can pay for both of us," Kertzner replied.

"Thanks for anything you can do," Edwin said.

"Don't worry, kid, these things have a way of working out," Irv replied.

"May I ask you one more question?" Edwin asked.

"Shoot," Kertzner said.

"Based on the questions you asked, I get the impression you seem to think the bank's reluctance to handle this quickly is strange," Edwin said.

"You're a quick study. I'll get into all that later. Let me get your problem moving for now."

"I don't know how to thank you," Edwin said.

"Save it for dinner. I haven't done anything yet," Kertzner replied.

"Is your grandson really into basketball?" Edwin asked.

"Runs in the family, don't get me started. It could take all day," Kertzner said with a chuckle and hung up.

Edwin was still worried, but his spirits started to lift. His cell phone rang; it was Donna Lane. Bill Smith was in the dining room with the airline people and asked if Edwin could join them.

As Edwin approached the table where Bill and two women sat, Smith stood up. "Edwin Christian, allow me to introduce Candace Harst and Ann Tompkins."

Edwin extended his hand to each of the women with a smile.

"It's a pleasure. Thank you for taking the time to visit the St. George."

As he finished, Wally Callahan appeared and offered his hand to the women. After he was introduced he took Ann Tompkins on a tour of the hotel to assure her of the hotel's security. Candace Harst took over the conversation. She outlined how badly the other hotels in town wanted the business and how competitive they could be with the rates. It was obvious she knew the hotel rate and room demand issues as well as any hotel company CFO. Edwin was impressed. *She takes the fight to you at the beginning. Good negotiator.* She kept her eyes glued to his and showed a slight smile.

"You obviously know we want the business. We also want people, like the crews of International Air, enjoying the St. George. If we cut the BS and go to fifty-five dollars including tax and transportation, can we sign the agreement and have the chef prepare us something special for brunch?" Edwin asked, maintaining his smile.

Smith sat in stunned silence. The BS comment to one of the most important hotel room users in the world was almost too much for him to take. When Harst replied she would accept, he almost fell over.

Ann Tompkins and Wally Callahan arrived back at the table.

"How was your tour?" Harst asked as they sat down.

"The hotel is fine, security wise. And Wally's police stories are entertaining to say the least," Ann responded. Wally thanked her for the compliment, told Edwin he needed him later, and left.

I didn't know Wally was a lady's man.

With the business concluded, Edwin thanked them for their kind consideration and pledged that if he could be of any help, they should call him at the hotel any time. As he walked around the table to shake their hands, Candace put her hand on his shoulder, giving it a slight squeeze. He didn't know if he was being hit on or how to respond so he smiled like a little boy. It was the right response. She returned the smile.

While the business session was going on in the dining room, Paul Winters was taking a break in the bar from his post as a textbook salesman in a booth for the teachers' trade show. An attractive middle-aged woman walked in and sat across the bar from him. Camille Slater was the wife of a small-town high school principal. She wished she could travel more, but the big trip of the year was to accompany her husband to the annual school teachers' convention. It gave her a chance to catch some theatre, do some shopping, and eat in upscale restaurants. She ordered a glass of white wine. When she felt someone looking at her, she looked up and met the smile of Paul Winters. They struck up a conversation and Paul moved to her side of the bar. After the normal conversation of where you're from and why they were here, Paul began his sad story of life on the road. His boss was cheap so he had to watch his pennies and living out of a suitcase was lonely at best. As they finished their third drink, Camille put her hand on Paul's as a gesture of sympathy for his lonely nights on the road.

In fact, Paul spent very few lonely nights on the road. He had a talent for telling his story to any impressionable female bar inhabitant. He had no restrictions on his meal tabs; Paul Winters ate better than most general managers in five-star hotels. They both ordered a fourth drink to go. Camille left the bar first. Paul sipped on his drink for a few minutes and then asked Marty for the tab for both of them. Marty watched him leave, smiled, and shook his head. He had seen the out-of-town mating dance many times before.

Edwin walked to Jack Vincent's desk. Jack was on the phone. When he hung up he told Edwin he was touched. An attendee of the teachers' meeting had ordered flowers for his wife and was going to surprise her at lunch. Edwin asked if flowers would work on Lee. Jack told him to hold off. He didn't think she was the type to be pushed.

"I'm glad I asked you first. By the way, have you seen Wally around?" Edwin asked.

"He's out front with Slim. I think he's waiting for someone to show up," Jack replied.

Wally and Slim were outside the front door, talking and watching the mid-day traffic in front of the hotel.

"You wanted to see me?" Edwin asked Wally.

"Yeah, step into my office," Wally said as he started to walk toward the corner away from Slim.

As they neared the corner Wally told him his cop's sixth sense was giving him bad vibes about the room denying service. He had LeRoy coming to back him up and they would take a bill to the room as a way to get in. Edwin told him to be careful and that he'd be in his office if Wally needed his help.

chapter

TWENTY FOUR

Edwin went up to his office to wait to see if Wally needed his help. Five minutes later his cell phone rang. It was Wally setting up contact. He thought Edwin might like to listen in. Edwin heard the knock and Wally said, "Management. Just checking on your stay."

There was a long silence. Wally knocked again. A moment later a male voice answered, "Everything is fine. Thanks for your hospitality." The door did not open.

"Sir, we really have to talk," Wally said more authoritatively.

"My wife is sick. Please leave us in peace," the voice replied.

"Sir, it will just take a minute. Please open the door," Wally asked.

There was a long pause before the voice on the other side of the door replied, "I said my wife is sick. This will have to wait until a better time."

"I'm sorry but this can't wait. If you won't open the door, I'll have to," Wally replied.

Captain LeRoy pushed Wally to the side, away from the door. He wanted to be sure, if the person in the room responded violently, Wally would not be in harm's way. A hotel door will not stop a large caliber bullet. A couple of years before a housekeeper in another hotel had knocked on a guest room door. The crack-head drug dealer inside panicked and fired a .357 magnum round through the door. It took the jaw of the housekeeper half off. She lived, but it took two years of plastic surgery to make her look half-way normal again.

Edwin was getting nervous listening to the exchange. LeRoy motioned Wally to open the door with his key making sure he stood well off to the side of the door.

"Police. Open the door," the captain said.

Before Wally could insert the card in the slot on the lock, the person inside said, "There's no need for this. I'm opening the door."

LeRoy stood back, his badge out. The door opened slowly as far as the security latch would allow. A tall man in a bathrobe stood in the door looking at LeRoy.

"Well, if it isn't Agent Holloran, our federal protector," LeRoy replied. "So sorry to hear about your wife's illness."

"Cut the crap, Moose. What's this all about?" the federal agent asked.

"I was about to ask you the same thing. Your wife's your partner now?" LeRoy inquired.

"None of your business," Holloran said.

"Open the door, Agent. The hotel has the right to inspect the premises," the captain replied.

"Open the door, Steve," came a voice in the room.

The door opened and LeRoy entered followed by Wally.

"Senior Agent Watkins, you know it's against policy for you two to date," LeRoy said.

"Very funny, Moose," the man replied. "What's this all about?"

"You've been denying housekeeping service and there are two people, as I can see, in a room registered as a single. I think you owe the hotel some money for the additional guest," LeRoy answered. "Anyway, what are you two up to in a hotel room? Or should I guess?"

His eyes surveyed the room. There were two cameras with telephoto lenses on the bed, a small video camera and two recording devices with a variety of phone lines connected to them on the desk. "I'd say you're on surveillance. What's wrong, you didn't trust your first-grade teacher?" LeRoy asked, referring to the teachers' group in the hotel.

"Even though I don't like it, I guess I owe you an answer for the help you gave us on the Lobo drug busts last year," Watkins replied.

"It was our case all the way, but I felt sorry for you. I didn't want you to miss your bust quota and lose out on that fat government retirement," LeRoy answered.

"We sewed it up for you and you know it," Watkins replied.

"Whatever floats your boat, Bill," LeRoy said.

"So, what's the deal here? You shooting a training film?" Wally asked.

"We got a tip a drug ring was operating in the hotel. There's a lot of concern about kids in school getting drugs. To see if some of it might be from the inside of the school systems, we set up to watch," Watkins replied.

LeRoy took the hotel bill from Wally and looked at it. "According to this bill, you've been here for a week. The teachers just checked in. That means you were here during the bar owners' meeting. You afraid a stripper's going to sell drugs to kids in school?" he asked.

"We have it on good authority this hotel has catered to drug people for some time, whether they knew it or not," Holloran said.

"No way. We'd have known about it," Wally answered.

"Well, maybe you did know about it and just didn't do anything, or maybe someone here is making a little fun money on the side," Watkins interjected.

"I hope you can back that up. I know that's not happening on my watch," Wally replied.

"If the evidence we've gathered proves what we think it will, you might have to find another job," Holloran said, pointing his finger at Wally.

LeRoy knew Wally. Wally would like nothing more than to reach out and break Holloran's finger off and stuff it up the Fed's ass.

"So, when do we get to see all of this evidence, and why would a devoted servant like Mr. Callahan have to look for a job?" LeRoy stepped in front of his old partner.

"Because if the evidence connects the hotel to the drug activity, the federal government can and will seize the hotel," Watkins replied.

"I know these people, Bill. And I know they have nothing to do with any kind of drugs, so let's look at your evidence," LeRoy answered.

"Sorry, Moose. That's privileged information. We have to review it first," Watkins said.

"So, based on this evidence, when can my friends expect to hear from you?" LeRoy asked.

"It'll take time. If we decide to start seizure proceedings, it could take a few months," Watkins replied.

Over the open phone line, Edwin had missed a few words, but he got the gist of the situation and he was starting to sweat.

"While we're waiting, I think the federal government owes these honest business people a little money," LeRoy replied, handing the bill to Watkins.

"What's this?" Watkins asked.

"If we're going to do everything by the book, you owe these people the rate for the two people who used this room," the captain replied.

"That's outrageous, Moose," Watkins responded.

"I don't think that's the only thing that's outrageous here. Come on, Wally, let's let our law enforcement brothers get back to enjoying their honeymoon," LeRoy said. "You can pay at the desk on your way out. You can put it on that fat government expense account. The tax-payers are footing the bill."

As they walked down the hall, Wally Callahan spoke into his cell phone. "Edwin, where are you?" he asked.

"In my office."

"Order some coffee. We'll be right down," Wally replied.

Wally, John Moose LeRoy, and Edwin sat in his office talking about the federal agents and what it meant that they were there. LeRoy thought it was strange two government agents, one local and one from Washington, had been in the hotel. Edwin was concerned about the possibility of the seizure of the hotel. LeRoy told him to relax and made a call on his cell phone. He explained the situation to the person on the other end and asked them to make a call to Washington to call the guys off and see if they could find out who had pointed them to the hotel. He hung up.

"That should take care of it. I'd like to see the look on the agents' faces when they find out Lee Brown was talking to their boss," he said. "And more important, who put them on to the hotel? It wasn't a friend."

Edwin didn't know what to say. *I know she worked in D.C., but how connected is this girl?*

chapter

TWENTY FIVE

As Edwin, LeRoy, and Wally concluded their conversation about the federal agents, Wally took a call on his cell phone.

"That was one of my security guys. We got a lady in 802 claiming assault and the perp is being held in the room. And people always ask, 'Where's a cop when you need one, Moose?'" Wally replied, looking at the captain.

"Why not? I wouldn't want to shirk my public duties," LeRoy said.

"Go back to what you have to do and don't worry about the Feds. I have a feeling it will be handled," LeRoy said. He and Wally headed off to Room 802.

Donna came in with a phone message and, with a smile, told him to return it immediately. Edwin called the phone number. It belonged to Nancy Farrow at CC&A Bank. Ms. Farrow answered and asked him to hold for Mr. Forrest, the bank president. Forrest came on and started apologizing. He said there had been a mix-up by someone in the loan department and he would take care of everything immediately. He also thanked Edwin for all the years of business from the hotel.

You lying gutless wonder. He could tell Forrest wasn't enjoying this call. He guessed Irving Kertzner still had a good amount of clout at CC&A. Forrest said the papers would be over in a matter of hours, and the money would be deposited that afternoon. Edwin thanked him and told him he would have his controller, Chuck Castillano, handle everything. When he hung up, he went to Chuck's office. He explained the call from the bank and gave him Nathan Forrest's cell phone number, asking Chuck to handle it.

While Edwin was deciding Nathan Forrest wasn't telling the truth and was a stuffed shirt, Wally and Captain LeRoy were arriving at Room 802. Wally's security guy explained he came to the room when he had gotten a call from housekeeping saying a disturbance was taking place. When he got to the room, the door was not fully latched. He entered and found Mr. Slater, the registered guest, and the other man rolling around on the floor, fighting. Mr. Slater claimed he had returned from a meeting with the teachers' group and found his wife being sexually assaulted by the man who was now in handcuffs sitting across the room. The man was wearing a white shirt and slacks and was in his bare feet. His nose was bleeding and he looked confused and scared. The woman was sitting on the bed. The man Wally took to be Mr. Slater was standing next to her, throwing menacing looks at the man in the chair. On the bed next to the woman was an expensive arrangement of red roses.

"Aren't you going to call the police and get this scum away from my wife?" Slater yelled.

"Mr. Slater, I know you folks are upset. I'm Wally Callahan, director of security for the St. George. This gentleman with me is Captain John LeRoy with the city police department."

Wally called the front desk and found the nearest vacant room. He asked his security guy to take the handcuffed man to the room and Captain LeRoy would go with him. The security guard escorted the handcuffed man out. Wally continued to look around the room.

"Aren't you going to do something instead of standing there looking around?" Mr. Slater demanded.

"Yes, I am, Mr. Slater, but officially this is a crime scene. Assault is a felony and a very serious one," Wally said.

He watched Mrs. Slater's face. Her expression didn't change, but her eyes were almost clouded over and she moved them toward the ceiling as if she were praying.

If she was being sexually assaulted, Wally thought, *there'd be anger or fear in them.*

Mr. Slater continued to demand that Wally do something immediately. Wally made mental notes as he continued his evaluation of the scene. Something was missing. It took Wally a while to figure out what it was.

"Mr. Slater, if you want the outcome you expect, I need just a few moments more to evaluate the scene. I'm a retired police officer. I understand how these things work," Wally said.

It finally struck Wally: *There are no clothes visible in the room. If someone was being sexually assaulted, there would be clothes scattered around. Maybe this guy is a clean freak or kinky.* He went into the bathroom. For some reason, he picked up both toothbrushes and felt the bristles. Only one of them was wet. He left the bathroom and went to the door. The door and frame were freshly painted and showed no marks of forced entry. He noticed a suit coat and tie neatly hung up in the closet. A pair of men's shoes were neatly placed in the closet with socks in them. They were not in the same part of the closet as the other male clothing.

"Mrs. Slater, I understand you're in distress, but I have to get your words on what happened here," Wally said.

"What do you mean what happened here? She was attacked and you're upsetting her further by asking," Mr. Slater said.

"Please, Mr. Slater. I have to get her story," Wally said. "It will also have to be repeated to the police."

"It all happened very fast," she started. "Luckily, my husband came in before it went too far."

She explained, when she finished a late breakfast, she had gone into the bar and gotten a glass of wine to take to her room. She only got away without the children during the annual teachers' meeting. She took the occasion to totally relax. While she was in the bar, she noticed the man who had later come to her room claiming she had left something in the bar. When she opened the door, the man forced his way in and began talking about sex. She objected, but his size and the look in his eyes told her resisting was useless and she might be seriously harmed if she did. She was totally embarrassed and ashamed her poor husband had witnessed his wife of twenty-two years in this position.

When she was done, Wally said, "Thank you, Mrs. Slater. I know it's been a terrible experience. Mr. Slater, please take care of your wife. I have to check on the man in the other room. I won't be long."

He went to Room 805, where Captain LeRoy was saying, "Look, Sparky, I've been a cop for a long time and I've met people a lot tougher than you. Everybody's innocent. So why don't you save me and yourself a lot of time and trouble and tell the truth."

"Let me guess. You met the victim in the bar. You struck up a conversation. She doesn't get away very often, and her husband is totally non-sexual. You, on the other hand, are a real swordsman in a puppy dog costume. The lady needs her annual fling and you're just the guy to drive her wild. Mr. Non-sexual-but-married walks in and she yells assault. Of course, you're just so good in bed, that you're amazed she would tell a lie to save her marriage. How am I doing so far, Romeo?" Wally offered.

"Look, I'm innocent. I don't care what she said," the man answered.

"I asked you how am I doing?" Wally asked.

"You're close. When did she confess?" the man asked.

"She hasn't," Wally said. He motioned LeRoy to join him outside the room.

"What you just said matches his story almost to the letter," LeRoy said.

"It ain't the first time this Casanova has banged a married broad, but I think he's telling the truth," Wally replied.

He explained the one wet toothbrush and the clothes hung up neat and nice.

"You ever see an assault that neat and deliberate? He might think his equipment is bigger than Texas, but I don't think he's stupid. You find anything to prove different?"

"You always were better at sniffing things out. I'll go with your call," LeRoy replied. "Besides, whatever was happening had just gotten started. There's no physical evidence. They were in the room, but a good lawyer could make it he-said, she-said."

"I'll go try to convince Mr. Slater they're better off dropping it. I'm not sure he'll buy it," Wally said.

"There might be a way to do it. Trust old Moose," LeRoy replied.

For the next ten minutes, the two old friends went back over the evidence. As they talked, Wally couldn't get the look in Mrs. Slater's eyes out of his head. He explained it to LeRoy.

"The eyes show guilt. She's lying. If we give her a way out so she doesn't have to give up the marriage, she'll convince her husband it's the right thing," LeRoy answered.

"You really think so, Moose?" Wally asked.

"Come on, Pard. Twenty-two years married and living in a small town where your whole life is centered. She'll find a way," LeRoy said. "Believe me; she'll know how to play it."

"I'll go try," Wally said.

"No, I think it's my turn. The badge will help deliver it when I say my years of experience tell me it will be a long and drawn-out process with a lot of publicity in their local paper. Do me a favor and go make that guy feel like the slime he really is while I'm telling my story to the Slaters."

LeRoy returned to Room 802.

"So, do we go to the police station now and put that pervert away?" Mr. Slater asked.

"That might make you feel a little better, and I mean a little, but I think it would be a disservice to your wife," the captain responded.

He looked into Mrs. Slater's eyes. They looked hopeful for the first time.

"The man was attempting to assault my wife. I can't allow her to be abused without justice."

"What I'm saying, Mr. Slater, is what will come out going forward might be harder on your wife and your relationship than what happened here today. Let me explain," the captain continued.

LeRoy took the facts and created a series of scenarios that a good defense lawyer might use. He concentrated on the stress on Slater's wife and the embarrassment back home for both of them. The trial of the man would be drawn out and traumatic. He watched Mrs. Slater's eyes as he spoke: relief. LeRoy had given her the perfect out.

"I don't like this one bit," Mr. Slater protested.

"Honey, we live in a small town. Our love is there and perhaps this will strengthen it. I would rather spend my time worrying about you than worrying about what our friends and neighbors are thinking and saying," Mrs. Slater offered.

The husband thought a moment, "If that's really what you want. But I don't want you sacrificing your personal feelings for my comfort."

"It's not for your comfort. It's for us and our life together," she replied.

Son of a gun, she saw the opening and sold it, LeRoy thought.

"Well then, we can proceed with living and forgetting?" the captain asked.

"Yes, we can and thank you, Captain," Mrs. Slater replied.

"I'm still not sure, but I'll trust my wife and respect her wishes," Mr. Slater said.

The captain thanked them, confirmed that it was not a police matter anymore, and excused himself. He grabbed the perp's clothes on his way out of the room. He looked back at Mrs. Slater. She mouthed the words thank you. He went to Room 805.

"Put these on and get out of town," he said, tossing the clothes to Paul Winters.

"I can't leave town. I have to run our exhibit at the teachers' trade show," Winters replied.

"Tell your employer you got the plague or a fever blister, and your doctor told you the climate here isn't good for you. I really don't give a damn, but be out of the hotel in one hour," Wally warned.

"You can't do that," Winters protested.

"If he can't, I can, and don't try to steal the robe or the towels," LeRoy replied.

Winters went into the bathroom to get dressed.

"That worked out O.K.," Wally said. "Let's have lunch. My man can show the gentleman out. My treat, you like creamed capon?"

"Love food," LeRoy answered.

"Edwin is hoping so," Wally replied.

chapter

TWENTY SIX

Edwin went to Chuck Castillano's office to see if the bank loan was taken care of.

Chuck assured him the paperwork was on the way. He had gotten Forrest at his private club having lunch and didn't think Forrest appreciated dealing with a lowly comptroller.

Edwin had time before his meeting with Chambers and his brother so he sat down with the financial statements to refresh his memory. The numbers were depressing. He remembered the hotel in the good days. What really made him sad was that his grandfather had taken so much pride in the hotel and its success. It was a love relationship for the old man. Now, the new generation of corporate hotels was beating it down. He felt an obligation to change that, but he wasn't sure if it could be done. He realized he was not a hotel expert, just a guy who didn't mind a fight. As he sat thinking, Jack Vincent called.

"Afternoon, Boss. Thought you'd like to know your brother and Mr. Chambers just entered the bar," Jack reported. Edwin looked at his watch: five o'clock. They were early. He decided to wait before joining them.

Let them talk. It'll save the phone calls between them.

When he entered the bar, Marty looked up and pointed to a corner table. Edwin walked over and welcomed them.

"Thanks for taking the time, Henry. Good to see you. Thanks, Leonard, for setting this up. I'm sorry I've been so busy," Edwin offered.

"I guess you have been busy, little brother," Henry replied with a crooked smile. "Leonard was telling me some of the strange things that have been going on around the St. George. Some public officials seem to be taking advantage of the new ownership. I think they were afraid of grandfather," Henry paused. "He also told me you might need my financial help in the short-term." Henry was already on his second martini and was gleefully smug.

"I won't have to bother you with that. Mr. Forrest at the bank has arranged an immediate loan," Edwin replied. Chambers and Henry tried to hide their surprise. He could see their minds grinding to figure out how he had moved the bank to his side.

"As to the strange series of events at the hotel, Henry, A.D. has been out of the hotel actively for a year, and I'm sure Leonard has had a good control on the property," Edwin replied. "It could just be coincidence."

Edwin wanted to appear as naive as possible. Acting stupid had worked well for him in the past when he was unsure of a situation.

"So, how are you enjoying the hectic life of a hotel owner so far?" Henry asked.

"Actually, I'm loving it. There's never a dull moment and I love the people," Edwin responded.

When in doubt, smile. It drives them nuts.

Edwin asked how the construction business and the airport project were going. Henry went into great detail to explain working government projects meant you got your money at the end, but the Christian name would be on the airport for eternity.

So, you're losing your ass.

"Anyway, you didn't request this meeting to talk about construction," Henry said.

Marty came to the table and asked Edwin if he'd like a drink. "Thanks, Marty, I'll have a Sierra, and it looks like these gentlemen might want another. I'm buying."

"Leonard indicated you had some questions about the hotel I might be able to help you with."

"I'm curious about a few things. First, the hotel's business levels go up and down like the tides. We've cut a lot of costs, thanks to Leonard, but cash flow is still a problem. Where do you see the future of the hotel?" Edwin asked them both.

"Quite frankly, I brought Leonard in to manage the hotel as an interim measure. I didn't think the old man could take the sale of the hotel. I told you earlier, with the new competition in town and the age of the hotel, I think the only answer is to sell. The land might be worth more than the building," Henry replied. "What about you, Leonard? You're an experienced hotelier."

"Based on what I've seen and my experience, I don't see a future for the St. George. Older hotels either need a complete renovation and repositioning or they need to be sold," Leonard replied.

"What type of repositioning would the St. George need to be profitable?" Edwin asked.

"Not one you'd want to consider with your own money," Henry replied.

"How so?" Edwin asked.

Henry explained, even with a large investment in rehab, it would take a few years to make any money. The large companies can hold on that long; Edwin couldn't. If he put an upscale hotel brand name on it, the bigger companies would also want a larger management company to run it or they'd run it themselves. Edwin would lose control of the hotel. The only other alternative was to make it a lower cost provider, which it was now, and it wasn't doing well. It was time to sell and sit back with some money.

"So, if things are so bad, who would buy it?" Edwin asked.

"There might be several buyers. As I said, the land is worth a fortune," Henry replied.

Edwin waited to speak until Marty left after delivering the drinks. He didn't want the rumor of selling the hotel being broadcast around the property panicking the staff. When people think the ship is going down, they often jump for the first lifeboat. In this case, the lifeboat would be a job in a competing hotel. Edwin didn't want to see himself, as the comedian Woody Woodbury had said, being the captain of the *Titanic* trying to tell the passengers, "Don't worry, folks, we're just stopping to take on ice."

"So, you're saying I'm between a rock and a hard place?" Edwin asked.

"Either that or in deep doodoo," Henry replied.

I hate that cutesy snobbish stuff. Shit is shit between three guys in a bar.

"I appreciate your honesty and experience. For now, I have to think about it and just keep running this place, with Leonard's help and loyalty," Edwin said. He made sure to put resolve in his voice and emphasize the word loyalty.

"You asked and we responded in your best interest. I'm glad you got things worked out with the bank," his brother offered. Edwin could see the bank giving him a loan was puzzling Henry. He knew Mr. Forrest would be getting a call.

"Don't get me wrong. I appreciate your help and advice and I'll think very seriously about it," Edwin answered. He wondered in whose best interest selling the St. George really was.

"Leonard, I want to bring our old chief engineer Jake Jacoby back. I think this old lady needs some TLC on a daily basis," Edwin said. "I don't mean to take money away from Christian Construction, but I think we need daily oversight from a person who knows the hotel intimately," he concluded.

The chief engineer in a hotel is a key asset. They know every nook and cranny of a hotel. They know every wire, pipe, and physical problem and they're resourceful in keeping a hotel going. This is especially true in older hotels that have been renovated or added to over the years. A long-term, dedicated engineer has the knowledge of a mechanical engineer, a mechanic, a construction supervisor, and a caretaker.

Henry and Chambers didn't look happy. Edwin knew his brother sensed it was coming because of his conversation with Chambers. It was anger on their faces, not surprise.

"I'd think about that, Edwin. Using our men saves you the cost of a full-time staff, and you know you have to conserve wherever you can," Henry offered.

"I really do appreciate that, but I can hire a small maintenance staff to help Jake for the amount we're paying your company. At seventy dollars an hour for your highly skilled men, I can give him the backup he needs for a fraction of that. This place, how did you put it, looks like doodoo? If we have any chance of making it, we have to improve guest appeal. At least, I think that's what you call it," Edwin replied.

Now he saw surprise on their faces because he had a good idea of how bad Christian Construction had been sticking it to the hotel. That a guy, out of the jungles of South America, could pick up numbers that fast really surprised them. The thing that angered Edwin was that Henry had been palming money from his own grandfather's hotel to make himself look good with the operating results of the construction company.

"I honestly think you're going the wrong way, but it's your hotel," Henry said. Chambers held his opinion.

For you, maybe, Edwin thought, *but I don't think so.*

"Thanks for your time. I appreciate your help and your interest," Edwin said as he motioned to Marty. "Marty, I have to go. Please give these gentlemen whatever they want and I'll sign the check tomorrow. This is a personal expense on me. They've given me the benefit of their long experience and insight."

Edwin excused himself with the promise to think hard about what they had said and headed for the kitchen. He hadn't eaten all day. He was famished.

The chef and his staff were preparing the teacher's buffet.

"You look like hell," the chef said.

"I just had a meeting with Chambers and my brother," Edwin replied. He didn't have to explain any further. The chef said he looked hungry and cut a piece of prime rib and made a sandwich with French bread. He wrapped it and handed it to Edwin.

Greg Plank

"Go home and eat. You look like you could use some quiet time," the chef said. Edwin thanked him and left through the front door of the lobby. He ran into Slim Johnson.

"I can get you a ride in the limo if you can wait," Slim said. "I sent your brother home in it."

"No thanks. I'll walk," Edwin replied.

"Why the limo for Henry? His driver quit?"

"No, he just had the night off. It's a good thing your brother wasn't driving himself," Slim replied.

"Why?" Edwin asked.

"Marty called me from the bar when he and Chambers were leaving. Your brother had six martinis. Besides, if I got him a cab, he would have billed it to the hotel and the cabby would have heaped a big tip on the fare."

"Thanks for helping out," Edwin responded.

"Just what the doorman does when the doorman's doing door," Slim offered with a smile.

chapter

TWENTY SEVEN

The next day was uneventful. Edwin continued reviewing the hotel financial statements. He was relieved by the cash the bank loan provided, but he was still troubled by the hotel's poor financial condition. He also continued to be confused by the lack of help he had received from old family friend Justy LaGrange. The sudden attention by city and federal officials puzzled him. In late afternoon, he left his office and went to the lobby. Jack Vincent was on the phone. When he hung up he explained it was the police lining up the Tiger's Tail mission. Edwin told him to be careful and repeated the lobby would not be the same without him. Jack told him he had bigger things to worry about, like a special dinner with a certain lawyer.

"No big deal. A little creamed capon, some wine, and some nice conversation. The chef promised his best," Edwin answered.

Jack took on a fatherly tone and reminded Edwin he was the owner of the hotel. The entire staff wanted to put on their best for him; the dinner would be something special.

"Can't people mind their own business around here?" Edwin asked in frustration.

"Allow me to remind you, this is a hotel not a monastery. Everyone knows everything. Relax and appreciate their feelings for you. And, don't put your foot in your mouth at dinner," Jack replied.

Edwin smiled and went to the front desk, got a key for a vacant and ready room, and told them to put it out of service. It would not be rented to another guest. He headed to Room 430, showered, and dressed. At six-fifty, he went to the lobby and stood in the back near the elevators. At six-fifty-nine, Slim Johnson, looking like an admiral in the Royal Navy, entered the lobby, and called the bell staff together. They talked for a moment and then lined up. Slim was just inside the door and the six bell staff lined up in rows of three on each side of the entrance. It was a reception line for royalty. On Slim's command, they all came to attention.

What the hell is going on?

The door opened and Lee came in. Slim Johnson stepped forward and welcomed her. He presented her with a red and a white long stemmed rose. He looked toward Edwin and winked. Edwin wanted to die.

Talk about overkill. She'll think I planned this. Edwin hesitated for a moment and then started to walk toward Lee. He didn't know whether to rescue her or disappear through the floor. Half-way across the lobby, he saw she had the biggest smile he had seen. She was laughing with Slim. As Edwin approached, he heard her say, "Thank you, gentlemen, what a nice reception. I feel special."

Maybe I won't fire Slim and Jack after all.

"Good evening and welcome to the Hotel St. George, Ms. Brown," he heard himself say.

I'm screwed now, so I'm going with it.

"Charmed, Mr. Christian," she said, starting to giggle.

"What's so funny? I feel stupid as it is," he said without thinking.

"I'm not laughing at you. I don't know you that well, but I don't think you would plan it this way. Actually, I am charmed. Your people must care about you," she answered.

"In their own strange way, I guess they do. How about some creamed capon?" he offered.

"Charmed, Mr. Christian, totally charmed," she said again in an affected voice. He thought she was having a little fun at his expense, but he was afraid to ask.

When they entered the dining room, there were ten tables occupied, but the corner table was set up with flowers and the large candles were lit. As they approached the table, Pas Medvier, the French food and beverage manager, appeared. He was dressed in a tuxedo with tails and a gray formal vest. He welcomed them in French and Lee answered him in French.

"We have a special meal prepared for you. My Italian associate has been slaving all day. I hope it is acceptable for Chef Mazzari and me to choose the courses and serve them. Of course, the main entree is creamed capon as the lady requested," Pas said.

Edwin looked at Lee who was smiling and answered, "You're the pros and the hosts. Please proceed."

Pas Medvier asked them for their cocktail or aperitif preference.

After they gave their orders and he left, Edwin was silent, thinking about the grand entrance. He was wondering how big a dork she really thought he was.

"Don't be embarrassed by the welcome your people gave me. I felt like the little girl who wanted to be royalty," she said reading his mind.

"I'm almost sorry you liked it," Edwin answered.

"Why? I enjoyed it, really," she replied.

"Because, I didn't think of it," he answered.

"If you're looking for sympathy, I do feel for you. That could have been very embarrassing if I had acted embarrassed. I like your company because you aren't full of yourself. I wish I had the whole thing on video," she said.

"How bad was the look on my face?" he asked.

"I was waiting for you to hide behind the potted plants."

"I considered it, but you were too far into the lobby by then," he said.

Pas Medvier returned with their drinks. "To an unusual or good or unusually good evening and good health," he said.

Lee raised her glass, touched his, and took a sip. "And to fun and friendship," she said. "And that will happen when you learn to really relax around me. I think between the cops who knew me, God knows what stories they've told, and the lawyer thing, you still don't feel comfortable, and you're trying to watch what you say."

"You want the truth?" Edwin asked.

"The whole truth and nothing but the truth. It's that law thing," she said.

"What the hell? I hate cowards and liars. The truth is I was taken by your voice the first time I talked to you. I had to meet you and I was nervous the night you came to the hotel for our first meeting. Then when I heard about your background, I was a bit intimidated. Going to you for advice sometimes makes me feel stupid. Wrap that all together and I guess you've got a guy who would like to see you enough to be able to relax and be natural."

"How much is enough?" she asked as she put her hand on his.

"I'm not sure there is enough," he said and broke into a smile.

"We'll have to see, won't we?" she asked.

Pas Medvier served an appetizer of three pates followed with fruit. The wines were white and light. As they ate, they talked about the hotel. He listened carefully to her opinions. When the entree was ready, the chef came to the table with a special cart holding a tureen. "Lee, may I present Chef Luigi Mazzari or, if he really likes you, Lou," Edwin said.

"I like her already. She requested my favorite dish," the chef said. He placed the large warm dinner plates in front of them.

"I would have thought that something with tomato or a zesty sauce would be the favorite of a famous Italian chef," Lee responded.

"But that's the secret," the chef said. "You can combine heavy spices and vegetables and make a very good sauce. But the true art is to make a delicate sauce, like a white sauce, have a special character," Chef Mazzari answered and artfully served the creamed capon.

Before he could leave, Lee said, "Excuse me, Edwin, but I can't wait."

She picked up her knife and fork, cut a portion and placed it delicately in her mouth, closed her eyes and smiled. If you asked both men, they would have both said it was one of the most sensuous things they had ever seen.

"Wonderful," she said, "Just wonderful. It was worth the wait."

"Thank you, Ms. Brown. You're very kind," the chef replied with uncharacteristic exuberance.

When they had finished the entrée, she put down her fork and took a piece of croissant from the silver bread tray. "Excuse my lack of manners, but I have to do this," she said as she wiped up the last of the sauce on the plate and ate it.

Pas served a light pastry and fruit dessert with coffee.

"When do you have to leave?" Edwin asked.

"I saved the night so we could talk," she said. "I have to be honest. I've been trying to tell you I'm frustrated with our lack of a relationship."

Edwin held his breath for a minute. He was afraid he was going to get the 'I think we should keep it professional and be friends' speech.

After all, I'm calling her for advice, my staff is making me look like I'm fawning over her and the only time we've been out together, I break a guy's arm in front of her.

She noticed the puzzled look on his face and said, "I think my choice of words was poor. See, I'm frustrated, for the lack of a better word, that you haven't pushed harder. I'm, let's just say, used to being pushed. Hell, I'm used to being hit on and you haven't even attempted anything. Oh God! I don't even know what I'm saying," she said. She didn't look so happy anymore.

"I've been hitting on you since the first time I talked to you. I thought it would be better if I did it by asking for help or just being nice. I have a big case of awkward self-doubt, because I really don't want to overstep my bounds or your standards," he answered.

She took a sip of coffee to have time to think. "I do have a standard, but you might find it strange."

"You're not into bondage and leather or anything, are you?" he asked.

She laughed. "It's not that kind of standard, and, no, I'm not into the kinky stuff. So let me explain."

Lee started with her college days. She had been a party girl. Wild is how she described her social life. By the time she was a senior, she wasn't enjoying the parties and casual relationships anymore, but didn't know what she did want. On spring vacation that year, she spent time with her grandmother, who was more like a big sister and never judged her. One night, Lee confessed her wild ways and her confusion about her life. She told her things she would never tell her mother. Her grandmother listened patiently and then told her, the guilt she felt came from inside, and that people only feel the amount of guilt they accept for themselves. Her grandmother concluded Lee didn't respect the party side of herself anymore.

It blew her away. Her grandmother knew exactly how she felt. She promised herself she was going to take care of her inner person. Throughout law school and time in government, she dated, but hadn't slept with anyone since college.

"What's the strange part of your standard?" he asked.

"I'm going to ask you to take the full series of STD tests before we make love," she answered, looking for his reaction.

He put his head back and bit his lip as he stared at the ceiling.

"I'll take them too. I just don't want us to find something good and our pasts could come back to make it sordid or tragic," she said, almost panicked.

When he looked into her eyes, his smile was radiant.

"I wouldn't make love with someone who just came out of the jungles of South America without some assurance they're not lethal either," Edwin added.

"You're not put off?"

"I'm honored," he replied.

A beaming Pas showed up at the table with Marty Rosenbloom in tow. "Your drinks," Pas said as he put two snifters in front of them.

"Thank you, Pas. Hello, Marty," Edwin said.

"Just here to check on my girlfriend's martini and say hello," Marty said, looking at Lee.

"It was great, Marty. You're the best bartender in the world. How are you?" Lee asked.

"Not as good as you two seem to be," he said with a wink. "You kids have fun. I'll be in the bar if you need anything else."

"Thanks, Rabbi," Edwin said.

Edwin sat back and let his arms fall with a large sigh.

"You O.K.?" Lee asked.

"You don't know how O.K.," he said.

chapter

TWENTY EIGHT

While the creamed capon was being served, Jack was a few blocks away starting his adventure. The Tiger's Tail, originally a warehouse, was located in the entertainment section of town. Billy Caponi, the owner, had a big fight against the moralists to get it permitted. Fortunately, he was well-connected in town and made sure he was always a good citizen: he held fund raisers for charities, participated in civic projects, and watched the operation carefully. The club had a solid policy of "look but don't touch," and the dancers were not allowed to date customers. The convention bureau had been a quiet supporter of the Tiger's Tail, because it was well-known, and, although it was never mentioned in the brochures, it was one more compelling feature of the city when booking conventions.

The front of the Tiger's Tail was a large wall painted in tiger stripes. The door was fashioned like a tiger's mouth, complete with teeth and a red carpet shaped like a tongue. Thousands of pictures of guests had been taken in the doorway. The dancers could make fifty to eighty thousand a year, based on the number of lap dances they were able to give at twenty dollars a dance plus tips. Some dancers were the main bread-winners in their household with Mr. Mom staying home with the children. They also got a good amount of money placed in their g-strings by adoring customers.

The inside of the club was more sophisticated than many good-sized live performance theatres. Caponi spent time in Las Vegas studying the entertainment rooms in the casinos. He didn't gamble. His time was spent with the engineers who installed and operated the sound and light systems. Over the years, he had invested a few million dollars in lighting, staging, decor, and sound systems. The ceilings were thirty feet high with every kind of light imaginable. There was a large horseshoe-shaped bar with a stage in the middle and four additional stages at different levels around the cavernous room. The sound system was so sophisticated, five different songs could be played at once and not bleed over into the other stages' areas. There was also a private section for the guests who wanted the pleasure of a private lap dance without being seen by their neighbors, employees, or relatives. Every wall had twenty-foot-high mirrors, placed so that all angles of a dancer could be seen.

Jack had agreed to meet the undercover officers in the far corner of the bar at ten o'clock. He had taken great pains to be disguised enough to avoid detection by anyone he knew. He wore a turtleneck of muted gray, a black blazer, and dark slacks. They would help him blend into the darker parts of the room. He also had worn his best pair of four-hundred-dollar European sunglasses. Being a frugal person, he had paid ten dollars for them at the charity auction the hotel had for the employees each year. The hotel auctioned off the unclaimed items from lost and found and donated the money to charity. He had also used mousse in his hair to give a slight spiked look.

Jack arrived at nine-thirty, using a lowered voice and a slight Italian accent. He passed unrecognized by the two off-duty cop doormen he had known for three years of attending Have-It-Your-Way Thursday nights. He ordered a beer. He never drank from a glass in any bar. He leaned against the wall and waited for the cops to show up. Thursday night crowds were loud and festive.

At nine-fifty, Frank Wright and Bruce "Bubba" Hall entered the club and proceeded to the back corner of the bar. They took up a position five feet from Jack and waited for him. Jack joked loudly with one of the bartenders in his Italian accent to make sure the two cops noticed him. They didn't. For effect, he pulled out a large cigar, walked over to them and asked for a light. Bubba reached into his pocket for a lighter. Jack lit the cigar, said thank you and went back to his post. Jack watched the crowd and the two officers. At ten minutes after ten, they checked their watches, wondering where he was.

"Do either of you gentlemen know where I might find a cop?" Jack called to them from a few feet away.

They looked at him suspiciously until Bubba Hall said, "Pretty freaking good, Jack."

"Sorry, guys. But I just wanted to make sure I met your standards of disguise," Jack replied.

They decided the best vantage point would be the upper level in the far corner. As they crossed the floor, a tall female in a tight black dress, spiked leather choker around her neck, spike heels, spiked hair and black lipstick, fell in behind them. She was carrying a large black leather purse with silver studs decorating it. She looked like the queen of punk and blended into the crowd. When they got to the table, she slid in next to Jack. When Jack turned to look, her appearance made him jump.

"Holy crap, Carla, no wonder you don't date anyone in the department," Bubba said.

"You're scarier than the hookers we booked last night," Frank said.

"Jack, this is Carla Brunhower, I think," Bubba said. "She's in the intelligence division."

"I'd say charmed, but I'm not really sure," Jack offered with a smile.

"So, you're the concierge? Nice to meet you," Carla said.

"Don't get any ideas, Carla. Jack's gay," Frank said.

"No problem. I appreciate good manners, and I don't try to lay all my dates like you two." She smiled at Jack.

"I don't either, Carla. Conversation is often more satisfying," Jack responded.

"Spare me," Bubba said.

"O.K., boys, what are we looking for?" Carla asked.

Frank handed a copy of the security-camera photo from the hotel to Carla. He explained the two guys were in the St. George the night the second dancer was murdered. Jack saw them in here together one Thursday night with an older seedy-looking guy. The mission was to get his picture.

"You bring a camera in that knapsack of yours?" Bubba asked.

"Yep, brought the one for low light the department got from the military," Carla replied.

"You gonna get it out and ready?" Frank asked.

"You show me what you want shot and I pick up my purse like I'm looking for something and take the picture. It's fitted into my bag," she answered.

"I'm impressed," Jack said.

"I thought you needed a telephoto lens or something to get close-ups," Bubba offered.

"Guys are fascinated with long lenses the size of what you wish your manhood was," Carla replied.

Jack laughed; the two cops looked hurt.

"Too bad you're gay, Jack. You have a good sense of humor," Carla said to rub it in.

A server in a tiger outfit came up to the table. They all looked on in amusement as she picked up her tail to write the order. She had inserted a pen in the tail.

"Very unique," Jack said.

"What else can you do with your tail?" Bubba asked.

"For a big tip, I can probably think of a lot of things," she answered.

Bubba sat, wondering if he had just been solicited. When the server, appropriately named Kitten, left the group they split the room into four sections and each took one for observation.

"Where did you see them before, Jack?" Frank asked.

"They were over there near the corner stage. The one with the dancer with the flowers on her breasts, Candi Lane," Jack answered.

"The stage is named Candy Lane?" Bubba asked.

"No. That's the dancer's name," Jack replied.

For the next hour, the four watched. Being Have-It-Your-Way night, there were some wild characters and unusual outfits in the crowd. The dancers went from female to male to appeal to everyone. Frank was having trouble grasping the fact that male customers put money in the g-strings of male dancers and females did the same thing to the female dancers.

After an hour and fifteen minutes, Jack asked the cops, "Is there a code word if I see our guys?"

"No, why?" Bubba asked.

"Because the two young men just sat down at the last table in the second row of my stage area," Jack said.

All three of the cops turned slowly to look.

"Yup, looks like them from the picture," Frank said. Whenever a person approached the young men's table, Carla would take pictures.

"Maybe we should take a few pictures of the dancers to establish where we are," Bubba said.

"Yeah, and you'll put them on your personal web site to prove we were here," Carla replied.

"I don't think so. He has trouble with email," Frank volunteered.

"Very funny," Bubba replied.

Jack felt the mild tension and said, "I really admire you guys for being able to make fun of each other and not take it seriously. It must make the boring days easier to take."

Carla liked Jack's feelings for people. He was the first gay guy she had spent any time with, other than the kinky ones she had arrested when she worked the vice squad.

"Bogey at the table," Jack said.

It took the cops a moment to realize what Jack was saying.

"You think that's him, the older guy?" Carla asked. She turned her bag and the whirring sound of the camera came in small bursts.

"That's him. As I told the captain, he has a horror-show look," Jack replied.

"Either of you recognize him?" Frank asked.

"No, but Carla might have dated him," Bubba answered.

"At least he dresses better than you, Bubba," Carla replied.

"If he's a regular, maybe Billy Caponi knows him," Jack offered.

"The captain alerted Billy we'd be here. We can ask him on the way out," Frank said.

The scene continued for another half hour before the older man got up and left. Minutes later, the two younger men got up to leave. Bubba pulled a large roll of cash out of his pocket and peeled off a hundred dollars. He told Jack to wait and pay the bill; they were going to follow the suspects. They'd call him in the morning.

"You did great, Jack. You'd make a good cop," Carla said. She leaned over and instinctively kissed Jack on the cheek. The move was not lost on Bubba.

"Don't forget the receipt. I need it," was all Bubba said.

Jack stayed to clear the tab with Kitten. She was thrilled with the fifty-dollar tip Jack left. Jack was thrilled too. He had never left a fifty-dollar cash tip before, but it was city money. And he had never been kissed by a cop. As he passed the two off-duty cops working as doormen, he said, "Ciao" and waved. He heard one of the doormen say, "Who was that? I swear I've seen him before."

"Probably one of Caponi's strange Italian relatives," the other answered.

Jack laughed to himself as he enjoyed the walk home.

chapter

TWENTY NINE

Edwin woke at five a.m. as normal. He was unusually tired and couldn't decide if it was from the tension of the hotel's situation or because he and Lee had stayed in the bar until two a.m. Thinking a run might get mind and body working, he put in five hard miles, changed and walked to the hotel.

Slim Johnson was on the door talking with Leonard Chambers, who was holding a leash attached to a small animal with bows on its head. It was a pedigreed Pekinese that barked violently as Edwin got close.

"Sorry, she doesn't take well to strangers," Chambers apologized.

Edwin walked directly to the dog and bent down. "Aren't you looking good this morning," he said.

Chambers was trying to restrain the dog like it was a three-hundred-pound lion. At the sound of Edwin's voice, the dog started wagging her tail and pulling toward him. He put out his hand and the dog licked it. When Edwin reached out and scratched the dog's ears, she panted with appreciation.

"You must have something with dogs," Chambers offered.

"Yeah, dogs and women," Slim said.

"I only have trouble with jumbo-sized doormen," Edwin responded.

"Why don't you try scratching my ears?" Slim said.

Chambers stood silent, surprised about how casual Slim was with the hotel's owner.

"Well, it's time to get Miss Shana back to the apartment. I'll see you at the department heads' meeting?" he asked, in leaving.

"Ten o'clock in the board room," Edwin replied. "I'm looking forward to it."

"It will be a pleasure to have you sit in," Chambers said.

He wants to make sure I know he's running the meeting.

"Well that's one thing you've changed," Slim said after Chambers was gone.

"The meeting?" Edwin asked.

"Nope, the dog-walking ritual. Before you got here, I had to send a bellman up to get the dog and walk it. Since you've been here, I think Chambers is afraid to have hotel staff do his personal stuff."

"The walk will do him good," Edwin said. He patted Slim on the shoulder and entered the lobby.

Jack Vincent was sitting at his desk. He looked up, beaming as Edwin approached. When Edwin asked how things went at the Tiger's Tail, Jack gave him the full story from his costume to the way the cops bantered with each other. He ended with the fact they got pictures of the older man and were processing them.

"How did your night go?" Jack asked.

"The chef, Medvier and Marty were superb. Lee and I talked a lot. Nothing earthshaking," Edwin responded.

"Sounds encouraging. You're smart to take it at her speed," the concierge answered.

"I have a feeling with Lee; you better take it at her speed. Under that little girl voice there's one tough woman," Edwin offered. He didn't mention Lee's encouragement in starting a relationship.

When he got to his office, he turned on his cell phone. There was a message from Lee. She thanked him for a great evening and asked him to thank the chef, Pas Medvier and Marty. She also gave him the name of a doctor and a phone number if he wanted to get the STD tests done. He called the doctor and made an appointment for the next day.

It was now nine-thirty. He didn't think it was too early to call Irving Kertzner. He thanked Kertzner for the help at the bank and asked if he could get some advice. He went back over the conversation he had with his brother and Chambers, repeating what his brother had offered about putting more debt on the hotel to make it truly competitive, and he reminded Kertzner he didn't have that much liquid cash available. Kertzner told him he needed a consultant and he had just the right guy: Al McNerey. He passed on his number and told Edwin to tell McNerey he said to call. Edwin thanked him again.

"No thanks necessary and the name is Irv," Kertzner replied and hung up.

There was fifteen minutes left until the department heads' meeting. The number was a Chicago number. Edwin decided, even though it was early there, he'd call.

"Al McNerey."

"Mr. McNerey, my name is Edwin Christian. Irving Kertzner gave me your name and number."

"You must have a problem. Irv always has a way of getting me involved in them," McNerey replied, laughing. "What do you need?"

Edwin explained his inheritance of the St. George. Al knew the hotel and A.D. Christian. He was sorry for Edwin's loss. Everyone admired A.D. and his love for the hotel. Edwin went on to explain the entire situation and asked if McNerey would take on a consulting job. Al said he could do it in the next few weeks and he'd send a sample contract and give Edwin an idea of his fees so he could decide. Edwin said he'd just rather sign the contract and get going. If Irv thought he was good, it was good enough for him. Al agreed and asked for the past two years' financial statements and a cash-flow projection as soon as possible. Edwin took down his address and said they'd be out that day.

"Is there a good looking woman in this someplace?" McNerey asked.

"As a matter of fact, that's who suggested Irv to me," Edwin said.

"In that case, I'll have to charge you less," McNerey replied.

"My only condition is that we keep the possibility of a sale totally quiet," Edwin replied.

"No sweat. We'll just say you hired me to look at improvements the hotel needs to stay competitive," McNerey replied. "I'll see you soon."

The department heads were sitting at the large table in the boardroom. Edwin greeted them and took a chair at the side of the table next to Donna. The large chair at the head of the table was empty. At ten past ten, Chambers entered the room. Donna poured coffee for him. Chambers greeted everyone without making an excuse or apology for being late.

Rude bastard.

"This morning we have a special guest, as you all can see," Chambers said. "I hope we all behave ourselves in Mr. Christian's presence."

These aren't children. I know them better than you do. I'm no guest. I own the place, you pompous fool.

"So, as is customary, Mr. Mason, please give us the occupancy forecast for the next week," Chambers started.

Mason went through the next week, day by day. Sunday would be a slow night, but the hotel picked up on Monday with another meeting starting and occupancy held until Thursday night. That too would be low, but the hotel would do well over the weekend with the music festival in town.

"Mr. Smith, what is the group coming in next week?" Chambers asked the director of sales.

Smith explained the group coming in and the details. The one extra they needed was a special room for a bar where they'd supply their own liquor.

"We have to remember that every bit of revenue is important. I don't remember approving that," Chambers replied.

"Well, to get the sale, we had to bend," Bill Smith replied.

"I'm happy you got the business, but we have to keep the approval process in place and run a tight ship," Chambers said.

"Excuse me, but you weren't here, and Bill needed an answer so I approved it. I thought it was reasonable and assumed you would too. It came up at the last minute," Edwin said.

There was silence around the table. Smith looked at Edwin; everyone else looked at Chambers for his reaction. Edwin had lied. The arrangements had been made months before. Edwin figured Chambers wouldn't even check, but, even if he did, he didn't care.

"Very well. Let's get to the music festival this weekend. Do we have any of the bands staying in the hotel?" Chambers asked.

"We have one, the Midnight Mayors from down south," Mason offered.

"A black group?" Chambers asked.

"Why do you say that?" Wally asked.

Chambers looked at Donna Lane. If anyone hated stereotypes, it was Donna Lane, and everyone knew it. He realized he had just put a good portion of his wingtip shoe in his mouth. He tried to bail himself out.

"Well, in the deep south, the most politically powerful black person was referred to as The Midnight Mayor. I just thought there might be a connection," he said haltingly.

Having missed the point that, especially in a hotel, it shouldn't matter what ethnic group or race a guest was from, Chambers moved quickly to change the subject. He asked Wally if security could prevent any damage to the hotel during the festival. Wally told him he had off-duty cops assigned. Hotels were very careful about various entertainment groups. Some like to party and when the booze and other stimulants build up, they've been known to completely take a room apart. If they suspect a group might party a little too hard, they check with other hotels where a group has stayed to see what their activities included. The problem was, in a litigious and equal-rights country, hotels have to be careful about discrimination laws too. They have to be careful who they deny occupancy to. Another example of the innkeepers' legal tightrope.

"O.K. Let's move on to some cost areas. Mary, the overtime pay in housekeeping was over-budget for the Bar Owners group and it didn't look good yesterday either," Chambers continued.

"Unfortunately, we can't have it both ways," Mary began.

"Your point?" Chambers asked, challenging her.

There he goes again. Mr. Control Freak. Go get him Mary.

Mary said without the right stock of linen, they had to wash the sheets and towels and get them back in the rooms each day. If they had enough linen, they would have back-up, and could cut back on labor. Her voice was strong; she was not the type to back down. She knew she could have a job in another hotel on a moment's notice. Chambers knew that too and backed off.

"We've discussed this before. I'm sorry about the linen inventory, but we're tight on money," Chambers responded. "On that note I think we've covered everything. I just have one announcement to make about a decision I've made for the betterment of the hotel and for your needs. Jake Jacoby, our previous chief engineer will be joining the staff. We won't be needing as much help from Christian Construction anymore," Chambers said.

Chambers had taken credit for a decision Edwin had forced on him. Chambers smiled as if he had personally made their lives better.

Oh human curse, ego is thy name, Edwin thought.

Chambers adjourned the meeting. Edwin thanked him for the invitation to the meeting and went to Chuck Castillano's office. He told Chuck about hiring a consultant and told him Al would have full run of the hotel. He asked him to send two years of financial statements and the cash-flow projections to Al immediately.

"When Al McNerey sees the cash-flow projections he might wonder how he's going to get paid," Chuck said, shaking his head.

"How bad is it?"

"In a few months, we'll need a printing press for money if business doesn't pick up."

"We'll let Mr. McNerey help us make decisions going forward," Edwin said.

"You really high on this guy?" Chuck asked.

"I've never met him, but the gentleman that got the bank to loosen up recommended him," Edwin replied.

"If he humbled a bank president, he must know what he's doing," Chuck said, smiling. "I'll get the financials off right after lunch."

Edwin thanked him and headed toward the lobby. The thought of running out of cash worried him. The mention of Kertzner pushing the bank made him wonder, again, why Justy LaGrange, a very influential man and old family friend, hadn't offered any help.

chapter

THIRTY

Edwin caught Jack Vincent at his desk. "I'm surprised you didn't say anything at the meeting."

Jack replied, "Look, Edwin, no one listens to me and I resent being patronized by Chambers."

"Close up your desk, Jack. We're going to lunch."

Jack followed the instruction, and they went out the front door. Edwin asked Slim to keep an eye on the lobby. Edwin and Jack crossed the street and headed for Jimmy's. As they entered, Betty Sloan looked up from behind the bar. The place was crowded as usual with cops, newspaper people, construction workers and every type of person imaginable.

"Well, look who it is. I thought you were dead and here you come bringing in a young one with you," Betty said to Jack.

"I take it you've been here before," Edwin said.

"I was a regular as I was coming to terms with my sexual prefer-ence. It was too depressing to be alone at night," Jack answered.

They went to the back corner. Some customers looked at Jack with his concierge suit and lapel pins. They wondered if he was with the police or fire department. One swore he was with the Salvation Army. His friends insisted it was the wrong season for the bell-ringers to be out. They placed their order with Betty.

Edwin got right to the point, "What's really bothering you?"

"It's probably unfair, but a lot of people are worried about their jobs because of the hotel's condition and the type of business we're doing. I guess we're all looking to you to change things and things aren't moving very fast," Jack answered.

"I'm taking my time. I really don't know what to do right away," Edwin answered. "Any advice?"

Jack thought for a minute. "You asked so I'll be honest. I'd get rid of Chambers and Mason. If you're serious about turning the hotel around, the old time department heads could do it better than anyone if they had the chance."

"I know that, Jack. I've retained a consultant to help. He'll be in next week."

"You thinking of selling the hotel?" Jack asked.

"Not if I don't have to. You got any more suggestions for the short term?"

As they ate, they talked about the little things Jack thought would improve the hotel and morale. They were finishing when Jack's cell phone went off. As he listened to the voice on the other end of the line, he looked very serious. He said they'd be right there and told Edwin there was an incident involving a young man in the hotel. Wally thought they could help.

When they got to the hotel, Slim Johnson intercepted them and said Wally was waiting in Room 720. When they got to the seventh floor, a startled couple from the teachers' convention was standing in the hall next to Room 718.

"We could have been killed," the man said as they approached.

"I'm sorry, folks. Allow me to check with my director of security. I'll be right back," Jack replied.

They entered Room 720 through the partially opened door. Wally was standing near the bed holding an empty vodka bottle. The young man was lying motionless on the bed. He had cuts on his hands and head from broken glass. The room was trashed. Broken furniture, lamps, and the bedside table were scattered around. Across the room, the flat screen television was no longer on the wall. It was smashed on the floor.

"It looks like the kid got drunk and went berserk. There's some crack cocaine on the bed, but it doesn't look like he got to that before he passed out," Wally said. "I think the kid's a novice drinker, and the booze flipped him out. When the chair over there hit the wall, the impact must have knocked the mirror over the bed down onto the bed in Room 718 next door. Good thing it missed the couple."

"Is he dead?" Edwin asked.

"No, he's just passed out," Wally replied.

"Crack and a gut full of booze. Do you think he was trying to end it all?"

"This might suggest it," Wally replied. Wally handed a hotel envelope to Jack. "It was sitting on the bed." Jack read the note inside out loud. It was addressed to the boy's parents.

> You know I've always wanted to be a chef. To have my own restaurant. You never listened. You wanted me to be an engineer so I could take over the family business. I've spent my entire life playing the sports you wanted me to play. I busted my butt to get A's in subjects I didn't understand and hated. I only dated girls you approved of. The daughters of your friends and only ones in your social circle. I finally see no value in living my life for you. I'm going to control my life for the first time.

Jack finished it and said, "Makes you wonder about some parents and their self-interest. Scares the hell out of you. I'm glad the couple next door are O.K. That mirror is heavy. I helped pick it out."

"What's next?" Edwin asked.

"I wanted to make sure he's not in alcohol poisoning, so the paramedics are on their way. I notified the police, and they'll be here soon. With the note, the overdose of booze, and the drugs, I think I can get them to put him in psychological observation for a few days if you don't press charges. He's obviously a danger to himself in his present state of mind."

"He seemed like a nice young man, Boss," Jack said.

"No use screwing his life up any further. We'll forget the charges, but make sure they check him out thoroughly. The kid obviously has some big problems," Edwin said. "Do you think he got the booze from the hotel? He's obviously underage."

"No. The bottle doesn't have our inventory stamp on it," Wally replied. To keep the staff honest, hotels apply special markings to liquor when it is received. It helps stop some industrious employees from bringing in their own bottles and selling their booze at the hotel's expense. It's not a bad personal business, if a person can pull it off. No overhead like rent and the hotel supplies the ice, mixers, and glassware.

"Good thing he didn't have a gun," Edwin said.

"You have no idea how bad that could have been. A few years ago, a guy's gun went off in a room across town. They found the bullet four rooms down. It went right through the sheet rock walls and missed two sleeping guests on the way." Wally responded.

"What a pleasant thought. Let me know what else we have to do. It'll be a pleasure handing a bill for the damages to his parents. I'll let you two gentlemen take over from here. Thanks for handling it," Edwin said, as he left.

Out in the hallway, the couple was getting a lot more vocal.

"I didn't think I was staying in a war zone," the man said. "I've been teaching in public schools for twenty years and nothing like this has ever happened. Now we come to a good hotel and almost get killed."

"Sir, I understand your feelings, but we have no control over all of the actions of our guests. Would you like medical attention? The paramedics are on the way," Edwin said.

"I'm not injured, I'm shocked," the man said. "And look at my poor wife. This is going to cost you."

Jack came out and explained the situation with the young man. He told them the hotel would move them right away and all of their charges would be on the house. The guest said he had seen the young man earlier in the elevator with what looked like a sports bag. Jack told him the police might want his statement. The guest said his wife's brother was a cop, and he'd be glad to help. He was calming down and looking forward to a nice dinner on the hotel. Jack called down for a bellman to move the couple. The couple asked if the mirror could just be removed. They loved the room and wanted to stay in it. Edwin thanked them and went back in the room with Wally and the boy. Jack joined them.

"I think they'll be O.K. It might not have been so bad if it wasn't that they were staying in Room 718," Jack said.

Edwin looked puzzled. Wally smiled and said, "718 is the room with the canopy over the bed with the mirrors in the canopy and on the walls. It's a romance room. O.K., it's a sex room for couples and newlyweds. The guy's away from home with the wife, and they're just getting into the mood. He's feeling pretty good and the mirror falls on them, killing the excitement. That would upset anyone I know."

"Wally, you're pulling my leg again," Edwin responded.

"Not really. Wally has a good point," Jack interjected.

Edwin looked at both of them trying to determine if the joke was on him. The two men swore it might be the main reason for the couple's real displeasure. Edwin suddenly understood why they wanted to stay in the room, and decided to let the subject drop.

Since Jack had spent time talking with the young man during his stay, Wally asked Jack to stay until he woke up and the paramedics and police got there. Edwin said he would contact their lawyers in case there were any repercussions. Jack was still wondering if the young man was trying to drink himself into a quiet end. Wally thought, even though hotels have their share of suicides, they couldn't be sure that this was an attempt. That would be up to the psychologists.

"You're taking this pretty matter of fact. Is this just another hotel happening?" Edwin asked, Wally.

"Happens more than you might think. A friend of mine was on his first hotel job right out of hotel school as assistant night manager at a big hotel. A guest jumped from the twentieth floor and landed on the canopy over the front lobby entrance. The night manager took the young guy up to the mezzanine floor and demanded he go out on the canopy and get the forty bucks out of the guy's pocket to pay for the room he had rented."

"No way! What did your friend do?" Edwin asked.

"Jobs were tough to get, so he went out on the canopy and got the money out of the guy's pants. He ended up with the night manager's job two years later," Wally replied.

"At least he got even. You and Jack take over. I'll go call our lawyers," Edwin said.

"Any particular lawyer?" Wally asked. Jack tried to hide his smile.

"We've been using the same firm for years," Edwin replied, weakly.

"Seems like we've been using them a lot more lately."

"Thanks for your personal interest, Wally. I'm sure you'll try to keep the rumors down. That goes for you too, Jack," Edwin said, smiling as he left.

When he got to his office, Edwin dialed Lee's private line. He gave her the details of the incident and mentioned Jack was going to notify the parents. She told him to let the police do it. If Jack did, it might implicate the hotel. Jack could call later and offer the hotel's services to the parents when they came to get their child.

"By the way, do you think a toga party for our first public date would be inappropriate?" Edwin asked.

"What are you talking about?" she replied.

"Daphne's having a literacy fund-raiser in two weeks, and the theme is Greek to celebrate knowledge. I think I should have a date," he said.

"I haven't been to a toga party since college. Unfortunately, it was in my wild days and I don't remember a lot of it. It might be fun," she replied.

Her comment about her wild days made him momentarily jealous. He made it pass by reminding himself they hadn't known each other then.

"I better get back to Jack. I'll call you soon," he said.

When Edwin informed Jack of Lee's advice, Jack said he'd notify the front desk to get in touch with him at any hour if the parents called.

"Thanks, Jack. That's nice of you. Keep me informed," Edwin said.

"It's the hotel business, Boss. We take care of people."

chapter

THIRTY ONE

Jack and Wally had taken over the handling of the drunken incident with the young man's parents. Jack said he had now met two control freaks that made Chambers look like Santa Claus. Wally had interceded, and in his 'let's get serious here' way, convinced them any attempt to go after the hotel or its staff would result in a legal backlash and publicity back home. Wally also told them, none too delicately, they were guilty of gross mental harassment in the way they raised their son.

Jack took the positive approach and tried to convince them that the parents of famous chefs were probably very proud of them and their financial and critical success. The parents lightened up as time went on. When their son came back to the hotel, after his three-day psychological observation period, he both thanked and apologized to Wally and Jack. It got so emotional; Jack and even Wally got a little choked up. They shared hugs and promises to stay in touch. Jack got special pleasure seeing hard-nosed Wally show some tenderness. He decided it would be a bad idea to share that with anyone else or for him to bring it up to Wally in the future. The young man had also gotten an apology card for the couple in Room 718.

Meanwhile, Edwin was focused on the hotel's financial position. He didn't trust Chambers and knew he had to face the money situation sooner rather than later. He also waited for the STD test results from the doctor. He didn't know what he was going to do with them when he got them. *You don't just call a girl up and say, "Hey I'm clean, let's get it on."* Another dinner would be the best way to ease into the subject.

Repeated calls to Justy LaGrange about the capital account from the will got nowhere. Justy was suddenly hard to get hold of. The old family friend's actions puzzled Edwin, but he didn't want to get Lee involved. The only other thing he could think of was to ask Ann Baxter for help. He had gotten control of the philanthropic account, so he called her and invited her to lunch. Edwin met her in the dining room. They sat at the corner table and talked mostly about A.D.

Finally Edwin decided it was time to explore the capital account question. "I can't understand why I'm not getting any reaction from Justy."

"It was a complicated estate, but I'll look into it," Ann said.

"I don't want you to stretch your loyalties or get into trouble."

"Don't worry, I'm a big girl."

"I'm concerned because A.D. was more detail oriented than Microsoft and wouldn't leave anything to chance. The only reason I can think of is that Henry might benefit through the repayment of the mortgage if I have to sell the hotel. Money is a big motivator for Henry and I don't trust him," Edwin explained.

"Oh. Maybe it's clearer than I thought," Ann said with a startled look.

"What do you mean?" he asked.

"Never mind. Let me look into it," she said.

"I appreciate it, Ann, and I need two more things. The first is a copy of Chambers' contract."

She said she'd fax it over when she got back to the office.

"The second is in this envelope," he said as he handed her the envelope. "It's $50,000. A.D. left it in a special account and instructed me to give you a total of $250,000 in five installments based on your needs. He told me to thank you for the special things you had done for him."

She wiped a tear from her eye and said, "I'd give it all to have him back."

At about two that afternoon, he got Chambers' contract. It called for him to be paid one-hundred and twenty-five-thousand dollars per year. He also received a bonus of ten percent of whatever expense savings he could produce. All of his living expenses were paid for. If terminated, Chambers got all payments and the use of similar accommodations. There were four months left on the contract. It was written completely favoring Chambers' interest. Even the usual clause of "termination for cause" was missing.

An hour later, Wally Callahan and Captain John Moose LeRoy showed up. They weren't having any luck finding out who the older man in the Tiger's Tail pictures was. The case was getting old and LeRoy was concerned. He thought the only way to get some traction was to press Mason, but he didn't know anything about the young man that would be helpful. Edwin related a conversation he had with Mason. He was brought up by a hard father who had little regard for weak people, especially women. Edwin had seen some guys like this in the service. He also didn't think Mason could take a lot of guilt.

They decided to have Jack take Mason along on his regular tour of guest rooms. In well run hotels, different levels of management tour guest rooms regularly, checking the condition of the rooms. When they got to the fourth floor the murder room would be open and Wally and the captain would be waiting inside. At LeRoy's instruction Room 441 had been left the way it was after the murder and had been sealed. LeRoy and Wally headed to Room 441. The room smelled musty. LeRoy wanted it that way and told Wally not to turn on the air conditioner or open the window.

After waiting ten minutes in the room, they heard Jack's voice coming down the hall through the partially opened door. Mason slowed his pace as they approached Room 441.

"Let's look in this room, looks like they unsealed it," Jack said. "Maybe you can make some suggestions to get it back in service quicker."

"I'd rather not," Mason replied.

When Wally heard Mason protesting, he stepped out of the room.

"I've got someone here I want you to meet, Robert," Wally said and grabbed his arm.

Seeing the security director come out of the room, Mason's eyes widened and his mouth dropped open.

"Robert, this is Captain John LeRoy of the police department. He has a few questions he thinks you can help him with," Wally said.

For the next fifteen minutes, the captain and Wally alternated asking questions.

"Robert, we're really trying to help you. It's in your best interest to cooperate," Wally repeated several times.

Mason insisted, "I don't know anything about what happened in this room."

"Robert, do you understand your Miranda Rights?" LeRoy said and read them to him. Mason continued to claim he didn't know anything.

"I want to show you something," the captain said as he pulled a picture out of his pocket.

Mason looked at it in terror. It was the picture from the security camera of him and his friend from the Merrill entering the lobby of the St. George.

Mason said, "That must be the night I came back to the hotel to pick up my cell phone."

LeRoy showed him the picture from the Tiger's Tail. Mason's mind was now mush. He took a deep breath and began, "I know Stephen Mallory from hotel school. We hang around together and on some nights we go to the Tiger's Tail. That's where we met Armand deCoste. He's the older guy in the picture. He bought us drinks and talked about how he had done some of the best adult movies in circulation."

The third time they saw him was the night of the incident. DeCoste met them and said he had found some talent and needed them to test her out in a threesome.

"He wanted to get a hotel room and do some preliminary filming. Mallory said we couldn't go to the Merrill because the hotel was full," Mason said.

Of course, LeRoy knew the real reason was Mallory and deCoste had done their thing before in the Merrill.

"I took them to the St. George, because deCoste promised the sex would be something I had never experienced. I've never been with any experienced women. DeCoste had a camera. We did a three person sex scene. I got nervous as the sex got rougher. I made an excuse and left," Mason explained.

He said that was it. He didn't know anything about a murder. When he saw the room out of service, he assumed they had messed it up and he didn't want to get fired so he kept quiet. That was probably true: All those who knew about the murder had been sworn to silence by LeRoy.

"O.K. Robert. I think I believe you. What I'm going to do now is quietly take you to police headquarters and get your official statement. Is that O.K. with you, Robert?" the captain asked.

"Yes, sir."

"One more thing, Robert," LeRoy said. "If you tell anyone about this, and I mean any of this, and Mallory or this scumbag deCoste leave town or cover their tracks, I'll make sure you do time for accessory after the fact in a murder. Do you understand what I'm saying and how serious that is?"

"Yes, sir," Mason replied. The blood was starting to come back into his face.

Wally escorted Mason back to his office and told him he'd be back in a few minutes. He went upstairs to meet the captain in Edwin's office, where LeRoy was on the phone with Detective Bubba Hall. He was explaining what they had just learned and instructed him to get some West Coast vice squads on the phone and see if they had anything on Armand deCoste.

After the captain hung up, Edwin asked, "You sure Mason had nothing to do with it?"

"He got his rocks off, he's naive and stupid, but I don't think he even knew about the murder," LeRoy replied. "Just keep the room totally vacant and treat Mason as you normally would. We don't want him feeling too guilty and doing something stupid."

He thanked them both, told Wally he'd see him soon and left.

Edwin sat in his office thinking about Chambers. *What's really the connection between Chambers and Henry? How does Justy LaGrange fit into the whole thing?*

chapter

THIRTY TWO

Over the next two days, Edwin spent little time at the hotel. He wanted to give Chambers, who knew Edwin was irritated, a chance to follow up on the hotel's physical condition. Edwin wanted to see if he'd do anything on his own to improve the hotel or wait for Jake Jacoby to show up. Edwin did go in each morning to read the daily report and the security reports. It didn't surprise him that people did strange things away from home. Wally Callahan was good at his job and really understood human behavior. Luckily for the errant guests, the hotel seldom had to call the police. The hookers were a challenge, but Wally and his staff handled them: head them off in the lobby and leave the john in his room wondering what happened to his date. The domestic situations were harder. When people drink more than they're used to, the hostility appears like a bear woken early from hibernation. Some of the real aggressors were the women. The guests, both male and female, propositioning the room service wait staff were also fairly easy to handle.

He stopped by the kitchen for lunch and to see how the chef and his crew were doing. Andy Scott was leaning on the wall to keep from falling over he was laughing so hard. The chef and Pas Medvier were sitting at the chef's table complaining to each other. The mixture of French and Italian protests, and apparently foul vocabulary in both languages, kept the entire staff amused.

"Don't stop the fun on my account," Edwin said as he walked up.

"I think they're planning an assassination," Andy answered. "Maurice Solomon, the local food critic, is in the dining room."

"That a problem?" Edwin asked.

"It might be. He's the one who noticed the liverwurst instead of the goose liver in the Beef Wellington at that big function," Andy answered.

"Did he write it up?" Edwin asked.

"No, but he promised to be back to see if we'd repented," Andy replied.

Three things can kill a hotel's food and beverage operation: lousy food, lousy service, and an outbreak of food poisoning among a couple of hundred people at a well-publicized banquet.

"Why don't you two go out and say hello?" Edwin asked.

"That would be the worst thing we could do. It'd look like we were begging," the chef answered. "We're better off staying here and doing our best to make everything perfect."

"Keep your friends close and your enemies closer," Edwin said, heading for the dining room.

"Fools rush in," he heard Pas say.

Solomon was sitting at the corner table. He had a pleasant smile on his face as he looked over the menu. For some reason there were quite a few other customers in the dining room.

At least it looks like we're doing some business.

"Welcome to the St. George, Mr. Solomon," Edwin said.

"Thank you. You're new here. You take over the dining room from the mad Frenchman?" Maurice asked.

"I thought I should welcome you personally. I'm Edwin Christian. I recently took control of the hotel. It's nice to have you with us," Edwin said.

"You're the grandson. Now I remember," Solomon replied. "A.D. and I used to meet at Jimmy's. We both were hooked on corned beef. Sit down. You don't want to go back to the kitchen and listen to Mazzari and Medvier complain about me being here."

The conversation started with A.D. and the history of the hotel and continued into Maurice's experiences as a food critic after he had retired from the hotel business. Maurice mentioned his love for cooking. He loved to work with meats and had bought every grill or smoker ever invented.

"In that case, why eat in the dining room? I've got a butcher shop and a big kitchen back there. Why don't you cook for both of us?" Edwin asked.

"If you can get that past the Italian and the Frenchman, I'll cook you something special. Them too, if they can swallow their pride," Maurice answered.

Edwin went to the phone on the hostess stand and called the kitchen.

He explained his idea. Then, "No, I'm not crazy. I don't think Maurice would tell anyone you surrendered your kitchen to him. Wait a minute." Edwin called to Maurice, "If the chef invites us in, do you solemnly swear you will not tell a soul?"

Maurice Solomon crossed his heart and nodded his head yes.

"He swears, Chef. We'll be back in a few minutes."

"I don't think I want to hear what's being said in the kitchen right now," Maurice said.

"Why did you pick today to visit the hotel?" Edwin asked.

"I had forgotten about it until I saw your brother at the art museum. He said I might find some interesting changes in the place. So, here I am," Maurice answered.

"How thoughtful of him," Edwin said. "I'll have to remember to thank him."

When they got to the kitchen, the chef and Medvier were standing by the cooking line with their arms folded in front of them. A white chef's coat and hat were on the chef's table.

"Thank you for the invitation, Chef Mazzari and Mr. Medvier. I don't often get into the kitchens," Maurice said.

"It was the boss's invitation. We've been busy in here," the chef responded.

"Where would you like to start this little adventure?" Medvier asked.

Edwin explained Maurice was a meat specialist and introduced him to Andy Scott. Maurice remembered Andy's brief career in football. They left for the butcher shop talking sports.

"You really are nuts, aren't you?" the chef asked. "You know what that guy can do to us in a two-paragraph piece?"

"Not much, if he's the one doing the cooking," Edwin replied.

The chef and Medvier smiled for the first time. A half hour later, Andy and Maurice returned with a small platter of meat. The chef and Solomon cooked for the next half hour. By the time the meal was done, they had both learned something.

"Chef Lou and Pas, I really do appreciate you allowing me to cook with you," Maurice said. They all shook hands and Edwin walked Maurice out, complimenting him on the meal.

"That Edwin's got guts, but he works things out," Pas said.

"He got them from his grandfather," Andy said. "That man had more than anyone I know. I don't think the kid will let his mouth put his butt any place he can't get it out of."

Outside, Edwin put Maurice Solomon in the hotel limo for his ride back to the newspaper. When he got to his office, the message light was blinking on his private phone.

"Edwin, this is Ann Baxter. The capital account cleared escrow this afternoon. You can contact the bank to get whatever money you need transferred. Thanks again for taking care of A.D.'s wishes in my behalf. It was very generous of you both. See you soon."

Yes you will Ann. I want to find out how you did that in a day.

As he remembered her semi-shocked reaction when he voiced his opinions at their luncheon, Vinnie DeTesta came in.

"As you instructed, I told your sister she could have any extras for the function she was willing to pay for. She called you an ignorant tightwad," he laughed. "Actually, her verbiage was a little stronger."

"I'll talk to her. How are we doing with getting the vendors to put up some stuff?" Edwin asked.

"Pretty well—they're not putting stuff up, they're selling us the stuff at cost, but, every little bit helps. Especially when you're dealing with Daphne Christian."

chapter

THIRTY THREE

When Edwin entered the lobby, he saw a familiar figure looking at the ceiling and taking notes on a large pad of paper.

"You waiting for the ceiling to fall down?" Edwin asked.

"Probably isn't the only thing that'll fall down around here," Jake Jacoby grumbled.

"I've noticed. It's good to see you back, Jake," Edwin said.

"Good to be back, I think," Jake replied. "I can't believe this place could go downhill so fast."

"What're the biggest problems you've found?" Edwin asked.

Jake explained he couldn't find any permits or city inspection reports for the elevators and the fire protection system. That was against the law. He also found some of the main standpipes that carry the water to sprinklers and fire hoses in the hotel turned off.

"Who would have done that?" Edwin asked.

"I don't know, but they'd have had to know something about high-rise plumbing," the engineer replied.

"Thanks, Jake. You've got full control of the place. Do what you have to do."

Edwin went to Castillano's office and signed the bank account cards. "And by the way, could you look up the past few months of bills from Christian Construction? I'd like to see what they were working on."

"After our talk about it, I pulled them up to look at the amounts they charged again," Chuck said. "They worked on the back doors. They replaced some carpet in the Regal Suite and they did some plumbing work in some of the pipe chases."

"That's very interesting. Thanks," Edwin said as he left.

He was looking at the previous night's sales report when his phone rang. When he answered it, he was sorry he had.

"Well, if it isn't my tightwad little brother."

"Nice to talk to you too, Daphne," he replied. "How may I help you?"

"You can tell those clowns who work for you that the literacy event is an important happening for the hotel. It's not a bowling banquet," she said, her voice rising in volume and pitch.

"I understand many of the suppliers have chipped in and the menu is superb," Edwin replied.

She ranted on about all the things Vinnie and the chef had said no to. When she realized she was getting nowhere, her tone changed, "It's really all about the honor of the Christian family. It will be a tribute to A.D. if we do this thing right."

God! She must think I'm stupid. The seductress is trying her wares on me and using her dead grandfather as a self-serving wedge. He told her the idea of making it a tribute to A.D., who had only finished the seventh grade and loved to read, was a great idea. He would chip in some money for some little extras if she and Henry would. She and Henry could be at the head table and say a few words and Daphne could be the mistress of ceremonies. *There's no way she's going to miss an opportunity to grab the microphone on the stage. Especially, with her new body showcased in a toga.*

"I'll tell my team of clowns they'll be hearing from you. I'm sure they'll make it special and protect your good name."

"Well, I better work on it. Thanks, I guess," she said and hung up.

The rest of the day went fairly well. The only entertainment happened at the front of the hotel as Edwin arrived to ask that the limo pick Lee up for their dinner. The infamous rogue limousine driver from the other day had reappeared with two other drivers with limousines to protest Slim's denial of their comrade's rights in a free country. Wally made a call and fifteen minutes later, three city tow trucks showed up and hooked up to the limousines. The drivers had refused to get out. As Edwin came out to the front of the hotel, the three tow trucks were departing with the drivers still in the limousines. They were honking their horns and yelling obscenities about the evil pigs that were persecuting them. Slim and Wally were standing on the curb waving goodbye to them.

"You boys having fun?" Edwin asked.

"Just cleaning a little crap out from in front of the hotel," Slim replied.

Edwin asked Slim to have the limo ready at six-forty-five. He would go with the driver to pick someone up.

"Gee, think I can guess who?" Slim asked with a broad smile.

Edwin didn't answer and went back inside to see Jack. He told him he needed some romantic flowers delivered to the Rappoli's restaurant for dinner. Jack said roses were trite and not appropriate for this stage of Edwin's romance. He suggested Gerber daisies.

"I'll go with your call, Jack. You've had more experience with this stuff than me," Edwin said.

"From both sides of the plate, my boy, from both sides," Jack smirked.

At six-fifty, he picked Lee up. She was curious about the dinner and continued to ask questions. He gave her no satisfaction and just smiled.

This lady likes to be in control. I hope it's worth the wait for her.

Inside the restaurant, the entire Rappoli family came out to greet them. The other patrons looked on, wondering who this special couple was. As they walked to the back corner, Edwin fell behind

Greg Plank

Lee. Adele Rappoli whispered to him his flowers were waiting. He told her to hold them until after dinner.

Papa Rappoli cooked special dishes and the family served them along with the appropriate wines. When they finished Adele placed the flowers on the table. Jack had once again gone overboard; the arrangement was huge. Edwin had to move around the table to be able to see Lee. The other customers were now staring at them and smiling.

"What's this?" Lee asked.

"I couldn't think of any other way to give you the envelope there in the arrangement," Edwin said. He was starting to think the whole thing was an idea gone crazy. He started to sweat as she opened the envelope and began to read the medical report on his lab tests. She smiled and then began to chuckle.

"What's so funny? I think that says I passed," he said.

"Yes, it does, but I would have taken your word for it," she replied as she reached for his hand.

"A little overkill?" he asked sheepishly.

"No. It's cute," she said. "I really feel bad now. I didn't do as good."

Edwin knew she was looking for his reaction. "In the first place, I'm sure we can work past that. In the second place, I think you're jerking my chain and it almost worked."

"I am jerking your chain. You made me wait for tonight, guessing all the time." She squeezed his hand with a wide smile. "I think we need to take a trip. Maybe a long weekend."

He was initially disappointed, but quickly realized she wanted it to be something more than a clothes-tearing roll in the hay.

"You pick the place and I'll clean up some things at the hotel so I can get away. That should take a couple of days."

"There's a special place off the North Carolina coast. You get there by boat and there are miles of beaches to walk and not many people around," she replied.

"It sounds perfect. I think we need someplace quiet," he said.

"I might over-think some things, but we should get to know each other in more than just the physical way," she replied.

"If we're serious about a relationship, you can't over-think it," he said.

"You're either the best liar in the world, or you have a feminine side," she said.

"No lie. I've just spent a lot of time with Jack. He's big on sensitivity."

chapter

THIRTY FOUR

Edwin was at the hotel by seven a.m. He entered through the back door. The Dumpster area had been cleaned up and the back doors had been painted. He started in housekeeping with Mary and visited every department head and told them he had hired a consultant named Al McNerey to help figure out how to improve business. The chef cautioned him Chambers' ego would blow when he heard. Edwin already expected an explosion.

In the executive offices, Chambers was waiting for him. He knocked once and went into Chambers' office.

"Good morning, Edwin. Donna tells me you have something important to talk about," Chambers said.

"As you know, I have little formal experience in hotels," Edwin started.

"I think you're catching on pretty quick, and you have me to bounce things off of," Chambers responded.

"I've decided to hire a consultant to give us an outsider's opinion," Edwin started.

Chambers sat quietly for a moment. "Who is this consultant?"

Edwin told him about McNerey and started to explain McNerey's background.

"I know him," Chambers interrupted. "Quite frankly, he doesn't have any more experience than I do." Chambers' facial expression was changing like a fast moving thunderstorm.

"It's nothing personal," Edwin replied.

"Look, I came here to do a job. Since you've been back, I haven't had the opportunity to do that," Chambers said. "If this is a matter of trust, you haven't spent the time to get to know me. You may think this isn't personal, but it will undermine my stature."

Edwin suddenly hoped Chambers would get mad and quit. He decided to give Chambers' ego a little nudge. "It's not a matter of trust in your expertise. But, it is a matter of trust in where your loyalties lie."

"What the hell does that mean?" Chambers asked.

"It means I believe you're loyal to the person who hired you," Edwin said.

Chambers' voice was shaky as he said, "You come in here with a bunch of boyhood memories. Now you question my loyalty to the hotel. How dare you?"

"I dare because I own the place. The financial burden rests on me, unless you have a source of capital to help out," Edwin responded.

"What I do have is a contract," Chambers shouted.

"I'm aware of your contract. It says I have to house you, provide maintenance, and pay you. It does not say I have to listen to you, give you any control, or kiss your ass."

Chambers was speechless. Edwin was certain the man wasn't stupid enough to void the contract by quitting. He might later regret it, but he made a decision on the spot. "I'll honor all the terms of your contract. However, I will provide your living quarters at a different location in the city. As of this moment, you have no active duties or authority in the hotel. I think you'll agree it's best for you to move out."

"You're actually firing me? If I could fight this I would. You're also affecting my reputation in the industry," Chambers retorted.

"Don't worry, Leonard. I'm not putting out a press release. Henry might need some help in construction. You already have a strong relationship with him," Edwin said. "I'll instruct Chuck Castillano to make sure your expenses and salary are covered on a timely basis."

"You're making a big mistake. You have no respect for experience or my hard work and efforts," Chambers said.

"The mistake may take time to be proven. If you want respect, call my brother," Edwin said and left the office.

He stopped at Donna's desk and told her Mr. Chambers had decided to leave. He asked her to get him a good real estate agent and a mover. He also asked her to clean out Chambers' office at the appropriate time.

Donna looked surprised but only said, "Certainly."

"I have a consultant to meet," Edwin said. As he turned for the door, he noticed the light on Chambers' phone lit up on Donna's console. He asked her to have the big desk in Chambers' office moved down for Jack at the appropriate time. He also asked her to do a memo on Chambers' decision to leave and to thank him for his leadership in the memo.

"You really want to say leadership?" Donna asked.

"Why kick a guy when his ego's just been gored? Live and let live," Edwin said.

He left Donna with a smile of respect on her face and headed for the lobby to see if Al McNerey had arrived. Jack Vincent waved him over to his desk.

"Morning, Boss. Your consultant's arrived," Jack said.

"Great, where is he?" Edwin asked.

Jack told Edwin he was in the suite upstairs. He added that McNerey had gotten in early and taken a cab instead of the limo. When he checked in he carried his own luggage and tried to take a regular room and not the suite. When Jack had asked him about it, McNerey said he was here to work like everyone else and didn't want to look like a big shot. Then he told Jack to call him Al. The look on Jack's face was total admiration.

Greg Plank

Jack dialed the Van diver Suite and handed the phone to Edwin. When McNerey answered, Edwin said, "Al, this is Edwin Christian. Welcome to the St. George." Edwin listened for a minute and replied, "My office is on the second floor in sales and catering. I'll meet you there when it's convenient. Thanks for coming."

When he got to his office, he asked Maryann to show Mr. NcNerey in when he arrived. Five minutes later he heard laughter in the reception area. A moment later, Maryann entered his office followed by a man in a blue suit and a silk tie with elephants on it.

"Mr. Christian, Al's here to see you," she said.

Edwin was startled by the introduction. *She's calling him Al?*

"Sorry about the informality. Nice to meet you, Al," Edwin said, extending his hand.

"What are you sorry about? The Al thing?" McNerey inquired.

"Well, that and carrying your own bags," Edwin responded.

"Hell, Maryann's my new best friend. It's a people business. As for the bags, who's going to be really honest with me if they think I feel I'm above them?" McNerey said.

Maryann chuckled as she left the office. Edwin instantly liked Al McNerey.

McNerey accepted a Diet Coke and pulled out his copy of the numbers he was sent.

"Any preliminary thoughts?" Edwin asked.

"Just one. Why are you in the hotel business? A young guy like you can do better in sales. If you really want to get beat up, try boxing," McNerey replied.

Edwin looked confused; Al told him to relax. He explained the numbers had led him to a conclusion, but he wanted to tour the hotel and meet the people before he said anything. The tour started in the sales office and ended in the lounge. With each person Al met, he asked questions about the numbers. It was obvious Al knew the hotel's financial statements as well as the auditors. He also showed his understanding of each person's area. With Bill Smith and Vinnie DeTesta he talked about all of their markets, from corporate to SMERF, which is social, military, ethnic, religious, and fraternal groups.

With Pas Medvier he discussed the high banquet volume keeping the food cost down because there was less waste, higher volume, and the ability to charge a little more. With the chef, he talked about his own Italian mother and Irish father to break the ice. When Andy showed up, Al talked about Andy's football career and told him he thought he was one bad dude on the field. Andy and the chef smiled throughout the entire conversation. He told each person he met to call him Al. Every person he met in the hotel loved Al McNerey.

Next, they went into the dining room and then the bar. Marty Rosenbloom was setting up for the day's business. When Marty asked how Al got to the St. George, Al told him that Irv Kertzner had put his name in.

"Hell of a guy," Marty said.

"You know Irv?" Al asked.

Marty told him they had shared some frozen ground during the Battle of the Bulge in World War II. He hadn't seen him since. They spent the next ten minutes laughing about some of the things Irv had done in the hotel business. The tour continued up through the floors as they looked at the available guest rooms. They returned to Edwin's office.

"When do I get to meet your general manager?" Al asked.

"I don't think that will be necessary. I fired him this morning," Edwin replied.

"What's his name?"

"Leonard Chambers," Edwin said.

"Lenny the Lasher. No wonder this place is tight on costs and repairs," Al replied.

"You know him?" Edwin asked.

"I don't know who hired him, but Chambers is known as the guy to bleed a hotel when you're waiting to sell it," Al said.

"My brother hired him when my grandfather got sick."

"And your brother suggested you sell the place." Al said. "If your brother hired Lenny, he was thinking of dumping this place the day he did."

They agreed Al would spend the rest of the day walking around and talking with the staff.

"One last question for today," Edwin said. "If sell is the right conclusion, I'd never sleep again if it was torn down or not run as a hotel. Can I protect against that?"

Al thought for a minute and a smile crossed his face as he said, "Little old ladies in tennis shoes."

"What?" Edwin asked.

"Little old ladies in tennis shoes. The ones who hug trees, volunteer at the library and are bugs on preserving history," Al answered.

"Preserving history?" Edwin asked.

Al explained the hotel qualified as a historic building. If Edwin could get some people who wanted to preserve history to push for certifying the hotel as historic, a developer or owner could never live through the publicity if they wanted to change the place. There might also be some tax advantages.

"You know anybody who can put you in touch with the society ladies?" Al asked.

"As a matter of fact, I'm related to one. She's not a little old lady. Saving her grandfather's dream and the press it will get her would make her day. Hell, it would make her year," Edwin said, thinking of a raging Daphne.

"Perfect," McNerey said.

chapter

THIRTY FIVE

As Edwin walked to the hotel the next morning, he thought about the dinner the night before with Al McNerey. They talked only briefly about the Hotel St. George. The conversation was more about Al's international travel and Edwin's travels with the military. Al explained how the hotel business had begun to change in the late sixties. Since then many of the individually and family owned companies had sold to conglomerates and many who had held on to their companies went public. The hotel business was now more about real estate and earnings than the operating of hotels for the pure love of it. Companies realized, like the fast-food companies, they could gain fees from selling their name to independent business people without having to invest large amounts of capital and incurring debt. Franchising grew quickly. The need to grow as public companies also brought segmentation to the industry. Understanding that consumer demand and tastes were changing and not everyone wanted a large full-service hotel, the companies developed limited-service properties. They were cheaper to build and didn't have the large labor costs of full-service hotels. The name motel came from combining the words motor and hotel. The lower cost of construction in limited-service hotels and motels and the availability of a brand name to help market them brought first-time hotel owners and operators into the business. Today, many of these first-time owners and investment groups, originally from India, have grown from one motel to thirty or forty properties with strong and respected brand names. They're hard working and very focused. They have also educated their children, who now are deep into hotel and other business ownership. If Edwin were to sell the St. George, he might well be negotiating with more than one of these groups. Being very astute business people, they were all well versed in negotiating to get the best deal possible.

When Edwin got to his office, the memo on the departure of Leonard Chambers was on his desk for signature with a note from Donna. She had made the lunch appointment with Lee Edwin had requested. The executive office would be cleaned out by five o'clock and the real estate agent was meeting with the Chamberses to help them find alternate living space. He took the memo on Chambers over to Donna's office. As he entered, her phone rang. She answered it, listened and said, "He's right here, Jake. I'll put him on."

"Hey, Jake. What do you need?" he asked. He listened for a moment. "I'll meet you there."

After he hung up, he asked her to show the memo to Chambers out of courtesy. He told her the fire marshal was downstairs and Jake needed him. She told him to tell Jake all the required inspections he had asked for were scheduled for the next day.

Edwin met Jake in the lobby. Jake started by telling him the guy waiting in the dining room was the head marshal. He was wondering why the top guy would show up and had a bad feeling it was not a normal visit. The coincidence of the closed valves on the fire system bothered him. Edwin told Jake about the inspections that were ordered for the next day and suggested they go face the music. The fact that the second top person from a city department was suddenly taking an interest in the hotel bothered him. The fire marshal and his assistant were sitting in the dining room drinking coffee.

Jake introduced Edwin, "Fire Marshal Sparks and Vice Marshal Taylor, this is the owner of the hotel, Edwin Christian."

"Welcome to the Hotel St. George," Edwin said, extending his hand. "Jake tells me you have a few matters to go over with us. Please forgive my ignorance, but I haven't been here long."

"Ignorance can lead to some serious problems, especially concerning human safety issues," Sparks started. "Vice Marshal Taylor has a list of some very serious violations."

"Please, if you have the time, let's go over them," Edwin said.

"We normally send them in written form, but, in this case, they're serious enough to shut you down immediately," Sparks replied. "Shamika, why don't you go over the most serious ones?"

Shamika Taylor opened her pad. The first two items were the lack of inspections on the fire safety system and the elevators. She listed the lack of inspection tags on various equipment and some interesting, in her words, repairs done to fire alarm control panels.

When Shamika was done, the fire marshal said, "On some of these, you face considerable fines and the possibility of immediate closure until they're remedied."

"I appreciate your concern and your comments," Edwin replied. "We have the common good of the public at heart and we share a common idiosyncrasy."

"What's that?" Sparks asked.

"My grandfather and I have been the brunt of some well-placed jokes. The name Christian, when you run a bar and have plenty of beds upstairs, is funny to some people. The name Sparks must have afforded you some of the same type of poking fun comments in your line of work," Edwin said with a smile.

Shamika Taylor was smiling for the first time. Sparks was expressionless. Jake Jacoby sat horrified. The boss was joking in the middle of a potentially catastrophic situation. *This guy's fearless and has connections downtown or he's a complete nut case,* Jake thought.

As the fire marshal raised his hand to scratch his nose, Edwin could see the bottom of a tattoo. He guessed it was the lower end of the U.S. Marines' coat of arms.

"Semper Fi," Edwin said, pointing to Sparks arm.

A smile finally crossed Spark's face. "Semper Fi. Yeah, I've taken my share of crap about the name."

For the next five minutes the conversation switched to the Marine Corps. Sparks had served in Vietnam on two tours. Edwin told him about his time in special reconnaissance. As the conversation was ending, Jake interjected how Edwin's father had died in a chopper crash in Vietnam.

"Could be I hitched a ride or two from him," Sparks said. "Let's go back over the list and see where we can help you."

"I don't want any sympathy, I want to do the right thing," Edwin said.

"That's what we're going to do. We're Marines," Sparks replied.

"In that case, may I ask why you showed up today, unannounced?" Edwin asked.

Sparks gave Shamika a dollar and asked her to get him a paper. She took the dollar and left the table. When she was gone, Sparks explained they had a call from city hall that someone familiar with the hotel had reported some serious violations, including the water supply to the fire system and the lack of inspections. He had asked his assistant to leave because he shouldn't be discussing the call with the violator.

Edwin gave Sparks a quick history of his ownership and some of the things that had been happening, including the fact that he had fired Leonard Chambers and brought Jake back to handle the maintenance instead of contracting the work to Christian Construction. He concluded with the fact that all the inspections were scheduled for the next day.

"When Ms. Taylor gets back, follow my lead. I can help you here, but you have to do exactly as I say," Sparks said.

"Not a problem, and thanks," Edwin replied.

"Don't thank me yet. It's going to cost you some overtime for your people," Sparks said.

Shamika Taylor returned. For the next half hour, the four went over the list. Sparks was demanding in his requests. Edwin understood Sparks could not appear to be doing a favor for a fellow Marine. They would have to have a regular fire watch set up with every floor visited every twenty minutes until the fire safety system and the elevators were inspected and passed. This would also include the kitchen until the hood over the cooking lines had been cleaned and the fire suppression system certified. The other items were not major and could wait for normal repair, but it had better be sooner than later. Shamika Taylor took lengthy notes.

"Can we get this written up and back to them today?" Sparks asked Taylor.

"Yes, sir. I can have it delivered by the close of business," she replied.

Jake explained how they would provide proof of the fire watches by coding special card keys and recording them being used every twenty minutes in the housekeeping closets on each floor. Sparks liked the idea. Edwin thanked them and leaving the check open so they could have lunch on him, he and Jake headed for the elevator.

"Think we dodged a bullet there?" Edwin asked.

"That wasn't a bullet; it was a freaking nuclear bomb. That guy has a lot of power. Good thing you were a Marine," Jacoby replied.

"Just a lucky guess. What saved us was your comment about my father. I was upset when you brought it up, but in the end, it meant something to Sparks. Good thinking," Edwin said.

"I almost crapped when you brought up the name thing," Jake said.

"We had nothing to lose. We were guilty and they knew it. I just wanted to break the tension and show we're human. With a name like Sparks in his business, he had to have taken a lot of crap on the way up. Probably still does," Edwin replied.

"He ain't going to hear it from me," Jake said.

"Me either—unless we're both drunk. There are probably some very funny stories there."

"You got more guts than me," Jake said and headed off to work.

Edwin was livid at the possibility Chambers or his brother or both were part of the violations and had made the call to the fire marshal's office. He considered calling Justy LaGrange to see if he could sue Christian Construction for professional negligence, but figured that for whatever reason, Justy had all but abandoned him. *I'll get even with dear Henry one of these days.* In Donna's office, he asked her if Chambers had seen the memo. She replied he was out looking for a place to live. Edwin took the memo, signed it, and asked her to post it in the appropriate places.

"My pleasure. Don't forget your lunch," she replied.

chapter

THIRTY SIX

Edwin called Robert Mason to see how things were going. Mason said he was nervous but holding up. Edwin tried to reassure him he believed his story and thought the captain did too. Edwin told him to stay busy to keep his mind off of his troubles. He thought working the desk and dealing with people would be perfect.

"It'll keep your mind off of the negative things," Edwin offered. "Do you see where I'm going with this?"

"I don't think I need more stress right now," Mason replied.

"That's exactly what you do need, a different kind of stress. If you sit there looking at your reports, too many thoughts will cross your mind," Edwin said.

"That sounds like an order, sir," Robert replied.

"You're very perceptive, Robert, and don't call me sir. Call me Boss. It's friendlier and less military," Edwin said.

"Thank you, uh, Boss," Mason replied, his voice less stressed, and he sounded sincere.

Greg Plank

Edwin asked him about the check in of The Midnight Mayors rock band. Robert replied that Music Corp would check in this afternoon. Edwin told him he wanted to know about the band. Robert replied Music Corp was the band and explained many famous people and entertainers use or are assigned fictitious names when staying in hotels. It protects their privacy while they're in their room or enjoying the dining room or bar.

"Are you coordinated with Wally on the timing of their check-in and room assignments?" Edwin asked.

"Wally's been in here twice today. He gave me a security radio so we can stay in touch. I think he assumes I report to him," Robert replied.

"Good. He can help you in more than one way," Edwin said. "Now go help the guests."

"Yes, Boss. And," Robert said, pausing, "thanks for the help."

"No big deal. Have a good day," Edwin said and hung up.

He went to the kitchen to check on lunch. Andy Scott put his large arms around Edwin in a hug, Edwin almost disappearing in the huge man's grasp.

"My main man. And he is da man," Andy said.

The others looked on, puzzled, as Edwin tried to extract himself from Andy's grasp.

"To what do I owe this heartfelt expression?" Edwin asked.

"Gather round and listen up everyone," Andy bellowed.

The entire kitchen crew, the dining room staff who had heard the summons, and Mary Rodriguez and two housekeepers, who were in the back hall, gathered around the big butcher.

"I have a very important announcement to make about our fearless leader here," Andy said. Edwin looked more embarrassed by the moment.

"We have been liberated from the jaws of tyranny and dictatorship. The wicked king and queen are leaving the building thanks to my little buddy, I mean Boss, here," Andy announced.

"You mean the Chambers are leaving their chambers?" Edmunds, the sous-chef, asked.

"Yup. Donna just posted the notice, effective immediately. The Boss canned the bastard," Andy said, lifting Edwin's arm up like a winning boxer.

The entire kitchen broke into cheers, whistles, and applause.

Edwin raised his arms and asked them to quiet down. "I appreciate your gratitude, but Mr. Chambers was motivated to explore better opportunities."

"Motivated by your size-eleven shoe, you mean," the chef said.

"Well, anyway, you're still my hero, Boss," Andy said, patting Edwin on the shoulder. "I'll be humming For He's a Jolly Good Fellow all day."

Everyone in the kitchen thanked Edwin, which only embarrassed him more, and went back to work happier than they'd been for quite a while.

Edwin told the chef about the lunch with Lee and Al McNerey. The Chef told him he'd make it special. "You just enjoy your lunch. I might even come out there just to see what Lee's wearing today. I'm her favorite chef you know."

"You're also a dirty old man."

"No. I'm Italian. It has nothing to do with age," the chef protested.

"That's what I meant. It comes naturally," Edwin said.

As Edwin entered the lobby to find Al McNerey and wait for Lee, every employee he passed smiled at him. The girls and even Robert Mason, behind the front desk, waved and smiled.

They've obviously read the memo. Edwin approached Jack Vincent's desk, where Al McNerey and Jack were talking. Jack looked like he just won the lottery.

"You heard, I suppose. No hugs in public," Edwin said to Jack.

"What he said was, if you bend over, he'll kiss your butt in the middle of the lobby," McNerey said to Edwin.

"As inviting and perverted as that sounds, having Chambers leave is really no big deal," Edwin replied.

"Not to you maybe, but it's July fourth to a lot of people," Jack said.

Jack waved toward the front door. Edwin turned around and saw Lee entering the lobby.

"Afternoon, gentlemen," she said. "The flowers were perfect, Jack. Roses would have been trite." Jack looked at Edwin with an I-told-you-so smile.

"Lee Brown, this is Al McNerey," Edwin said, giving Jack an 'O.K-Mr.-know-it-all' look.

"Lee. It's a pleasure. I understand you know Irv Kertzner," Al said as he stood up to shake hands.

"Yes. I'm a big fan of his," she replied, smiling.

"So am I. Lunch will be interesting," Al said.

In the dining room, after the three were seated at the corner table with the drink orders already taken by the hostess, Edwin asked, "Al, you got any hotel questions for Lee as our attorney?"

"Yeah, I do, but in the interest of time, may I send you my legal questions and you can get someone to compile the answers?" Al asked. Lee happily agreed.

As they ate, Lee and Al exchanged Irv stories as Edwin listened. Irv was a very unusual person — a great businessman with a touch of endearing eccentricity.

After forty minutes of laughter, Lee asked, "Al, what do you think about the hotel?"

Edwin was a bit irritated she would ask questions about his hotel. Then he remembered the 'both in control thing' he and Lee had discussed and decided he should take it as a sign of genuine interest and concern. Al recognized the look on Edwin's face.

"With Edwin's permission, I'll answer the question. Because I think you two are an item," Al said. "I watched your reaction to each other when Lee showed up at Jack's desk."

"Al, how many years have you been married?" Lee asked.

"Forty plus, to the same woman with one dog, two married children and two new grandchildren," Al answered.

"See, Edwin, people who have been through it, understand relationships," Lee said.

Edwin looked at Al McNerey for help.

"Don't look at me, bro. You're hung, man," Al said.

"I think I am, Al, I think I am," Edwin said.

"Damn right you are, Winnie," Lee said.

It was the first time anyone, other than his grandfather in affection or his sister mocking him, had called him Winnie. He realized he liked it coming from Lee.

Al never answered Lee's question about the hotel. The rest of the conversation was about relationships and honesty. When they got to the lobby, Al thanked Edwin for his hospitality and reassured him he was doing the right thing. His report would take everything into consideration and be totally honest. He had six hours until his flight and was going to look at the competitive hotels in town on his way out.

"I'll look at the St. George as if I owned it," Al said.

"I can't ask more than that. Thanks for coming. I'll get the limo to take you around," Edwin said.

Al declined. He thought the limo would bring too much attention at the competition and he wanted to look around unnoticed. Lee excused herself saying she had to get back to work. She gave Al a hug and thanked him again.

The lobby was filling up with music fans. As Edwin walked toward Jack's desk, the Chambers came out of the elevator. Mrs. Chambers saw Edwin and started to approach him. The look on her face was pure hatred. Leonard Chambers took his wife's arm and headed her toward the front door before she could reach Edwin.

"I think Chambers just saved your life, or maybe your manhood," Jack said.

"I'll bet she could do some serious damage with that look on her face," Edwin replied.

"She and Daphne would be a match," Jack said. "Kind of makes severe PMS look like a minor mood swing."

"Some people have it all the time. It's triggered when you tell them no. It affects men too. They just call it ego," Edwin said.

"Speaking of Daphne, Vinnie DeTesta said to tell you he has her latest list of specialties for the benefit. He wants to go over them with you," Jack said.

"I can hardly wait," Edwin replied.

Edwin went up to the offices and sat down with Vinnie. Daphne's list was two pages long. Edwin looked it over. She had requested seating on pillows on the floor and very low tables to give the ancient Greek feel. Edwin grimaced. The rest of the list was pretty simple until he got to the last item. Daphne wanted four African American males to portray Greek slaves who would carry her in on a divan for her grand entrance. Edwin nixed the slaves and just shook his head in wonder that his sister could be so out of touch with reality. He instructed Vinnie to get a cross section of football players or weight-lifters to do it. He also said the seating on pillows was out. They didn't need some drunks in togas rolling around on the floor. When Edwin asked what the requests would cost, Vinnie told him about thirty thousand dollars.

"It's worth my ten grand just to get this over with. I'll call Daphne and give her the bad news about the seating," Edwin said with a sigh and went back to his office.

He called Daphne at home. He got her on the tennis court. When he explained her requests were fine with the exception of the special floor pillows seating, he could hear her tennis racket hit the ground. She was insistent; the seating created the mood. He explained that older heavier women and men in togas did not have the agility to sit on the floor with any amount of modesty. It was also a huge liability factor. Daphne calmed down a little and said she would practice sitting down herself to see how bad it was.

"Practice well," he said. He could imagine his sister lying on the chaise longue with the young stud tennis instructor making advances. *She doesn't need any practice for that.*

He was interrupted by a call from Wally Callahan asking him to come to the lobby. When he got there, he saw a commotion at the front desk. Wally motioned for him to go in the bar.

"What's up?" Edwin asked.

Wally explained the smaller man making the scene was the band manager for the Midnight Mayors band. He acted like he was managing the Beatles. The other guy was their security man. He thought he was Rambo. They showed up with ten groupies they were claiming were equipment people and were demanding five additional rooms.

When he was told that the hotel didn't have the rooms available, he demanded to see the hotel manager.

The band's manager was five-feet-eight and wearing his hair in a tight ponytail. Six of his fingers held heavy gold rings. Wally led Edwin over to the group and he introduced himself as the owner. The band manger unloaded on him, demanding the extra rooms. Edwin held his ground: There would be no extra rooms. He kept his eyes on the security guy who was six feet tall and was really built.

Wonder if he's packing a pistol inside that lumpy-looking sport coat? The equipment and lighting people don't look old enough to get working permits.

When Edwin wouldn't give in, the band manager decided to take his offer of rooms for the groupies in a hotel where the St. George was holding overflow rooms.

As Edwin turned to leave, the security guy remained planted so Edwin had to go around him. He scowled at Edwin as he walked past him.

When they got to the elevators Wally said, "Those folks are trouble. The equipment and lighting people will be sneaking in here tonight. I'll have my guys keep a special watch."

"The real trouble is the security goon. You think he's packing?" Edwin asked.

"Yeah. I'll get his I.D. and call one of my police buddies to run him. Mr. Muscle might have a record, which makes carrying a weapon a felony."

"You're a devil, Wally."

chapter

THIRTY
SEVEN

The music festival weekend was as loud and boisterous as antici-pated. The hotel was filled with people of all ages wearing tee shirts and hats decorated with the logos and artwork of their favorite musi-cal group. The bar and dining room were doing record levels of busi-ness. Edwin took the time to relax and see Lee. They jogged together and Lee talked Edwin into going to the music festival in the after-noon. As they arrived at Exposition Park, a gentle rain started. As the rain increased in intensity, the well-trodden soil turned to three inches of mud. The humid air kept the pot smoke from the crowd near the ground. The beer flowed freely. The combination of drunks falling in the mud and people high on pot growing increasingly rowdy was becoming too much to take. They decided it was time to go, and headed to Jimmy's for a casual dinner.

The place was full of the usual eclectic crowd. They ordered corned-beef sandwiches and onion rings. He picked up his sandwich, looked at her, growled, and took a huge bite, chewing it with a lust à la *Tom Jones.*

"You really that hungry or are you practicing for the honeymoon?" the voice asked from behind him.

Lee almost spit out her onion ring when she started laughing. Captain John LeRoy was standing behind Edwin.

"Don't worry. I won't tell Wally you eat in heat," the captain continued. "He's down at central booking."

"You arrest your old partner?" Edwin asked, trying to recover.

"He's filling out an arrest statement about the security manager of the Midnight Mayors' band," LeRoy replied.

"Did you get him on a firearms violation?"

"It's a little more than that," the captain answered.

"I'll buy you a beer. I've got to hear this," Edwin said.

LeRoy sat down and Edwin motioned to Betty Sloan for a beer for the captain.

The captain took a sip of beer and explained the evening's happenings at the St. George. Wally had run the band's security guy's record: he was on probation for a felony assault conviction. Wally had instructed his team to keep a special look out for the Midnight Mayors and anyone who tried to visit them. Luckily, the new CCTV security system had been installed and was in the test phase. Wally couldn't call the cops and just go up to the guy, with no reasonable cause, and frisk him for a gun. So he watched the cameras on a regular basis and told his people to call him if any strangers showed up on the band's floor.

The rain had cancelled the remainder of the day's music festival, and the band came back to the hotel. Within an hour seven different pizza deliveries had been made to the band's floor. All of the delivery people were in uniform. One of his security guards observed that once the pizza was delivered, the delivery people never left the floor. Wally got curious, thinking about the groupies, and went up to check. Unfortunately, he went alone, thinking his other security people would be nearby on their regular floor checks if he needed them.

He knocked on the door to the band's suite. When the door opened, Wally could smell pot, and saw several young girls in various stages of undress. When the band's security man recognized Wally, he shoved him back out the door. He pushed Wally down calling him a fat bastard and threatening to beat him to a pulp. While Wally was ducking the muscular man's shoves, C.A. Mullins, a guest in the hotel, heard the commotion. C.A. was a nice guy from the mountains who had brought his wife to the music festival at her urging. He would have rather been at a car show or playing golf. They were enjoying a movie and eating room service. Being six-feet-eight and weighing in at two hundred and forty pounds, C.A. was enjoying a triple order of fried shrimp when his dinner was interrupted by the noise in the hall. When he got into the hall, he saw a younger man trying to beat the crap out of an older man with a limp. When the younger man indicated he didn't care if the older man was the director of security for the hotel, C.A.'s basic country respect for authority and fair play kicked in. He grabbed the younger man from behind by the belt and neck.

By the time Wally gathered himself, one of the off-duty cops showed up to find Wally a little dazed and a large man holding the muscular younger guy against the wall by the neck. The guy's feet were not touching the floor, and his eyes showed he was having a hard time breathing because of the large man's grasp on his neck. One finger was dangling at an abnormal angle, having been dislocated when the younger man tried to pull his pistol out on C.A. Mullins. You just don't do that in proper Southern society. When you do, it has a way of upsetting the locals. Mullins was waving the gun in the man's face and saying, "I hope you really didn't intend to use this on my friend or me."

Wally took the gun from C. A. Mullin's hand. "Thanks for the help. I think you can put him down now."

"Do I have to? This guy's trash."

"Yeah. I think he's had enough," Wally replied. He had the off-duty cop cuff the guy, and call the police.

Wally asked Jack to comp the Mullins' stay and move them to the suite, as soon as he threw the band out and the suite was cleaned. He then walked down the hall and knocked on the door to the suite.

Wally informed the band manager they had thirty minutes to get off the property. The band manager protested. Wally explained what had just transpired in the hall, and told him he could be an accessory after the fact and so could the band. He added if there were any under-aged people in there and, by chance, any illegal substances, he was in deep trouble. Wally's Irish temper was evident, and the band manager decided leaving was the best option.

When the cops escorted the band's security man out of the hotel, the band and their groupie friends were standing on the curb in the rain, trying to decide where to go for rooms. C.A. Mullins had returned to his room and finished his shrimp. Wally had gone to the police station to give his statement. He took a CD copy of the security system's recording of the event with him as evidence. Wally had sustained no injuries, except those to his pride.

"Think we should have let them off that easy? There were underaged girls in there and probably some pills along with the pot. Too bad we can't let the girls' parents know what their children are doing," Edwin said.

"Interesting point. I'll talk to the D.A. and see if we can subpoena them as witnesses to the gun. If they are underage, the subpoena will go to their parents. We'll have to subpoena the hotel where the girls were staying to get their names. It might be a wild goose chase, but we can ask," the captain replied.

LeRoy finished his beer and said, "I better go check on Wally. I don't think he got hit, but you never know."

"Wally thinks he's the toughest guy around," Edwin said.

"He isn't as tough as C. A. Mullins. My guys said the band's muscle looked like he'd gone ten rounds with Ali," the captain said.

"Another exciting night at the St. George," Lee said.

"Like Jack says, welcome to my world," Edwin replied.

When they left Jimmy's, the rain had already stopped. They walked to Lee's apartment. After talking outside for a while, they decided it was a good night to get some sleep. Edwin walked home.

On Sunday, Edwin stopped by the hotel to check on Wally. Slim Johnson was outside talking with a couple. The man towered over

Slim. He remembered Captain LeRoy's description of C.A. Mullins and guessed it had to be him.

"Morning, Slim. It looks like you finally hired a bodyguard," Edwin said.

"I'm just talking to some special guests," Slim responded.

"If these nice people are the Mullins, they're very special guests," Edwin said.

"Mr. and Mrs. Mullins, this is Edwin Christian. He's our owner," Slim offered.

"Nice to meet you, Mr. Christian. You own a very interesting hotel. More action here than we get in the mountains back home," C.A. Mullins said.

Edwin shook hands with C.A.; his hand totally disappeared in the large man's muscular paw. "The Hotel St. George, Wally Callahan, and I owe you a debt of gratitude. Thank you for helping out last night," Edwin said.

"Shoot, no problem. We don't like folks like that back home either," C.A. replied.

"I don't know how often you come to our city, but you'll be our guest anytime you can," Edwin said.

"Last night was enough. Jane loved the suite so much, I think she's going to make me renovate our home," C.A. replied.

"The suite just reminded me to motivate him a little," Jane said, smiling.

"And Momma can motivate, believe me," C.A. said.

"Where are you folks headed?" Edwin asked.

"We're off to the airport. Headed home," C.A. said.

"Slim, why don't we have the limo take the Mullins to the airport?" Edwin said.

"You don't need to fuss over us. We can take a cab," C.A. said.

"Trust me, it's the least we can do," Edwin said.

Slim motioned to the limo driver and the large stretch pulled up in front of them.

"Y'all have been very nice. If you get to the Georgia Mountains, let us repay the hospitality," Jane said.

"You near the Ranger camp?" Edwin asked.

"Right down the road. You know it?" C.A. asked.

"I spent a couple of months there in training. Beautiful country," Edwin replied.

He said his good-byes as Slim picked up their luggage and put it in the limo.

As the limo pulled away, Slim said, "Nice people. I wish all the guests were that way."

Edwin left Slim at his post and went looking for Wally. He found him sitting at the chef's table having coffee with Pas Medvier.

"Well, at least you look like you're no worse for the wear," Edwin said to Wally as he approached.

"The guy never laid a hand on me, but it's a good thing C. A. Mullins is one big quick guy," Wally offered.

"I'm just glad you're alright," Edwin said.

"Yeah, without Wally we'd have no one to test the donuts for the dining room," Pas said.

"Very funny, Frenchman," Wally said.

"Looks like things are back to normal. I'll see you gentlemen tomorrow," Edwin said as he left.

chapter

THIRTY EIGHT

The last few days had gone pretty well. Chambers was gone and the staff was in a much better mood. Edwin was excited about his trip with Lee. When he got to the hotel, Jack informed him Bill Smith, Pas Medvier, Chef Mazzari, and Vinnie DeTesta were waiting in the boardroom with Daphne. After the normal greetings, Vinnie handed out an outline of all the arrangements, and, in a politically astute move, asked Daphne to lead them through the list.

She liked her role as queen. The meeting went well until they got to the seating arrangements. Daphne again pushed for the pillow seating with low tables on the floor. Pas Medvier asked them to follow him into the ballroom. When he turned on the lights, a low table with six pillows around it on the floor appeared in the center of the room.

"Shall we?" he asked, pointing to the table, "Ladies first, of course."

Daphne was wearing a knee-length skirt. Determined to win her argument, she proceeded to sit down with no assistance. As her rear end met the pillow, she fell backwards. Her skirt jumped up to her waist, and a run appeared in her panty hose. In an effort to be a gentleman, Vinnie sat down. The rip in his pants was loud enough for everyone to hear. Daphne had to roll out of her sitting position onto all fours to get up.

"O.K., I guess you were just trying to help. We'll go to chairs," she said, still red-faced from her tumble.

The remainder of the meeting was civil, and Daphne maintained her air of royalty. She was impressed when Vinnie told her about the athletes he had enlisted to carry her in, and reminded her to put her make-up on a little heavier because the large spotlight would be on her as she gave her tribute to her grandfather.

The rest of the day was uneventful compared to the last few weeks. The only exception was a call from Captain LeRoy, asking for a meeting with Edwin, Wally, and possibly Robert Mason the next day at ten. Edwin agreed and told Donna to remind him.

The next morning, he expected Al McNerey's report. His curiosity consumed him as he took his morning run. When he got to his office, Donna told him Al McNerey had called. The report would be there in the early afternoon. Al asked that Edwin wait to call him until he had read the report and thought about it.

At ten sharp, Wally and the captain entered the executive offices.

"We've found out who Armand deCoste is from the guys on the West Coast. It didn't take long, even though his real name is Warren Lewis and deCoste is an alias. We got lucky. The West Coast guys have a Facial Biometric System supplied by a North Georgia company named Alive Tech. When they enter your picture in the system, it picks your face out of the computer files in seconds. It doesn't matter how many aliases you have. It brings them all up. We didn't have a fingerprint. If they didn't have that system it would have taken days or weeks to look through mug shots. That would have been a lot to ask. Lewis is a small-time porno operator on the web, and in some local movie stores and clubs out there. He came here because the heat was on him for some alleged rough-sex films," the captain explained. "They're sending us his file and a copy of the film. If either of our victims are in it, we've got him. How's Mason holding up?"

"He's nervous, but coping," Edwin said.

LeRoy asked them to call Mason to the office. He wanted to use him to get his friend from the Merrill over to the St. George so he could sweat the guy before he knew deCoste was in custody and clammed up. Mason looked scared when he saw the captain.

"Don't worry, Robert. I'm here to help you end your worries, if you cooperate," the captain said.

Robert Mason sat down, and, as the conversation went on, he relaxed. The meeting lasted a half hour and ended with Robert Mason agreeing to call his friend when deCoste was in custody.

Edwin was nervous as he waited for McNerey's report. It arrived at two-thirty. He closed his door and began to read. McNerey had assembled an impressive amount of information. There were occupancy and rate comparisons to the competing hotels; an analysis of the future of the market; commentary on the cash-flow analysis; and the financial statements. Like a reader who can't wait to find out how the story ends, he turned to the conclusion before he had digested all of the numbers.

Al McNerey's conclusion was in the first sentence. Sell the hotel before the earnings dropped more and took the selling price down with them. There was also the real possibility that the bank would foreclose, sooner or later. Edwin's first instinct was denial. Selling was what he did not want to do. He read on through McNerey's rationale for his recommendation. The hotel did not have a chain to help market it. To get a brand name or to compete on its own, a very large amount of money would have to be put into the hotel to bring it up to par with the competition. Based on the numbers, Al didn't think Edwin could get a loan on the property. He would have to use personal cash, or bring investors in and possibly lose control of the hotel.

The location of the hotel, the basic building, and the parking made the hotel worth more than the numbers showed, at least to the right purchaser. That would be an individual or a company that wanted to invest the money to make it a five-star property that would get a much higher rate and make money.

Edwin's denial turned to resignation and then acceptance. He was depressed as he thought about the loyal employees. He had been so keen on reading the report he had ignored the cover letter McNerey had included. Al McNerey had recognized his dilemma. The letter contained three paragraphs that lessened Edwin's depression. The hotel would, after the loan was paid off, bring a good price, leaving more than a few million dollars for Edwin. It was Edwin's money and he could do with it what he wanted. Al suggested one thing could be payments to the staff for their loyalty. He could also stipulate that the key employees must be given the option to stay for a year or more. It would be a hard sell to the buyer, but they'd probably want the employees based on what Al had observed of their talents and knowledge. The third paragraph of interest was Al's restatement of the historical-building angle that would make it hard for anyone to purchase it and change its use.

Al McNerey had covered all the bases. Edwin decided to think about the entire situation and consult Lee during their trip. That night, he sat alone in his loft and wrote a list of questions he wanted to ask McNerey.

The next day it was raining when he woke. Running in the rain has a special peacefulness to it. He pushed himself hard as he thought about selling the hotel.

When he got to the hotel, there was a message from Captain LeRoy. He was coming over again at nine. When the captain arrived with Wally, Edwin was going over Al's report.

"You get what's-his-name?" Edwin asked.

"Picked him up last night at the Tiger's Tail. The movie the West Coast cops sent shows a woman who looks a lot like the girl we found at the Merrill," LeRoy replied.

There was a knock on the door. It was Robert Mason.

"Robert, we're in the home stretch. We picked up Armand deCoste last night. He hasn't had a chance to alert your friend. Can you get him over here?" the captain asked.

"I guess I could ask him to lunch. We've been talking about it for a while," Mason said.

"Good. Call him now. When he gets here, we'll meet him in the lobby. I think interviewing him in Room 441 would be appropriate," LeRoy instructed. Mason made the call. They agreed to meet at noon in the lobby of the hotel and Mason and the others left the office.

Edwin dug out the list of questions he had written for Al McNerey and called him. Al was his usual upbeat, patient self. He could tell by the tone of Edwin's voice he was still concerned.

"Edwin, this is not a death sentence. It happens all the time in business. What we have to do is address your concerns, and minimize any impact you feel is serious. So, ask me your questions," Al said in a fatherly tone.

Edwin's first question: What would the selling process be like and what could he do to lessen the concern of his employees? Al told him he would suggest two brokers. One was in Phoenix and one was in Denver. They were both ex-hotel people, and would understand his concerns and try to work through them. Regardless of how they handled it, prospective buyers and their teams would be coming through the hotel and would want to see all of it, and ask questions of the staff. This would intensify if a buyer was ready to make an offer. There was no way he could hide it from the staff. That's why he had suggested loyalty payments to the key staff members. It would keep them around and lessen their concern. They would also work to keep the line employees positive and keep them working at the hotel.

Al told him to gather every legal document attached to the hotel. That would include all contracts, service agreements, and licenses. They would be needed before a sale could be closed. Finally, he told him to tell the important members of the staff what was happening in private, and include what he had decided for loyalty payments.

Al could still sense the confusion and concern in Edwin's voice. "Edwin, trust me. You'll get through this, and I'll be there every step of the way. Everything, including the employees, will come out O.K.," he said.

"I'm just trying to get used to the idea that I'm losing my grandfather's first love," Edwin replied.

"You're not losing it. You just won't own it, but it will go on. The hotel business has changed. Nothing lasts in its present state forever," Al said.

Edwin thanked him and told him to proceed. He also decided, even if he ended up with nothing, that the loyalty payments to the staff would be substantial. His conscience began to feel a little lighter.

chapter

THIRTY NINE

At noon, Stephen Mallory, front office manager of the Merrill Hotel and friend of Robert Mason, entered the lobby of the Hotel St. George. As Mallory crossed the lobby to meet Robert, Captain LeRoy and Wally rose from the large chairs at the concierge desk and walked up on either side of him. The captain showed his badge and said they had a few questions for him. Mallory looked at Robert with a puzzled expression and tried to turn to leave. The two men grabbed his arms.

"What's the matter, you don't like to talk?" Captain LeRoy asked.

"I don't have anything to talk about," Mallory replied.

"Bull. Follow me," LeRoy said, and he and Wally escorted Mallory to the elevator.

As they walked down the hall toward Room 441, Wally could feel Mallory tense up. Wally opened the door and they walked in. Mallory's face registered fear and the sweat on his forehead was obvious.

Captain LeRoy did the talking. After reading Mallory his rights, he started with questions about Mallory's friendship with Warren Lewis, a.k.a. Armand deCoste. Mallory referred to their relationship as casual, that he didn't know much about the man. He had gotten some free sex through him, and that was all. When LeRoy asked him about the murder at the Merrill, Mallory said he didn't know anything about it. He only knew a room had been taken out of service. He suspected something, but was afraid to talk to deCoste about it, become involved and lose his job. He never considered murder; he only thought deCoste might have messed up the room after he had left. It was the same story Mason had told.

For the next two hours, LeRoy grilled Mallory hard. Mallory's story never changed. Mallory finally said he would have to consult a lawyer and refused to answer any more questions. The captain told him not to leave town or contact deCoste or Robert Mason. He was not going to arrest him, but he could get a warrant in a matter of minutes in a murder case. LeRoy and Wally escorted a nervous Mallory downstairs and out of the building.

After Mallory left, they went in to see Mason. They explained the situation, told him not to worry and not to contact either of the other two men. Wally would bring Edwin up to speed.

Saturday morning, Al McNerey called and told Edwin he had asked the two brokers to make arrangements to visit the hotel on the Q.T., to look around. It was strange to have two brokers on a deal, but the two had worked together before. Sam Apistol, the broker from Phoenix, and Robert Baisch, the one from Denver, would be contacting him for their visits. He explained Sam was an ex-hotel company president and hotel owner who liked the desert and a certain brand of vodka. Baisch had similar credentials and lived in Denver, because, being an ex-surfer, he loved to ski. The main purpose for their visits was to get a consensus on the selling price of the hotel. Pricing it too low would leave money on the table, and pricing it too high would prolong negotiations and scare some potential buyers off. Some brokers might inflate the price to make Edwin believe he could get more just to get the listing contract. These two guys were not that type.

Edwin explained he would be out of town for a few days next week. Al thought that was a good thing. Apistol and Baisch would make their own reservations and act like regular guests. Edwin was anxious the process was starting so quickly, but he was thankful Al was moving it along – dragging it out would be worse.

Edwin had spent the afternoon checking on the arrangements for Daphne's big party. Tonight would be interesting with Daphne acting as the queen of charity. He was impressed that, with all the details, decorations, and pressure from his demanding sister, the staff was acting like it was routine. Every time he thanked one of them, they replied, "no big deal."

Lee arrived at the hotel at five-thirty with a medium-sized suitcase. When Edwin got to the lobby to greet her, Slim, Jack and Wally were sitting around Jack's desk joking with her. He could hear her laughter across the lobby as he approached.

"These gentlemen hitting on you, Miss?" Edwin asked.

"Boss, you're so territorial," Wally said.

He thought about saying "Only with my woman," but decided Lee was not the type to be referred to as a possession.

"No, I'm just trying to protect the innocent from three dirty lechers," he replied.

"Leave me out of this. She's wonderful, but not my type," Jack said.

"Well, that really narrows the field a bunch," Slim said.

"Yeah, and it takes a lot of sensitivity out of it too," Edwin said.

"Now, Edwin, they're sensitive in their own way," Lee said.

"In that case, I might not want to be labeled as sensitive," Jack said.

"I think we better go before these three take over our night for a shrink session. But, on second thought, that might be better than the party," Edwin said, offering her his hand.

"Don't worry about him gentlemen, I feel your sincerity," Lee said as she left.

Edwin escorted Lee up to one of the two-bedroom suites so they could change into togas for the party. Just after they got there, there was a knock on the door. The room-service server put a tray on the cocktail table explaining Marty had asked him to deliver it. The tray contained a martini for Lee and a bourbon for Edwin. He signed the check and thanked the server.

"I could get used to living in a hotel," Lee said.

"We can talk about that next week," Edwin replied.

"Promise?" Lee asked, smiling.

"Yeah, but it's not the conversation you're thinking of," he answered, thinking of the sale of the hotel.

Lee pouted for a moment, puzzled, but decided it would be better to wait than to pry. They each went into a bedroom and changed into the togas. When they met again in the living room, all Edwin could think was *Wow*. The toga revealed more of Lee than he had ever seen. She had the body of an athlete and the toga showcased it. And she didn't miss his well-muscled frame. *Now that's a hunk,* she thought, as she asked him to turn around to model the toga. *Great butt,* she smiled.

They finished their drinks and went to the ballroom, now transformed into a Greek circus. Young college art students lined the entrance like Greek statues. Their skin was completely covered in bronze paint and they wore transparent togas. They were frozen in their positions. Daphne was standing in the doorway in a greeting line of her board of directors of the literacy society. Her toga was more of a mini-skirt with a bib top. Her large breasts stood out proudly. She greeted them warmly, and Edwin introduced Lee.

"I'm so happy to see my brother has maintained some of his once impeccable taste. It's a pleasure to meet you, Lee," she said, gushing and smiling.

"Thank you, Daphne. It looks like you've arranged another unique affair," Edwin replied.

The line was building at the door. Edwin took the opportunity to move into the ballroom.

"Nice dig," Lee said.

"You noticed my sister's way of insulting people in a civilized manner. She's got a thing about men, and it's not good," Edwin said.

"Passive-aggressive-teenage-syndrome. Some women never get over it," Lee said.

They found a table in the back of the room and sat down to watch Daphne's circus. Some live animals were being herded around the room and wine was being poured from earthen jugs. The red fabric from the BOOB convention covered the walls and ceiling; lights moved behind it making it look like flames. Changing pictures of ancient Athens were projected on the fabric behind the head table. They met some of the attendees Daphne sent their way who just had to meet the young owner of the hotel. The pot-bellies on the men were not completely hidden by the togas, and the trophy wives of some were enjoying their new bodies their husbands had invested in. The older and less statuesque women wore a lot more cloth in their togas.

Just before dinner was served, the mayor, Phil Jackson, came over and greeted them. He welcomed Edwin back to the city and talked about how good it was to have the St. George as a famous hotel in town. He asked how owning a hotel was going.

"Pretty well. Some of your more important city officials have been by to visit. They're very concerned with public health and safety," Edwin answered. He could tell by the look on the mayor's face, he wasn't missing Edwin's message. The mayor brushed it aside with a weak comment and left quickly. Justy LaGrange came over to say hello. Edwin was still irritated by the old family lawyer's lack of help on the money issues with the will.

"How's retirement going?" Edwin asked.

"I'm not retired. Where'd you get that impression?" Justy replied with a puzzled look.

"When you didn't return my phone calls, I just assumed it," Edwin said, looking him in the eye.

"I thought Lee was handling things. Sorry if I gave the wrong impression. I hope things are going well now. Wonderful affair tonight," the lawyer replied, trying to change the subject. He was having a hard time maintaining eye contact.

"Lee's been very helpful and things worked out," Edwin said.

Justy's wife noticed the tension and made an excuse to end the conversation. Lee looked confused, but held her questions.

The local business people at their table spent the entire dinner asking questions about the hotel business. Lee was enjoying his answers. She knew he was making a good number of them up as he went along. Just before the meal was served, the lights went low and a spotlight shown on the main entrance to the ballroom. Trumpets played as the four athletes carried Daphne in on a divan, taking her to the head table. She went to the microphone. "Let the games and the good times begin," she said.

The people at Edwin's table marveled at the lamb entrée and the unique fruit and vegetable dishes the chef had prepared. Edwin asked a server for a pen and wrote a note on his napkin for his sister asking her to bring the kitchen crew out after dinner to thank them. The server delivered the note to Daphne at the head table. She looked toward Edwin with a questioning look. He shook his head yes.

After dinner was served, Daphne took center stage and introduced Henry. It was obvious he was not a fan of going to the gym. Henry's comments started with his grandfather's love of education and reading. He told the story of A.D.'s limited education and his struggle to be successful. After the first few comments, Henry managed to get his remarks around to the great government of ancient Greece and how today's challenges for the city and the state mirrored those times. He ended with the point that good people with strong diplomatic and business skills were the answer.

Henry's first campaign speech. What a self-indulgent snob. And he's had too much to drink already, Edwin thought.

Daphne took the microphone next. Edwin listened carefully to see how many words she slurred. Her remarks were loving and thankful about A.D. She thanked all of the contributors for their support. The audience gave her a standing ovation. Daphne then called the chef and his crew out of the kitchen to be thanked for a "wonerful" dinner.

Edwin knew the wine had kicked in. As Daphne moved her arm to put it around the chef, her left breast was freed from her toga. The chef took a quick peek and then fought to keep his eyes on the crowd.

Unfazed by her partial nudity, Daphne placed her breast back in her toga and said, "There's no limit to what I'll do for charity."

The audience broke into laughter and applause. Throughout the rest of the night some of the husbands with trophy wives encouraged them to repeat Daphne's boldness. Edwin was surprised at how many took the bait.

"You want me to try?" Lee whispered in his ear.

"You don't have to. You've got boobs and brains too. You've got them out-classed. It wouldn't be a fair contest," he said, and kissed her on the cheek.

"You've got more class than they do too. Thanks for the right answer," she said, hugging his arm and smiling.

They were enjoying themselves until Henry stopped by their table. "Your staff did well, Edwin. I'm impressed. Hope you've thought about what I said about this place," Henry said in a boozy voice.

"I'm thinking about it, Henry. I really am," Edwin replied.

"Well, I hope your judgment of people gets a little sharper as you go along. Chambers was the right man for the hotel, and Mrs. Martinez is the wrong woman to take care of Mother," Henry said.

Edwin thought for a moment. "You're welcome to your opinion, brother, but I've been picking people who would keep me alive for years. The basic characteristics I look for are honesty and concern and an ability to think for themselves. Maybe the standards in the construction business are different," he replied with a hard look.

The comment made Henry take a boozy, unsteady step backward. "That was uncalled for," was all Henry could say.

"I'm not ten anymore. I can tell friend from foe. Good night," Edwin answered. He took Lee's arm and left.

"You're really into this honesty thing, aren't you?" Lee asked.

"Especially with the people I care about," he replied.

"That's one of the things I like about you."

"What are the others?" he asked.

"You've got a very cute toga butt for one," she said.

He couldn't stop smiling as they talked to Marty in the bar. For the next hour, they discussed their coming island trip.

chapter

FORTY

The day had finally come for the trip to Feral Island, North Carolina. Edwin picked a smiling Lee up in the hotel limo at six a.m.

"You look happy. Excited about the trip?" she asked.

"Yeah, but that's not why I'm smiling," he answered.

"What's the smile for, then?" she asked.

"Your luggage. I expected to see you with ten bags like most women," he replied.

"I thought you knew I'm not like most women. I learned to pack for the international trips with the government. We were on the move a lot, so we didn't want a lot of bags. It also helped with security," she said.

"I'm impressed. And I don't think you're like most women," he said.

"I knew you didn't. I just wanted to jerk your chain," she said as she got into the limo.

The flight to North Carolina was pleasant. The plane had to circle once as the airport police and the natural resources people removed a deer from the runway. They caught a shuttle service to the dock at the Wilmington River. Feral Island is only accessible by boat. They boarded the "Sea Stallion" water-taxi for the forty-minute trip through the salt marshes and sound to the island. When they arrived at the Dunesgate Inn, one of two inns on the island, Edwin was impressed. The inn had been built in 1918 by Reginald Faust, one of the railroad barons of the day. This wealthy class of people had built a variety of large homes and some resorts along the Southern Coast of the United States as winter refuges from the cold North. Faust was a very social person and enjoyed flaunting his wealth. He built Dunesgate with thirty rooms for his guests and three cottages for the employees. He brought a variety of friends and business associates to the island to enjoy special weeks that his wife planned. The inn was built of North Carolina pine. The fifteen fireplaces were made of native stone from the North Carolina Mountains. When Faust died, almost penniless from the Great Depression, Dunesgate was auctioned off. A local tobacco grower, who had a love affair with the wild horses of Feral Island, bought it and converted it to an inn. The broad porches and light-blue wood trim gave it almost a fairy tale look. The inn stood out against the lush vegetation of the island and was immaculate. The island had been designated as a nature preserve by the federal government. It was an ecological wonder, with wild horses, miles of pristine beaches, and hundreds of species of birds, animals, fish, and reptiles. The island got its name Feral from the horses that had swum ashore from wrecked Spanish galleons 500 years before.

The greeting and service were remarkable. He could see his department heads fitting into the inn's total feel of hospitality. It made him proud, although he thought Wally Callahan would have to mind the wild horses to fit his personality. When they checked in, he was surprised to learn Lee had reserved a two-bedroom cottage.

"Don't worry. I reserved the cottage because I wanted to look proper. Plus, if you decide things aren't going well, we can still be friends and enjoy the rest of the stay without feeling awkward," she said.

They changed into beach clothes, got a picnic lunch, and walked to the beach. They found a lonely dune and ate. The rest of the day, they walked the beach, wading and swimming. At one point, a wild horse appeared on a dune. They stood and watched it. The horse shook its head, but stood there proudly looking back at them as if he was welcoming them.

"I think he approves of us being here," Lee said.

"You know him too?" Edwin asked.

"Why do you ask?" she replied.

"You seem to know everyone. It wouldn't surprise me if he was a bodyguard or something," Edwin answered.

"I've got the only bodyguard I need. Although, sometimes, he's as stubborn as that horse probably is," she said.

The horse let out a snort and shook his head.

"I think he's either a chaperone or he's jealous," Edwin said.

"No, I think he's just agreeing with me," she replied.

That night they ate in the main dining room. The chef did a special entrée of crab cakes that were unbelievable. They agreed Baltimore might have just moved into second place in the crab world. The wine, from Dunesgate's sizable collection, relaxed them. Edwin had been careful not to get sunburned. A sunburned lover is not always an attentive one. *Although rubbing the lotion on your partner could have its benefits.*

The next morning, Lee was asleep when Edwin woke at five. He quietly got out of bed, dressed for the beach and left Lee a note that he would meet her for breakfast at eight. He went to the inn and inquired about horseback riding.

"I'm sorry, but the only horses we can ride here have two wheels and pedals. I'd be more than happy to get you one, Mr. Christian," the young guest service agent said with a smile.

He was surprised she knew his name. The service at the Dunesgate Inn was very personal, very warm, and very professional. He must have looked surprised, and the young woman caught it.

"The wild horses can be territorial with other horses. If we brought some outsiders in for the guests to ride, they might not appreciate it. Horses are a little large to be disciplining and trying to explain things to," she said.

"They must all be men," he replied.

Greg Plank

"Not necessarily," she said with a wink. "Can I get you a bicycle?"

He thanked her, but declined. He walked to the beach and ran for what he thought was five miles down and back on the beach. The thin sliver of sunlight, rising over the water, almost mesmerized him. He sat down on a dune near the trail to the inn. He was as happy as he could ever remember. In fact, he had never felt this deeply warm and content before. He thought about last night in the cottage. He had been awkward at first. Lee took the lead, touching him with a soft loving touch. She cuddled him until he relaxed. Then, she took him on a physical journey he had never been on before. From softness to boldness and on to body-shaking moves of passion. They rode their emotions up and down, around caressing corners, diving into breath-stopping gasps. It had been the ultimate dance of living. At the height of it, he felt their souls touch. At the end of it, he felt them bond as they fell asleep.

His first thought as he awoke was he now knew what love was. He understood the delicate balance of physical passion and unselfish caring. He sat on the dune, his mind locked on last night. He smiled, not forgetting one second or one touch of the journey. He was startled when something touched his shoulder.

"Best horse on the beach," he heard the familiar, soft voice say from behind.

He turned around. Lee was smiling as she sat down next to him. He put his arm around her and kissed her. "Couldn't sleep?"

"Not without you."

They sat in silence smiling and touching, as they watched the sunrise. Not far away, the horse from the day before appeared from the trees. The large animal surveyed the beach, his gaze fixed on them. He snorted and shook his head.

"Think he was peeking last night?" Lee asked.

"If he had, he'd be sitting next to you," Edwin replied.

"You're romantic in the funniest ways," she said.

"And you, my love, in the most surprising ways," he replied.

It was the first time he had used the word love. It felt good. He looked for a reaction.

"You think two people can make a life out of funny and surprising?" she asked.

"Sure as hell beats comfortable and familiar," he said, smiling.

"We can try those in the old-age home," she said.

"I don't think age will change anything. Modern medicine will keep up with our feelings," he replied.

"I truly hope so," she said.

The horse continued to watch them. They decided to see if they could buy him, name him First Time, and run him in the Kentucky Derby.

They went back to the inn, showered and went to breakfast. When the server took their order, Lee asked for the largest breakfast on the menu. Edwin decided to do the same.

When the server left the table, Lee said, "I know I ordered enough for both of us, but the salt air and great lovemaking have made me very hungry. I'll have to learn how to curb my appetite with you around."

"I'd rather you just keep burning calories with me," he replied. "I'm available twenty-four hours a day."

"What about the twenty-fifth at ten a.m.?" she asked, laughing.

He reached over to the empty table next to them and took the pen off of the signed breakfast check another couple had left. He wrote "25th @ 10 AM" on his hand.

"What are you doing?" she asked.

"I didn't have a calendar to write it on," he replied.

She took the pen and did the same. "Promises are promises. I keep mine."

They held hands as they waited for breakfast. Afterward, they sat on the front porch and read the newspaper. They took coffee back to the cottage and dressed for the beach. After a long walk, they sat down on a lonely dune.

"I told you I had something to talk to you about. Actually, I really want your opinion," he said.

"Shoot."

He spent the next fifteen minutes bringing her up to date on the financial situation at the St. George. When he was done, he told her his only choice was to sell it.

"I feel so sad," she said. "It must hurt you to even think about it."

"That means a lot to me. Thanks," he said. "Now I want your take on the whole thing. I've been alternating between total guilt and depression."

"You want the legal opinion or the gut opinion?" she asked.

"The gut opinion," he replied.

"First of all, it sucks for a lot of reasons. The two main ones are your feelings and the great people in your hotel family," she said.

"If I lose it, everyone loses. If I sell, a lot of jobs might be saved. They're good people, and McNerey has given me a plan for them," he said.

He explained the loyalty payments to the staff.

"You'd give up that much of your own money?" she asked.

"What do you think?" he asked.

"I think I love you, as long as you don't change," she replied.

The next few days went quickly. They explored the island, walked the beach, and looked for the horse every day. He kept coming back to stand and watch them. The morning they left, they walked to the beach and waved good-bye to First Time. He shook his head and snorted.

"I think he's going to miss us," she said.

"I think he's going to miss you more. I'm sure he peeked," Edwin replied.

chapter

FORTY ONE

Edwin had dropped Lee off at her place and gone home. The memories of their time on the island kept him awake until one a.m. He was tired and went directly to the hotel without his daily run.

"Morning, Boss. How was the trip?" Slim asked.

"Great, Slim. Very relaxing," Edwin replied.

"What a shame," Slim said, putting a sad look on his face.

"Am I going to get that from everyone until I spill all the details?" Edwin asked.

"Probably."

"I'll show slides at the department heads' meeting," Edwin said.

"Excellent idea, Boss. Things have been a little boring around here."

"Slim, I didn't take a camera. Sorry for the disappointment," Edwin said as he smiled. "But it's good to see you."

"We'll all be very disappointed, sir," Slim said.

"Get over it," Edwin said as he entered the hotel.

Jack Vincent looked up with anticipation on his face.

"Morning, Jack. No, you're not getting any details on my trip. It was very relaxing," Edwin said.

"Is that relaxing enjoyable? Relaxing stimulating? Or just relaxing?" Jack asked.

"All of the above, but that's all I'm saying. How was the hotel while I was away?"

"Normal and uneventful. Business was surprisingly good. It's nice to have you back," Jack replied.

"It's nice to be back. Thanks for taking care of things," Edwin said.

When he got to the executive offices, Donna Lane was at her desk going over some forms. She welcomed him back and told him McNerey had called. He thanked her for not asking for the details of his trip like the others, and went into his office and called McNerey. For the next fifteen minutes, Edwin listened as Al reported on the findings of Sam Apistol and Robert Baisch, the two hotel brokers. They had agreed on an asking price; it was fair and would move the sale of the hotel.

Al explained the selling process. People would be looking at the hotel, and asking a lot of questions of Edwin and the staff. The offers, if people decided they wanted to buy, would range in price and terms. Al encouraged Edwin to get the cleanest sale he could, and avoid taking back any notes, or paper, in the sale. It should be an all-cash deal, so he could get out without worrying if he would ever get all the money should a buyer default or fail. Then he gave Edwin the good news. At the asking price, Edwin would net twenty-five million after taxes. Al had already figured in the three years' salary to the long-term employees and bonuses for the regular staff along with the closing costs.

"That's a lot of money for a dumb retired Marine," Edwin said.

"I figure you'll find something good to do with it. If you agree, I'll send the sales listing contract today," Al said.

"I've thought hard on this. Send the papers. Let's get on with it," Edwin replied.

In conclusion, Al told him to get busy gathering all contracts, licenses, permits and anything else that would come into the legal side of the sale. Al thought the sale would happen quickly, because of the potential and the location of the hotel. He reminded him to think about the historic building idea, and get it moving, if he wanted to make sure the Hotel St. George lived on as a hotel. Edwin promised to call the next day, when the documents were ready, and hung up. He called Lee on her cell phone and asked her to start gathering the legal documents. He also invited her to dinner.

"I'll have a lot of money when it sells. I'd like to think about what we can do with it," he said, putting emphasis on the word we.

"I've thought about that too. I really don't care, as long as we do it together," she replied.

"Does that come with a prenuptial agreement?" he asked.

"With that much money at stake, I think it should and I can do one," she replied.

"Good—then you can watch me tear it up. I've got this thing about trusting certain people," he said.

It was time to start the process with the staff. He would talk to them individually and have them sign confidential agreements for the loyalty payments.

No time like the present, he thought and invited Donna in. She sat, stunned, as he explained the loyalty payments and his putting a no cut clause in the agreement for one year for the employees. She argued he didn't have to give away a lot of money to assuage his guilt. He replied it wasn't guilt, it was A.D.'s money, and he would want it that way.

The rest of the day, he walked around the hotel and delivered the same news to the key members of the staff. He was amazed. All of them had almost the same reaction as Donna. They were a hotel family. None of them held a grudge or questioned the necessity of the sale. They were also universally surprised and appreciative of the loyalty payments and the potential employment agreements. Jack and Marty were the only ones with a different slant.

"With three years' salary and you with some money left over, we can start something really interesting. Ever thought of a bed-and-breakfast?" Jack asked.

"You going to do the breakfast or the beds?" Edwin asked.

"Depends on who's in the bed," Jack replied.

With Marty it was slightly different. Marty should have been a cop or an interrogator. After Edwin had finished his conversation about the sale, Marty asked, "So, the Greek and the Denver guy are the brokers?"

"How did you know that?" Edwin asked.

"Kid, I'm Jewish, which makes me an authority on anything real estate and I'm your rabbi," Marty answered.

"There's got to be more to it than that," Edwin said.

"O.K., I've got these two guys in the bar trying to act like they don't know each other. The Greek guy has three older couples at the bar wetting their pants with laughter. The Denver guy knows more about baseball than Willie Mays. But they both ask how the business in the bar is going, how the hotel is doing, and when it was last upgraded. I didn't put it together until now, but I know people," Marty answered. "Hey, thanks for the loyalty thing. It's the biggest tip I've ever gotten."

"You earned it, Marty. You earned every penny of it," Edwin replied.

The next evening, Edwin picked Lee up in the hotel limo and took her to the family home. From the moment he introduced Lee to his mother and Mrs. Martinez, he was left out of the conversation. His mother wanted to know all about Lee. She explained her career with the government, and even put in some of the details about her tougher assignments. Mrs. Martinez traveled between the kitchen and the porch, bringing wine and cheese and cooking dinner all at the same time. The three women became a sorority in the first hour. His mother had no trouble communicating with Lee, and insisted she sit next to her. Every time she looked at Edwin, she smiled her approval.

When Edwin heard a sports car pull up in front, he excused himself and went to the door to greet Daphne.

"I've been a very good girl around Mrs. Martinez. I even cooked dinner the other night so she could go home. I've also sent a personal note to all your hotel people. It was a great occasion. Did you see my picture in the Sunday Society Page? The hotel got a wonderful mention."

"Thanks, Daphne. The staff enjoyed the event and Mother and Mrs. Martinez seem very happy," Edwin said.

"You're not as thick-headed as I thought. This is a happier place," she said, and she affectionately touched her brother's face.

"That's not really why I wanted to talk with you. I have a favor to ask," he said.

"I guess I owe you one. What can I do?"

He explained the sale of the hotel and his desire to keep it a hotel. He asked if she could help on the historic building designation.

"If I can save the Arkwright Building, the hotel should be a snap. I'll get you an application tomorrow. I'm the Historic Committee chairperson this year. I can have the thing moving quickly, and I can start getting some press about it," she said.

"I wouldn't want to mention the sale in the press," he said.

"Of course not. The press is to make people aware of how important the Hotel St. George is to the community," she replied. "Trust me, I'm a great crusader."

"I have no doubt. You're also a pretty cunning strategist," he said.

"I take that as a compliment," she said.

"I meant it as one. Oh. I've brought a guest for dinner. She's out with Mother," he said.

"The little girl in the toga, I presume," Daphne replied.

"Why would you guess that?" he asked.

"Winnie, I've been married twice. I can read a man's eyes. Especially the I'm-in-heat look," she replied.

"It's more than that."

"I sincerely hope so. The heat thing doesn't last long, and you've got this loyalty thing," she said with a smile. "Let's go so I can get to know her."

"Only on the condition that you don't tell any embarrassing stories about my youth," he said.

"Not tonight. I'll have plenty of time for those," she said. She took his arm and pulled him toward the porch.

Maybe Daphne is getting more human. Then he reminded himself you watch the teeth, not the wagging tail, when you face a dog you don't fully know. They joined the others. He finished preparing dinner, as the four women talked and laughed on the porch. Mrs. Martinez made a fuss over him cooking and doing the clean-up, but she didn't argue hard. Edwin felt a family kind of happiness. As Edwin and Lee prepared to leave and she went to the bathroom, the other three all hugged him and gave their approval.

"Don't screw this up like I did. I think you're lucky you've got a really good person," Daphne said.

Edwin could tell she was sincere. Her teeth weren't showing. In the limo on the way back Edwin asked Lee what all they had talked about.

"Just girl stuff. You didn't think we talked about you the whole time?" she asked.

"No, I wasn't asking that," he replied.

"Yes you were, and yes, you were the high point of the conversation, and I still love you."

The next morning, Edwin signed the sale listing agreements and sent them back to Al. He called him to tell him.

"Edwin, you're doing the right thing. You'll have a lot of life and a lot of happiness," Al assured him.

"Life is already getting a lot happier. Just let me know what to do next," Edwin replied.

"Get ready for the Greek and the ex-surfer to show up with some very interesting people. Unfortunately, some of them might be arrogant or pushy. The two of them will guide you through the process," Al replied.

His cell phone beeped while he was talking to Al. When he hung up with Al, he retrieved the message: Ann Baxter. She wanted to remind him, when he got close to a sale, he should call her at home and set up a meeting.

chapter

FORTY TWO

For the next four days, Edwin spent his time getting ready for the prospective buyers. Lee had gathered all of the documents the law firm had, and Donna Lane met with every department head, gathering any agreements or contracts they had signed in behalf of the hotel. The total of all the paper filled fifty folders. They put it all in the boardroom. It would be the "war room" for prospective buyers and their due diligence people to use in evaluating the hotel.

Robert Baisch called to set up bringing representatives from a large hotel company that wanted to do a five-star hotel in the city.

"These guys will be super-critical of the hotel and the operations. They have a high opinion of their own hotels. They run great places, and deserve the reputation, but everything they find, to weaken your confidence, could help them drive the price down. You might want to prepare your staff not to take anything personally, and not to argue. I'll do that," Baisch explained.

"I'm not looking forward to all this," Edwin replied.

"Don't worry. It's the business equivalent of a mating game. I'll be there tomorrow. Call me Bob and act like we're long-term friends. Tell them I speak for you. It'll make it easier. I don't have any emotional attachments in the deal," Baisch said.

Edwin called a department heads' meeting for the afternoon. He explained the situation, and what Baisch had told him about handling the prospective buyers. They were to follow Baisch's or Apistol's lead. He also told them some possible buyers might visit the hotel as guests, to observe it before they came officially. Everyone should watch all of the service people in the hotel, and have them on their best manners with positive attitudes. They decided to tell the staff Bill Smith had some important meeting planners looking at the hotel over the next few weeks.

The next morning, Bob Baisch showed up at eight a.m. Donna showed him into Edwin's office.

"How'd you get here from Denver so early in the morning? You take the red eye?" Edwin asked.

"Nope. I stayed at the Merrill last night. I wanted to see the competition. It's a good hotel, but this town could use a five-star," Bob said.

They went down to the dining room, had breakfast, and waited for the group to show up. They talked about Bob's international trips and compared notes on the places Edwin had been with the military. At ten, Edwin was paged to the lobby; the visitors had arrived. Baisch told him to sit tight. He would go meet them and bring them to the dining room. When he came back, he had three men and a young woman in tow. One was an acquisition specialist. He was wearing the most expensive suit. One was an operations person, and was the oldest of the group. The young woman was an auditor, who didn't look old enough to be out of college. The last one was an engineer with a lot of on-property experience.

The acquisition specialist pissed Edwin off in the first three minutes of the conversation. He sat adjusting his expensive watch asking insulting questions about the hotel's business levels, the aging condition, and lack of capital investment over the past eighteen months. Baisch picked up on Edwin's agitation.

"Mr. Christian is not selling the place because he's making a pot full of money. You've seen the financials. You're here to see if the location, which is A-plus, and the basic building will make money with your improvements and superior chain marketing. If you want to start nit-picking to lower the price from the get-go, it's not negotiable. If that bothers you, we can call it quits now and save a lot of time and bullshit," Baisch said.

The young woman flinched. The engineer chuckled, and the operations guy smiled and looked away. Baisch had cut to the chase and backed the specialist into a corner.

"Don't take me wrong. I'm just making observations," the specialist replied weakly.

"Then let's get you with the people you need to talk to, so you can get a first-hand look. We can meet again in the board room for lunch, and then proceed further," Baisch said.

Edwin was impressed. Baisch's calm and humorous demeanor covered a quick business mind and a large amount of intestinal fortitude. They split the team up. The specialist went to the boardroom to look over the documents. The engineer was introduced to Jake Jacoby for a tour of the hotel. The auditor was taken to Chuck Castillano to review the financials. Edwin and Baisch took the operations guy on a tour.

At one o'clock, they met back in the boardroom for lunch. The acquisition specialist led the conversation. He asked each of his team for their general impressions. The operations guy said, "We ought to hire all of their department heads, whether we buy the hotel or not."

"Ditto for Chuck the controller," the woman said.

"And you?" the specialist asked, looking at the engineer.

"This place might be a little worn, but Jacoby has all the mechanical systems in top shape. He's as good as I've seen," the engineer answered.

"So, we've got a great location, good staff, and lousy numbers. What's the problem?" the specialist asked.

"Simple. You've got a hotel with too many rooms to fill against the new competition. It has no chain affiliation, no frequent-travelers club, and no money to advertise. People are fickle when they can get points for their personal use from the big chains. You guys bring all that with you, and, if you take it upscale and combine more rooms into suites, you'll get the higher rate you need and you'll fill easier. It's a no-brainer," Baisch said.

"Sounds easy, but we have to put a good deal of capital into an upgrade. I'm not sure the numbers will work," the specialist replied.

"You're the first group in to look at it. Don't take too much time with the numbers. It might not be available when you're done," Baisch replied.

The specialist looked annoyed with Bob's comment and kept quiet through the remainder of lunch. Bob and the other three talked about the hotel business and how it has changed. The auditor was more interested in Bob's surfing days in Southern California. After lunch, the team stayed in the boardroom to look over the documents and compare notes. They worked until midnight, and left the next morning promising to get back with their interest within a week.

That night, Edwin invited Lee over for dinner with Bob. When the broker found out Lee read the sports page cover to cover each day and was a Braves fan, the conversation turned to baseball. Edwin sat listening and laughing as the two argued over who was the greatest player in each position over the last ten years. They went to the bar and Marty, Bob, and Lee finished the night debating the best players in baseball. Edwin watched as Lee used her legal interrogation skills against the two older men. He decided arguing with her was not going to be on the top of his list for life.

Two days later, Edwin got a call from Sam Apistol. He was bringing a group in to see the hotel.

"They're going to be tough. The father started the company. The son has a finance degree and is a strong numbers guy. They started with small motels and have been very successful. They're into upscale properties now. They've got a strong financial team and they're hard negotiators. We'll be there the day after tomorrow," Sam said. "I guess you know the drill by now."

"Yeah. I keep quiet and you do all the talking," Edwin replied.

"One exception this time. Make sure you mention some of the bigger franchise companies are after you to keep it and put a brand name on it. Let them think you're seriously considering it," Sam said.

"You want me to play hard to get?" Edwin asked.

"Kind of like that. These guys will be concentrating on getting the price down. At first, they'll make you feel you should pay them to take the hotel off your hands. Why shouldn't they? If you don't ask, you don't get. We don't want them to think you're in a must-sell position," Sam replied.

"Got it. I'll see you soon," Edwin said.

Two nights later, Edwin was in the bar talking with Marty. A man in a camel hair sports coat came up to the bar.

"Marty, how you been?" the man asked.

"Absolut on the rocks tonight?" Marty asked, already reaching for the bottle.

"Edwin, this is Sam Apistol," Marty said, realizing the two had never met.

"Nice to finally meet you, Sam. You guys go back a ways?" Edwin asked.

"Just a couple of weeks. See, there are four things you need in life. A good woman. Good kids. A good doctor, and a good bartender/rabbi," Sam replied. "Marty has completed my life."

Edwin and Sam ate dinner in the bar, talking with Marty about the hotel business until midnight. The next morning, Edwin got to the hotel at seven in anticipation of the group's arrival. He was foggy from the night before. He had never had that much vodka. He found Sam in the dining room doing his second crossword puzzle of the day. He had been there since six a.m. and was fresh as a new preacher on Sunday.

"The group checked in last night. We meet them at ten in the boardroom," Sam said cheerfully. "You don't look so good."

"Death by vodka," Edwin said, and chugged a large glass of orange juice.

"I forgot. You haven't been in the hotel business very long. You gotta learn to sip, son," Sam replied.

"I wish you'd told me that last night," Edwin said.

"Just don't forget the bit about the franchise companies. You'll feel better as the day goes on," Sam said, still working on the puzzle as he spoke.

At ten, they went to the boardroom. Three men from the purchasing group were there looking over the financials on the hotel. Sam made the introductions. The younger man was the son, and acted as chairman of the company. The others were the president of operations and the CFO of the company.

"Not very exciting numbers," the younger one said.

"That's why I'm considering my options," Edwin replied. "I either sell it or I take one of the franchise proposals on the table and put a flag on it to help market it."

Sam smiled at Edwin as if to say, "Well done. You got it in early."

"You really want to bet on putting the necessary capital in this place with no hotel experience?" the young chairman asked.

"I might be naive, but if you can make it work, I think I might too. Like you, I was brought up in this business, and the staff is the best in the city," Edwin said.

"No offense, but we've bought a lot of distressed hotels from people who felt the same way," the CFO interjected.

"With this location and these facilities, a little money and a little marketing will level the playing field. This city needs a hotel with charm, instead of the chrome and shiny paneled ones that have been built recently," Sam said.

"You must think the market's big enough or you wouldn't have wasted the airfare to get here," Sam replied. "Why don't we let you look around and see for yourselves?"

They left the CFO in the boardroom and brought Chuck Castillano in. Jake Jacoby took the president of operations around to look at the physical plant, and Sam and Edwin escorted the chairman through the various departments. Three hours later, they met back in the boardroom. For the next four hours, Sam and Edwin fielded questions from the group. The young chairman began the conversation, pointing out the elements they had observed as inferior or non-competitive. Sam and Edwin listened patiently and took notes. Fifteen minutes into the conversation, it was apparent to them they were into the Let's-knock-the-price-down game. At the thirty-minute mark, the chairman had completed his list of drawbacks at the hotel.

"You've brought up some interesting points," Sam said. "Let me go through them."

For the next fifteen minutes, the hotel veteran went over each point. He analyzed each one and concluded, "With your operational experience and company resources, they're all day-to-day operational issues, and not major cost items in the purchase of the hotel."

He saved their point about the physical condition of the building structure for last. "Your concern for the electrical and mechanical items is obviously a potential cost item in your renovation and upgrade of the hotel. We've looked at them and none of them are a serious problem. All of the systems — plumbing, electrical, elevators, fire protection, etc. — are all up to code. There are no surprises hidden behind the walls, and we'll be glad to certify that in the sales agreement. In fact, a major hotel company was here earlier and their head of engineering indicated the hotel was up to snuff," Sam said. He put his pen down and sat back, waiting for their response.

"We'll have to have an independent engineer verify that," the chairman said.

"We expect that to be part of your due diligence. Like I said, we'll be glad to certify the physical condition in the sales agreement," Sam replied.

There was no reason for further discussion, so the chairman moved on to the price and financing of the transaction. His first mention of price was twelve million under the asking price. He also wanted Edwin to take back a second mortgage of twenty million to make the deal move faster.

"If you're bottom-fishing, you're in the wrong lake," Sam said. "There's not ten hotels in the country in a location as good as this, and in a market that's crying for a five-star hotel. The price is fair, and that's what we'll settle for. As to taking paper back, Mr. Christian is willing to take the risk himself only if he operates the hotel. No offense, but if he gets out of the hotel, he wants a complete break. He's not keen on tying his financial future to a third party. If you want him to help finance the deal, lease the hotel from him, and you put in the capital improvements."

The group was silent as they thought over what Sam had said. They asked to be alone to discuss the situation. Sam and Edwin left them in the boardroom to talk. Two hours later, they had Sam and Edwin paged to the boardroom.

"We've talked it over. We're still interested, but we have to look at our financing options. That will take a couple of weeks. I take it all of these documents will be available for our attorneys to look over in the process," the chairman said.

"Of course. We'll even provide them with rooms while they're in the process," Edwin said.

They said they'd be in touch in the next three days to make the arrangements.

After they'd left, Edwin asked Sam, "You think they're really interested?"

"They won't waste a dime on lawyers unless they're serious," Sam replied.

"You're pretty direct in your negotiations. You kind of caught them in the cookie jar on the price," Edwin said.

"The art of negotiating this stuff is to get all the bullshit out of the way early. I was just moving them along. The second part of negotiating is to respect your opponent. They're good businessmen, they're successful, and they've played this game before," Sam replied.

chapter

FORTY THREE

Edwin's guilt about selling the hotel was still eating at him. The department heads were making him feel worse because there was no complaining or negative talk. They continued to do their jobs and were cheerful. He wondered if Custer's troops were that way just before the Little Big Horn. When he got to his office, there was a voice message from Wally Callahan. He wanted to bring Captain LeRoy in to meet at ten a.m. Edwin called him and agreed. Donna brought him a cup of coffee, and told him the lawyers from both groups that had looked at the hotel would be in over the next few days. She had taken it upon herself to schedule them on different days.

"Thanks. I would have forgotten that they wouldn't want to be here at the same time," Edwin said.

"Don't worry. I made it sound like there were a multitude of groups who wanted to look at the papers. It might whet their appetites if they think they're in a big competition," she said.

"You have a cunning side to you," he replied, smiling.

"Just intuition. Men like to compete, makes the prize seem worth more," she said as she left the office

At ten a.m., Wally appeared with Captain LeRoy.

"Wally tells me you're looking at selling the hotel. Bummer," the captain said.

"Not of my choosing. The market's changed. You have to move on," Edwin replied.

"I think the captain has some good news for you," Wally said.

"I could use some," Edwin replied.

LeRoy explained the murder was wrapped up pretty tight, and Mason was out of the woods. Warren Lewis, aka Armand deCoste, was very interested in a plea bargain. He claimed the victim asked for some rough sex and it got out of hand. They could go for murder-one, but all the evidence was circumstantial. Mallory and Mason could put him in the room and the fibers matched up, but there were no eyewitnesses. The D.A. was checking with the girl's family to see if they'd go along with murder-two. He wasn't sure they really cared; they hadn't even claimed the body. It would put deCoste away for a long time, but no death penalty. Mason and Mallory would come out O.K. They had sex, but that appeared to be all. Edwin thanked him for saving Mason. He would have a talk with the young man along with Wally and Jack. The guy needed a friend and he had to understand how big a bullet he had dodged. Wally agreed and the three men continued more pleasant conversation as they finished their coffee.

Later that morning, Edwin invited Robert Mason to his office. Wally and Jack were there waiting. Mason looked scared at first. When Wally explained the situation with Warren Lewis, and that Mason would only have to testify, he relaxed a bit. As the message sank in, tears came to Mason's eyes. Wally got a look on his face of "Oh Jeez" and turned away. Jack moved to the chair next to Mason and put his arm on the young man's shoulder.

"All I can think to say is thank you for sticking with me," he said, wiping the tears away.

"I think you have potential, Robert. Just don't blow it by hiding in doubt and self-pity. Get on with your life," Edwin said.

"I will, sir. I will," Mason replied.

"Good. Get back to work. We need the money. And don't call me sir," Edwin said. Edwin asked Wally to stay and Jack and Robert left the office.

"I read your security report from last night. What was the cross-dresser thing?" Edwin asked.

"Most of that comes from Jack, but I'll explain," Wally said.

A high-level executive entered the hotel with a very attractive woman. Jack noticed the gentleman went to the elevator immediately, without making eye contact with anyone in the lobby. The woman had a hard time keeping up with him in her high heels. Jack had helped check the man in and remembered he had asked for a single room. He paged Wally, because of the gentleman's behavior. Prostitutes can give a hotel a bad reputation and liability. Fifteen minutes later, Jack and Wally were standing in the lobby when the elevator doors opened and the woman came out, walking as fast as her high heels would allow. Seconds later, the gentleman came out of another elevator on a dead run. He was holding a towel around his waist.

The woman and the gentleman bolted through the front door before they could intervene. Fortunately for the gentleman, two beat cops were outside talking with Slim Johnson. As the two came flying out the door, the gentleman was yelling every four-letter word he had ever heard. The cops grabbed the woman as she tried to pass. The gentleman came running up with Jack and Wally ten steps behind. He spent the next two minutes telling the officers how the woman had tricked him into taking a shower before what she promised would be the most exciting experience of his life. She had taken his wallet, money clip and twelve-thousand-dollar watch, and luckily, he had come out of the shower just in time to hear his guestroom door close and saw his lady had departed.

The cops listened patiently and fought hard to stifle their smiles. Jack and Wally listened in amusement. As the gentleman was finishing his story, the larger cop interrupted, "Well, sir, allow me to introduce you to your real date tonight."

The other cop reached over and pulled up the woman's dress to reveal an ample and quite unexpected piece of anatomy inside the see-through lace panties. The gentleman stepped back in horror.

Jack's mouth dropped open; Wally lost it and burst into uncontrollable laughter.

The big cop continued, "Allow me to introduce Maxine Passion who's given name is Charles White. Charles is a well-accomplished socializer in our precinct."

Maxine didn't seem distressed. She, or he, had been a police informant on several occasions and had always gotten off clean from any money-making adventures with the innocent. The cop informed the gentleman he could take his valuables and return to his room or press charges and come downtown for a statement. The gentleman quickly decided to take his things and leave.

"Do we have one of your new security cameras covering that area?" Edwin asked.

"As a matter of fact we do," Wally replied.

"Good. You might want to inform the gentleman you have it on disc in case he changes his mind and wants to sue us," Edwin said.

"You're very devious, Boss, and you're learning very fast," Wally said.

"I'm learning from a couple of masters," Edwin replied.

"I'm flattered," Wally said on his way out the door.

Edwin was finishing his lunch in the employee cafeteria talking with some of the staff. His cell phone rang. Donna Lane told him Al McNerey wanted to talk with him. Edwin excused himself and returned to his office. He dialed Al's number. McNerey told him he had gotten a call from an off-shore industrial and investment group. They wanted to look at buying the hotel for their associates who visit the city often. He thought they might as well talk with them.

"What the hell? The more the merrier. When do they want to come?" Edwin asked.

"Tomorrow. They know we've had a few groups looking, and they don't want to miss the opportunity. I've pre-qualified them as best I can. They understand it's an all-cash deal and the price is firm. It'll be two of the bigger investors and their attorney coming. I've already emailed you their names," Al replied.

"Will Bob or Sam be on this one?" Edwin asked.

"This time you're on your own. You know the drill by now," Al said.

"Thanks for the confidence. I'll give it my best shot," Edwin said.

"Just don't let them know you speak Spanish until the end of your conversations," Al said.

"Why?" Edwin asked.

"You'll find out. Good luck," Al said and hung up.

The next morning at eleven, Jack Vincent called the executive office, announcing there were three gentlemen in the lobby asking for Edwin. Edwin asked him to put them in the dining room and went down to meet them.

"I'm Edwin Christian," he said offering his hand.

"Con mucho gusto, one of the men said as he introduced them.

Edwin let the Spanish comment go, remembering what Al had said.

The first man was the group's agent and attorney. The other two were investors. One owned a large exporting company, and the other was in real estate and commercial development.

"Welcome to the Hotel St. George. How may I help you?" Edwin asked.

"We would like to look around and discuss the sale of the hotel. Mr. McNerey may have told you we have great interest in a hotel in the States," the agent said.

"We have all of the financial information in the boardroom upstairs, and I can have my department heads show you around and answer any questions. I can also put you in rooms for the night," Edwin replied.

"We'd just as soon see the hotel together. Do you have time to show us around?" the agent asked.

"It would be my pleasure. Can I get someone to put your bags in your rooms?" Edwin asked.

"That won't be necessary. We have a short time here and will be leaving this afternoon," the agent replied.

Probably just on a fishing trip, if they're not staying long. "In that case, let's get started," Edwin said.

He escorted them through the front of the house first — the meeting rooms, bar and a cross-section of guest rooms and suites. As they toured the hotel, the men spoke in Spanish. Edwin tried hard to ignore the conversations and look stupid. The tour lasted two hours. They returned to the boardroom and Edwin ordered lunch from room service. The men looked through the assembled documents.

As they finished lunch, the agent told the other two in Spanish he had not found anything that would hinder a quick purchase. He also thought they could probably knock a few million off the price because of the financial condition of the hotel. He would convince Edwin that he had an urgent problem and they had available cash. He thought people in Edwin's position were impatient about money, and Edwin had not had the hotel long enough to have an emotional attachment to it. He didn't think Edwin really knew what it was worth.

"How will you manage the hotel?" Edwin asked. "Part of the sale is that the existing employees stay on contract for a while."

"We have an associate who has operated many large hotels internationally. He would welcome the local knowledge of your staff," the agent replied.

"If you'll leave us to meet alone, we'll see you before we leave about our interest," the agent said.

"I'll be in my office," Edwin said.

This is too easy. They'll never make an offer. There's something strange here.

He was talking with Jack Vincent about the incident with the gentleman and the cross-dressing hooker the night before when Donna interrupted him and told him the three gentlemen wanted to talk with him. When he got to the boardroom, the three men looked eager. They explained they were very interested and could close the sale in a very short time.

Edwin hesitated for a minute and then said, in perfect Spanish, "I'm really not impatient about the money, and I don't have to sell right away. If you're looking for a large price break, it's out of the question. I will also have to check out your operating person; to be sure he's the right person to lead my staff. I have an emotional attachment to them. They helped raise me in this hotel from childhood."

The three men looked at each other in surprise. Finally, the agent began to laugh and the other two joined in.

"Senor, your Spanish is very good," the agent said.

"Just something I picked up in school," Edwin replied.

"You have a South American dialect," the man said.

"I traveled a lot, and my teacher was from there," Edwin replied.

"We understand your position. We would like to buy the hotel. But we have to offer our partners some concession for putting up their money so fast. What can you do on the price?" the agent asked.

"I'll talk to Mr. McNerey and get back to you by tomorrow. I might be able to take something off the price to save you face, but it won't be nearly what you were thinking," Edwin said.

"We'll wait for your call. My cell number is on my card," the agent said.

The conversation lasted only a few more minutes, and the three men departed.

Edwin went to his office and called Al. He explained the strange meeting and the men's request. It didn't surprise Al. He'd dealt with similar groups before.

He explained the pros and cons of the sale. Edwin could wait and maybe get nothing. He could wait and end up in protracted negotiations with the buyer he chose. The first thing to do was check on the validity of the group's claim of funds, and being able to close fast. Al would check those things out and get back to Edwin.

"Talk to you soon. This sounds too good to be true, but you never know. I'll also ask them for the information on their operating guy. I've got some contacts down there," Al offered.

They agreed to talk within the next two days.

chapter

FORTY FOUR

Edwin called Lee and asked her to dinner. She told him she had planned to meet her parents for dinner.

"Are you afraid to introduce me?" he asked.

"Of course not. Where did that come from?" she asked.

"Then why don't you bring them to the hotel? If it's not too early to introduce your sinful side," he said.

"Believe me, they already know about you. The hotel will be great," she replied.

"Let's meet here at seven. Anything I should avoid so I don't make a liar out of you?" he asked.

"Just be yourself," she said.

He hung up and called the chef and asked if they could eat at the chef's table in the kitchen. Mazzari was delighted as usual. When Lee and her parents arrived at the hotel, Edwin was standing outside talking with Slim, who was explaining that the expensive piece of luggage the woman with the two dogs claimed he ruined when he got it out of the cab was damaged long before that. He had pointed the damage out to the lady before he removed it from the trunk. When she checked in, she claimed Slim or the bellman had done it. Jack Vincent handled her and filled out a claims report. She used the title countess and got verbally abusive when Jack informed her he would report it to the insurance company. She wanted cash on the spot. Edwin told Slim he'd look into it in the morning and not to sweat it. Slim smiled, opened the doors to Mr. Brown's car and escorted the ladies out.

"Welcome to the St. George. I'll keep your car here in a special spot. I just need the keys," Slim said.

"Edwin, this is my father Matthew and my mother Linda," Lee said.

"It's Mat and Linda. Just don't call her Lyn," her father said, shaking Edwin's hand.

"It's my pleasure to finally meet you," Edwin said awkwardly.

Lee picked up on it and said, "Don't worry. I haven't shared any sordid details."

Edwin blushed with embarrassment. Lee's mother put her arm around Edwin's and said, "Don't let her bother you, Edwin. She's got a smart mouth when she's nervous. It runs in the family. It was so nice of you to invite us."

Edwin liked her immediately. He could see where Lee's openness and casual honesty came from. He escorted them into the lobby and through the dining room to the chef's table in the kitchen. Chef Mazzari greeted them. He had a special fan set up to take away some of the kitchen heat. Pas Medvier showed up with a selection of wines. He and Linda had a brief conversation in French. Edwin heard his name mentioned while they were laughing, but didn't ask any questions. When Linda mentioned that her husband was a bit of a gourmet wannabe, the chef escorted Mat around the kitchen, ending up behind the main cooking line. Before long, Mat was dressed in a chef's uniform wielding a French knife doing fancy vegetable garnishes and joking with the chef. Edwin remained at the table talking with Lee and her mother. Linda became the interrogator. She asked Edwin about his military experience and international travels. She finally got around to his family. She knew his brother and sister by reputation and was curious about their relationships.

"Daphne is a social work in progress. She's growing old before she grows up, but it seems to work for her. Henry is the ultimate entrepreneur, but with an over-developed need for control," he answered. "The age difference and the early loss of our father kept us separated in spirit and viewpoint. I don't think we share the usual sibling love and concern."

Linda was impressed with his openness. "So, she's flaky and he runs on ego," she said.

"Mother, it's none of your business. That's not a proper thing to say," Lee said.

"The lawyer is objecting. She does that a lot," Linda replied.

"No more wine for you," Lee said.

"Lee. I really don't mind. Linda, you're right on. I stopped making excuses for people a long time ago," Edwin said.

"If this had been a test, you would have passed top of your class," Linda said.

"What do you mean test?" Lee asked.

"Mothers have their rights, when it's about their children," Edwin said.

"Where's your dark side?" Linda asked Edwin.

"Mother, you're really getting out of hand," Lee said.

"You mean what keeps me awake at night?" Edwin asked.

"Yes. What dark secrets are locked in your psyche?" she asked.

Edwin thought for a moment.

"You don't have to answer that. She was a psychology major in college and practices without a license," Lee said.

"My darkest secret is I have a tendency to be gung-ho in tight spots. When I am, I sometimes forget others might not be able to keep up. It can cloud my judgment. One night, on a classified mission in Africa, I got two of my men killed. You wouldn't read about it in the newspapers. Their bodies came home quietly. I set the mission up wrong, in my gung-ho state of mind, and they died from friendly fire. That's what really ended my interest in the military. I have to be very careful when I feel the adrenaline start to flow."

"That's why you went slowly with my daughter at first. That's why she wondered about your apology for taking on the two muggers," Linda said.

"I'm really not liking this, Mother," Lee said.

"You must have done well in psych class," he said, and smiled.

"I think it's time we had our first family dinner. Lee Christian has a nice ring to it," she replied.

"After tonight, there might not be any ring at all. Mother, you can really irritate and embarrass me," Lee said. She was almost in tears.

"A family dinner sounds good to me. That's if Lee still wants me in the family," he said.

"I wouldn't blame you if you didn't want to be, after the great shrink just got done with you," Lee said.

"The honesty of the Brown women attracts me. It's part of what makes a family. Let's have dinner," he said.

Lee squeezed his hand and smiled. The chef and Mat brought a veal dish, pasta, salad, and bread to the table.

"What have you been talking about, while we've been slaving in the kitchen?" Mat asked. "Notice the garnishes. The chef taught me some new tricks."

"He's a natural," the chef said as Mat beamed.

"So is Edwin," Linda replied, smiling at her daughter.

For the next hour, they enjoyed the food and talked about Mat's business career and Lee's childhood. Edwin kept thinking about family.

The next morning, Edwin took a longer run than usual. He replayed the dinner in his mind and decided he was more hooked than ever. When he got to the hotel, Slim was still upset about the lady and her luggage. Edwin stopped by Jack's desk to ask about it. Jack explained everything was O.K. He knew Slim had nothing to do with it; he was always very careful. Jack had gotten curious about the guest and did some digging. Last night he had to tell the supposed countess from middle Europe she could not take her two dogs into the dining room to eat at the table. She had the vocabulary of an uneducated gang member when she was excited. Jack checked her credit card again. It came up on a second search as stolen. When she had Smiley the bellman walk the dogs that morning, Jack told him to look for I.D. tattoos; they were expensive dogs. Smiley found the tattoos and Jack went online and checked a site for missing pets. The dogs were stolen. They belonged to a well-to-do woman in Connecticut. Wally called her. She was thrilled to get her little fur balls back. The police were on the way. Unfortunately, the hotel had to eat the Countess's four-hundred-dollar bill.

"How'd you figure all that out?" Edwin asked.

"Just experience. When 'Thou doth protest too much,' it often means thou hiddeth something. It was easy to check on her. Computers are wonderful," Jack replied.

"You really should have been a cop," Edwin said.

"No tips," Jack replied.

Edwin headed to his office chuckling to himself. Donna informed him the lawyers and an outside auditor for the large hotel company were in the boardroom looking over the documents. Edwin went to check on them. He introduced himself and asked if he could help in any way.

"You have everything here. I just can't get over the variety of signatures on some of your service contracts. We'd never let the employees sign for the hotel. It's letting the inmates run the asylum. You've got no control," the young auditor said in an arrogant tone.

You little snot, Edwin thought, and began to smile.

"Any of those contracts look out of line, price or terms wise?" Edwin asked.

"No, they're in line," the young man answered.

"Any of them look funny or unnecessary?" Edwin asked.

"Not really."

"It appears the inmates do a pretty good job of running the asylum. If you've got the right people, and give them a little trust, they do just fine. You have any other questions?" Edwin asked.

"Not right now. I think we've got what we need," the older lawyer said. He was smiling at the rebuff the younger man had received.

"Great. If you need me, Donna can find me," Edwin concluded.

When he got to his office, Donna handed him an envelope from Daphne. Inside was a copy of a press release about the hotel seeking historic status. There was a note attached asking him to call her. He read the release. It went into the entire history of the hotel, including famous people who had stayed there. He called his sister at the number on the note.

"Well, little brother, what do you think of the release?"

"I think your PR firm earned its money," he replied.

"What PR firm? I wrote that," she said indignantly.

"Then I think you missed your calling. It's very good," he said.

"If you approve, I'll get it in the paper. But I thought maybe we should have a little press gathering at the hotel. Maybe a small luncheon with a couple of people from the Historical Society and the press," she said.

"If that helps your cause, I'll have Vinnie call you this afternoon to set it up," he replied.

"You're not going to restrict the menu, are you?" she asked.

"Are you still being good at home?" he asked in return.

"Yes, I am. In fact, I must admit Mrs. Martinez is doing very well. I like her and Mother is doing better than she has in months," she replied.

"I'll tell Vinnie you can have any menu you want. Thanks for the help. The release is very good," he said.

"Thank you, but you're still a bit of a hard ass," she said.

"My sister taught me that," he replied.

Daphne chuckled and hung up.

The chef and Andy Scott, the butcher, were having coffee at the chef's table. Edwin poured a cup and sat down. He thanked them for the dinner for Lee's parents.

"Andy, you look a little out of sorts today," Edwin said to the big butcher.

"I told him about the sale. He asked and I didn't think you'd mind," the chef said.

"Andy, I'm sorry. I'll do all I can to help you. I'm also putting an employment clause in the agreement, so you all can stay," Edwin said.

"My man, don't be sorry. When it's third down and long, you gotta throw the ball. I've seen this coming for a couple of years. The new guys in town are nine-hundred-pound gorillas," Andy replied.

Edwin stood up and asked Andy to follow him to the butcher shop. When they were in private, Edwin told him he would be added to the confidential list of people getting three years' salary. Andy was speechless. He stood there staring at Edwin.

"I can do this, can't I?" Andy asked. He put his large arm around his boss.

"I'm sorry about the sale," Edwin replied.

"Hell. With three years' salary, how fast can we sell the place?" Andy asked.

"You want me to wear a for-sale sign out front?"

They walked back into the kitchen. The chef looked at the smile on Andy's face and knew what Edwin had done.

On his way back to his office, Edwin stopped in the sales and catering office to talk to Vinnie DeTesta.

"Vinnie, I have something special for you to cater," he said.

"For you?" Vinnie asked.

"Kind of, but you'll be working with Daphne."

"This is like a joke, right?"

"No joke. It's a lunch for the press and the Historical Society, maybe ten people. I'm trying to get the hotel on the Historical Building Register," he said.

"So just a few animals and she rides into the ballroom on an elephant or something," Vinnie replied.

"I really think she'll be good. Did you get the thank-you note from her for the charity thing?" Edwin asked.

"Yeah. I had it tested for anthrax before I opened it. Actually, it was surprisingly nice," Vinnie said.

"See? She loves you," Edwin replied.

"Loves to make me squirm just like anything else in pants," Vinnie said.

"Give her a chance. This is important. If she gives you any trouble, call me," Edwin said.

"Guess I've kissed worse asses than hers," Vinnie said.

"You're a team player, Vinnie. Thanks," Edwin said and left.

That night, Lee invited him to dinner at her place. He showed up with Gerber daisies in one hand and a toothbrush in the other. After dinner, they sat on the couch and talked.

"You really think you got those guys killed in Africa?" she asked out of the blue.

"Does that bother you and our relationship?" he asked.

"No, it just bothers me that it bothers you," she replied. "Could there have been a reason other than your judgment?"

"It was late at night. We were all tired and we all spooked in the dark. I just think, maybe, there were ten things I could have done to make the mission safer," he said.

"Promise me, we're not going to live a coulda, shoulda, woulda life," she said. "Guilt kills relationships in the end."

"I promise, I'll do my best," he said.

"I see I'm going to have to kick your butt."

"What a pleasant thought," he replied.

chapter

FORTY FIVE

When Edwin got to work, Slim Johnson was escorting the last of a senior citizens' group from a tour bus.

"It's strange for a group to check in this early in the morning," Edwin said.

"We picked them up from the Pickwick Hotel. They over-booked a group for today. When the front office manager called Mason for help, the kid was smart enough to offer a breakfast buffet and the tour guide snapped it up. The kid's starting to think on his own," Slim replied.

"How's everything else in your world?"

"I'm in love with Jack," Slim said with a smile.

"Interesting. Does your wife know?" Edwin asked.

"Let me rephrase that. I have the highest regard for our distinguished concierge and his detecting abilities," Slim said.

"It was pretty cool the way he handled the lady with the luggage," Edwin replied. "Why don't you give him a special parking spot in the garage as a thank-you? Make sure he knows it was your idea, and I approved it," Edwin replied.

Edwin stopped by the front office. "You thought on your feet, Robert. Be proud. That's what we've been talking about."

"Thanks. It felt good," Mason said.

Edwin sat in his office going over a list of questions the large hotel company's due diligence team had left. They wanted explanations for some of the contracts, and some additional back-up for the mortgage on the hotel. Donna stuck her head into the office.

"Sorry to bother you, but I have a strange-sounding man on the phone who won't give his name and insists on talking with you," she said. "I can get rid of him if you like."

"I'll take it. Maybe I can save money on my car insurance or something," he said, and picked up the phone. As he did, he looked at the caller I.D. panel. Nothing was showing on it.

"This is Edwin Christian. How may I help you?" he asked.

"There's an offshore group looking at your hotel. I know your situation, and I knew your grandfather. Take their offer. They can close quickly. It'll be worth it to you, especially with your personal attachment to the hotel," the voice said.

"May I have your name?" Edwin asked.

"My name isn't important. Taking the offer is. I have some information I can't divulge. Trust me. A.D. did," the man said, and hung up.

He walked out to Donna's desk. "That was strange. Do you have any idea who that was?" he asked.

"I don't know who it was, but the voice was vaguely familiar. That's the only reason I considered putting the call through to you," she replied.

"If you can think of anything else, let me know," Edwin said.

He called Al McNerey, and told him about the call. Al thought it was strange, but he had checked the group out and they seemed legit. They had done several big all-cash deals. He told Edwin to think it over and they'd talk soon.

Edwin sat trying to place the voice. He was puzzled, but he trusted McNerey. At noon, he decided to eat in the employee cafeteria. On his way, he walked through the lobby. Wally Callahan was welcoming an International Airlines flight crew. The flight attendants had seniority; they were in their late thirties and forties. Wally was glowing as he walked them across the lobby, explaining the special crew lounge and offering to answer any questions or recommend places to go on their layover. When he had placed them on the elevator, he walked back into the lobby.

"You trying out for the concierge job?" Edwin asked.

Wally got an innocent little boy look on his face. "I'll have you know, I'm very good with seniors, mature women, little children and pets. There's a softer side to my gruff police exterior."

"Jack probably feels threatened with your new customer-service skills." Edwin said.

"As well he should."

That evening, Edwin remembered the call from Ann Baxter telling him to contact her as the sale got nearer. He called her home number.

"Edwin, how are you? A certain attorney seems to be almost radiant lately," she said.

"I hope so. A certain hotel owner has a little glow too," he replied. "You told me to call when the sale of the hotel heated up. I think it's about that time."

"It sounds like things are moving faster than anyone thought. If that's the case, I must swear you to total secrecy before we meet," she said.

"This is the second mysterious call I've had today. Of course, I'll keep whatever it is in total confidence," he replied.

"I'm going on vacation next week, so we have to meet soon. How about tonight?" she asked.

"I'm at home. I can meet you wherever you want," he replied.

She told him there was a small coffee shop on Twenty-Fourth Street. She'd meet him there in forty minutes.

Edwin got changed and walked the four blocks to the Cafe Bean, got a latte and took a lonely table in the back. Ten minutes later, Ann Baxter joined him. He asked her if she wanted anything, and got her the tea she requested.

"This is all very curious, but we've known each other a long time. I guess you'll tell me why the secrecy," he said.

Ann told him she was on a mission of conscience and took two pieces of paper out of her handbag. When he had called about the special account being held up, she decided to look back over the entire will. Something about how the loan against the hotel was being handled, letting the construction company off the hook, bothered her. She had typed the original will and kept a hard copy, in a confidential file, which she did for all of her work. The first page she handed Edwin was a page from the will that she herself had typed. A.D. had initialed it. The second page was the one in the will that was distributed to everyone. She didn't think the initials were A.D.'s. She'd done his legal work for years. In the page from the original, the loan responsibility went back to the construction company. In the copy everyone received, the liability for the loan stayed with the hotel.

Ann told him to listen carefully. A.D. had come to Justy LaGrange when Henry was in college. He'd been caught in a scandal at college involving drugs as payment for students taking other students' exams and doing papers for them. A.D. couldn't bring himself to allow Henry to be charged and thrown out of school. He asked Justy to intervene with some friends who were high up in law enforcement and at the college. Justy did it for his old friend. A few years later, Henry needed help again. He threatened Justy with making the original fix public and possibly getting him disbarred. At the time, Henry had nothing to lose and Justy had everything to lose. She had a feeling the same threat had been used once again to get the will changed. She had a high regard for Justy and thought he would want to make it right if he could.

Edwin replied they didn't have much proof. "But I'm not a forensics expert and certainly not a legal expert," he said.

"You don't have to be either. You just have to be one very upset brother, and a good bluffer," she replied.

"I certainly qualify on those two counts. What do you want me to do?" he asked.

She explained if he could convince Henry he had proof, and would pursue him legally, Henry would be in a very uncomfortable position. She was certain she could convince Justy to do the right thing. If Edwin could be convincing enough about going public, Henry now had a lot to lose. He was an egomaniac, loved his public reputation as a mover and shaker, and he had his sights set on public office.

"I take these to my brother and press him," he said, holding up the two pieces of paper. "But then he could go to Justy and threaten him again and they circle the wagons. At least now I know why my brother, with the use of some of his political friends putting on the pressure, tried so hard to convince me to sell the hotel."

"Don't worry about them circling the wagons. I think I can convince Justy he did something with the will he didn't have to do. If you're willing to pursue it, I'll take care of Justy," she replied. "The last part is that no one, especially Lee, can ever know."

"I think I'm going to accept an offer on the hotel tomorrow. I'll go to Henry in the afternoon," he said.

"Call me at the office and give me two hours' notice. I want to prepare Justy. I'm sure Henry will be contacting him," she said.

"If this is going to destroy your relationship, I'm not sure the money's worth it," he said.

"In the end, Justy will thank us both. He's an honorable man," she said.

The next morning he called Al McNerey. Al had found no negatives on the offshore company. Edwin told him to draw up the paper to accept the offer. At eleven, Edwin called his brother and told him he needed his advice. Henry's ego made him bite. They agreed to meet at Henry's club at four p.m. He called Ann Baxter and told her.

"Just be as tough as you can, and think about all the things you can mention he'll lose if he doesn't go along with you," she said.

Edwin went on line and looked at the Christian Construction site for any information on his brother's activities. Luckily, Henry liked to list everything he had ever been involved in: charities, boards of directors, political campaigns, and organizations.

Thanks, bro, Edwin thought as he went over the lists.

At three-fifty-five, Edwin entered the upscale Commerce Club and proceeded to the reception desk. He asked the woman at the reception desk for his brother. She instructed an attendant to take him to the library bar where he would find Henry. Henry ordered another drink and Edwin ordered none.

"What can I help you with?" Henry asked. "You selling the hotel?"

"I am selling the hotel. The thing you can help me with is a paper problem," Edwin explained.

"Whatever I can do to help you sell that cash drain," Henry replied with a condescending chuckle.

"This is the paper I have a problem with," Edwin said. He unfolded the two pages from the will and slid them across the table.

Henry tried to play it cool, but his jaw tightened and his eyes grew noticeably wider as he looked at the two pages.

"What's wrong with these? They're identical copies of the same page," Henry replied.

"Nice try, but you know if you look at the second paragraph, it's worth millions to your company," Edwin said.

Henry looked briefly at the second paragraph on both pages. "One is obviously a draft. This is the one in the final will," he said, holding up the altered page.

"Bullshit. I think you and a certain attorney cooked the will to get you off the mortgage liability," Edwin growled.

"I don't know where you got these, but someone is feeding you a line," Henry replied.

"My source is impeccable. I'm in the process of calling in favors with some of my friends at the forensics lab in D.C. I think they can prove the initials on the supposed draft page are the real thing and the others aren't," Edwin said.

He was bluffing. But he thought he could always call in an old favor. He didn't know if they'd back up his assertion, but it was worth a try.

"So it's some old friend that will back you up? Your assumptions are false, libelous, and insulting," Henry growled.

"The old friend who will back me up is Justin LaGrange," Edwin replied.

Henry was shocked. He fell silent for a full minute.

"Justy already knows we're meeting. I also have the person who typed the original will. She's outraged at your manipulation of her boss and friend. I think you ought to think about what this will cost Henry Christian. Your company takes on the liability for the mortgage, as our grandfather planned, or I become your new press agent," Edwin replied.

"Just what does that mean?" Henry asked.

"It means, I tell your entire story. Indiscretion in youth. Cheating. Bullying a trusted friend who tried to help you. Fraud in the will. The list of what you can lose is rather long. It's on the Christian Construction web site if your memory needs refreshing," Edwin said.

He pulled out the pages he had printed off the Internet about Henry's proud public and philanthropic efforts. He began to read the long list of Henry's affiliations, credentials, and community service. As he read, Henry pulled out his cell phone and punched a number. Justy was not answering his private line. Henry left an urgent message and punched another number.

"Is Mr. LaGrange in, please? This is Henry Christian and it's urgent," he bellowed.

After a short moment, he said, "Ann, don't play games. Tell him I called. It's a matter that needs immediate attention."

"Tell you what, brother. You sign the paperwork to get the will back to its intended state and I'll forget prosecution, and my publicity campaign. You can go on with your political ambition and maintain your sterling reputation. I don't like the thought of you in control of public funds, but this may be a life-changing experience for you," Edwin said.

"Go pound sand, you ignorant bastard. You've got nothing," Henry replied.

"If I were you, I wouldn't be insulting our mother. What you have is twenty-four hours to declare your position or I start in the PR business. When this comes out, a few other people, like employees, past associates and others, might have a conscience-cleansing too," Edwin said. "I'll expect your call tomorrow morning so we can make the proper arrangements. And while you're thinking it over, consider someone other than yourself. The looks your wife will get at the spa while she's tightening her buns for you. The invitations from her society friends she'll miss. Your kids in the carpool for private school and the questions and looks they'll get. You're not the only one who has something to lose."

He left before Henry could answer. On his way back to the hotel, he called Ann Baxter and told her about his meeting. She told him Justy was nervous, but he wanted to do the right thing. They were preparing the paperwork to revise the will.

"Ain't honesty great? When in doubt, tell the truth. You sleep a whole lot better," he said.

"There were certain things A.D. said that stuck with me. That was one of my favorites," Ann replied.

"Thanks for the help. I know it wasn't easy," he said.

"Easy ain't always easy," she said.

"That's another one," he said.

chapter

FORTY SIX

Al McNerey sent the papers for the sale. Edwin met Lee for lunch at Jimmy's and asked her to look them over. She read them in detail, handed him a pen and told him to get on with it.

"This is still really sad," she said.

"It might work out better than I could have hoped. These guys can close fast and the employees stay," he said. "Eat your big sandwich and enjoy it."

"I ordered the salad," she replied.

"Lost your appetite?" he asked.

"No. Just want to be in shape. You might have a lot of spare time in the near future," she replied.

"And that means?" he asked.

"It means, I can take a break, and maybe we can go somewhere together," she said.

"Back to the beach?"

"We've been there. I've been thinking the mountains," she replied.

"I have a standing invitation to the North Georgia Mountains. I'll find the place this time," he said.

"No tents," she said.

"Slept in them for years. Never again," he replied. "Besides, cots aren't very romantic."

When he got back to the hotel, he asked Donna to call a department heads' meeting. At two, he met with all the people he had offered the three-year deal to in the Presidential suite on the top floor. He was nervous about what to say and how to say it. He remembered something an old friend had told him: Deliver the message with honesty, humility, and humor. He decided it was the way to go.

"We're meeting here, because I wanted this to be relaxed," he began.

He went on to tell them about the sale and that the buyers had agreed to the employment contracts for them. Al McNerey told him the operations guy was good. It was a very quiet meeting. He asked if they had any questions.

They had quite a few, but most of them were about what he planned to do, and not about their future. He almost broke down.

"For God's sake, I'm selling the place. Let's talk about you. I'm out of here and doing pretty well. Let's talk about how I can help you," he said.

"You can start by getting off the personal guilt trip you're on. You're getting very depressing," Jack interjected.

"Everyone has a job, and we've got a good money send-off. We couldn't have done that on our own," Chef Mazzari said.

"I thought you all signed confidentiality agreements not to talk about the pay-outs," Edwin said.

"Boss, you're running a hotel, not the CIA. You couldn't keep a secret here if the Secret Service was guarding it," Bill Smith said.

"What's left to be done?" Edwin asked.

"The going-away party. It's a tradition," Wally shouted.

"What about a theme?" Vinnie DeTesta asked.

Without thinking, Slim Johnson said, "Christmas! We've never had a Christmas party with you, Boss."

"It's September, Slim," Edwin replied.

"It's Christmas for us," Andy Scott said.

Everyone in the room agreed. Edwin thought for a moment. "On three conditions."

"Don't be a prude. What conditions?" Donna asked.

"Every employee brings their families. Second, we pick the slowest night possible, and third, we close reservations for that period, so everyone possible can attend," Edwin replied. "If there are any guests in the hotel, we'll invite them so we can close everything down."

"That's going to cost you a lot of money," Chuck the controller said.

"Maybe it'll prove A.D and I care more about you than the money," Edwin replied.

"That was never a question," Robert Mason said.

They all turned and looked at the junior department head. He suddenly looked self-conscious.

"I couldn't have said it better," Wally Callahan said, putting his large arm around Robert.

"As soon as I have the date of the sale, we'll get things going," Edwin said. "I'll ask Daphne to help in the planning."

"You want the Grinch planning a Christmas party? Or are you just torturing the chef, Pas and me for the last time?" Vinnie asked.

"Even the Grinch found his heart," Edwin answered.

"What the hell? It's Christmas," the chef said.

"Speak for yourself," Vinnie replied.

"Really. I think she'll get you to pull out all the stops. I want to celebrate the future. We're not burying the past," Edwin said.

He left them talking about the party and went back to his office. Ann Baxter had called to tell him he should go to Hollywood and start an acting career. Henry had called Justy LaGrange and verbally beat up on him. After he vented, he agreed to sign the papers, and change the will with no repercussions, if Justy agreed never to mention the past. The papers were being filed immediately, but as an assumption of the mortgage and not a change in the will. Henry wanted no record of his wrong-doing.

The next day, Edwin called Al McNerey and told him he needed control of the hotel for two weeks past the closing for the party. Al said he'd put a two-week lease in the agreement for a dollar. It wouldn't be a problem.

Edwin called Ann Baxter and invited her to lunch. She came over at noon. Ann thanked him again for handling the matter of the will so well.

"It's no big deal. Henry isn't a very strong person. He blows a lot, but he even hid behind Justy. He'll make a great politician," Edwin replied.

"What are you going to do?" she asked.

"I'm going to the mountains with a glowing attorney for a while," he replied.

"You ready to take her off the singles' market?"

"You really think she's ready for that?" Edwin asked.

"Men aren't very perceptive, are they?" she asked.

After lunch, he handed Ann another envelope. She opened it. "What's this? It's too much. Are you crazy?" she asked.

"A.D. and I want you to have the best vacation ever. It's the entire amount you were to get in installments. The extra is for putting yourself in the middle of something you didn't have to," he replied. "Take it and live well."

"I don't know what to say," she replied.

"If a certain attorney says no, you can say soft things to prevent my suicide," he said.

"That won't happen," she said. She leaned across the table and kissed him on the cheek.

For the next few days, he could never find a department head in the early afternoon. Daphne had called secret meetings to plan the Christmas party. Al McNerey accelerated the sale, and saw no reason it would not go through. The buyers were hot for the hotel, and even hotter to get their money into U.S. assets. Devaluation of their currency was looking like a good possibility.

The days seemed to go slow. Slim was still chasing rogue limo drivers with a vengeance, and Wally had caught another pervert flashing a room-service person. This time it was a middle-aged female guest taking off her robe and offering some special services to Rudy the server. Much to the woman's disappointment, Rudy declined. When she was confronted, her only comment was, "What kind of people do you employ here?"

Rudy's sly reply: "She looked like my mother."

The operations director for the offshore group arrived to get oriented to the hotel. Edwin took him to the sales department, and introduced Israel Merced Santos to the staff. He had a good amount of experience and related well with them. After the first day, Edwin gave him full run of the hotel. Three days into the process, Edwin and Israel had lunch.

"You have a great staff. Maybe the best I've ever seen," Israel said.

"They'll be loyal to you, if you let them do their jobs and you treat them well," Edwin said.

"I better treat them well. I've been talking with Mary Rodriguez. She doesn't mince her words. I'd hate to make her angry," he replied, smiling.

"She's a keeper. She'll be your most loyal supporter," Edwin said.

"I don't doubt that," Israel replied.

Two attorneys for the purchasing group arrived and spent three days in the boardroom going over the contracts and hotel paperwork. They found no surprises and said they were satisfied. Edwin continued to question the sale. His guilt kept gnawing at him, but time was passing quickly and he was determined to go through with it. It was the best option for everyone.

The next day, Edwin was summoned to the ballroom. Daphne introduced him to five members of the Historical Society and five members of the press. He didn't understand why the television people were there. He didn't think the story of the hotel would be compelling on television. When he saw the extravagant luncheon Daphne and Vinnie had planned, he was surprised the national media wasn't there. After lunch, Daphne took the party on a tour of the hotel, pointing out facts and some architectural features that had been state of the art when the hotel was built.

When the affair was done, Daphne asked, "How'd I do?"

Greg Plank

"Let's just say you have me wanting to stop the sale and open the place as a national shrine. You were great," Edwin replied.

"I'll send you my bill in the morning."

"I honestly expect you to. You did a lot of work on this. Thanks," he said.

"It won't be a big one, but I need the money to start my new public relations company. You've convinced me I have a talent," she replied.

"It takes some of us a little longer to find our calling. I'm still looking for mine," he said.

"I think yours is about five feet tall."

Two weeks and one day after McNerey told him of the offshore group's desire to buy, Edwin found himself in the boardroom with five attorneys, two bankers, and Al McNerey. The closing took five hours. There were constant calls between the banks and some of the companies that had contracts with the hotel. The title company had messed up the title-search documents and a messenger had to bring new ones.

Edwin was nervous throughout the meeting. Al McNerey and Justy LaGrange, who had shown up in person, kept taking him outside, trying to calm him down. Every time Justy tried to apologize for the will and mortgage incident, Edwin alternated saying, "Forget about it" and "Henry's a bastard. I don't blame you."

At five p.m., the bank in New York called. The funds had been received and were deposited. Justy handed Edwin a pen, and told him to sign. When he had signed the master document, he looked at his signature. It was shaky, almost illegible.

"That's it. The Hotel St. George is sold. Congratulations to you all," Al said.

Edwin felt like he wanted to throw up, but graciously shook everyone's hand and thanked them. Al and Justy escorted him to the bar. Marty already had the drinks waiting.

"I feel empty," Edwin admitted.

"Move ahead," Justy said. "You've got a lot of good ahead of you, and the money to make a difference."

300

"Yeah, but I think it was Satchel Paige who said something like, 'Don't look over your shoulder. Something might be gaining on you,'" Al offered.

The bourbon calmed Edwin down. He called Lee and invited her to his place. That night, she was warm and comforting. He finally felt relief as he fell asleep in her arms.

chapter

FORTY SEVEN

The day of the farewell Christmas party was a Sunday. The staff and families began arriving at two-thirty. At the department heads' request, Edwin had not gone in the ballroom for the past two days. He spent time with Jack and Donna on his special part of the evening.

"It's all set for six o'clock or thereabouts. Just follow our instructions when you get to the stage. I'll tell you when," Jack said.

"After you give the employees their envelopes, we're ready. The key will not open the trunk that will be on stage. You know the words that will. When they're said, a small pop will open the chest," Donna reminded him.

"Got it. Thanks, I hope," Edwin replied.

"The grand finale. I love it," Jack said.

"Just make sure the damn thing opens. I'm embarrassed enough," Edwin said.

"Jake will be there with a crowbar, just in case," Donna said.

Edwin met Lee in the lobby. She was wearing a Christmas dress of red satin.

"Well, Mrs. Claus, you look great. Nobody told me to dress up," Edwin said as he kissed her.

"You look nice in your blazer. Besides, you're the host," she replied.

When they entered the ballroom, Daphne greeted them dressed like a Santa's helper. Slim Johnson and Andy Scott were both dressed like Santa Claus. The chef wore his black chef's hat with a Christmas wreath on it. Pas Medvier, Chuck Castillano, and Clarence Edmunds were dressed in Christmas outfits from their native lands. Marty was dressed as one of the wise men as were Bill Smith and Vinnie DeTesta. Jack and Donna had changed into reindeer costumes, and Wally Callahan and Robert Mason were dressed as shepherds. There was a large buffet filled with Christmas food. There were also jugglers and a face-painting station for the children. Christmas trees, a manger scene, games for the kids, an ice-cream stand, and two bars for the adults were scattered around the large room. Artificial snow was on the floor, along with a Teflon skating area, and a petting area for the kids with two lambs, rabbits and a small deer. Three photographers circulated, taking instant pictures for the kids and families.

"Unbelievable," Edwin said.

"My first professional assignment as a public-relations executive," Daphne said.

"I'm sure I'm getting billed for this," Edwin replied.

"Not for my services. This is an early Christmas present," Daphne replied. "I take it you approve of all this?"

"It's wonderful. They're all having fun," Edwin said. "Just one question: Why two big Santas?"

"They both wanted to be Santa and none of us were big enough to argue."

"Good point," Edwin said.

"Come on. There's some special people here for you," Lee said and took his arm to guide him around the room.

His mother and Mrs. Martinez were there. His mother was having more fun than the kids. Captain John Moose LeRoy and some of his men were there with their families. Betty Sloan from Jimmy's and Billy Caponi from the Tiger's Tail, Fire Marshal Sparks, and Shamika Taylor, his assistant, were talking in the corner. Edwin stopped and talked with them all.

The party got louder and more furious as the children opened presents and played with them. Electric cars and trucks sped around the floor. Balls and remote-controlled airplanes filled the airways of the two-story room. Finally, Jack came and got Edwin. It was time for his speech. As he approached the stage, his palms got sweaty. He had decided there would be no good-byes. He nervously took the microphone. The activity in the room came to a stop as the band played a loud chord. He cleared his throat.

"As you all know, the St. George is passing into different hands. Actually, it's not. It's passing into new ownership, which is a good thing. You've all got jobs, and you've met your new boss, Mr. Santos. He's a good man. The St. George is still in the hands of the people who care the most about it. That's all of you. The most important thing I can say is thanks for all you've done. From the time I was a child in this hotel, many of you have lovingly accepted the burden of helping raise me, and I am a better person for it. The three wise men brought gifts to the first Christmas. Vinnie, Marty, and Bill, our three wise men, which is a bit of a stretch, are circulating among you with an envelope for each of you. A small thank-you from A.D. and me. If you can have Christmas in September, you can have Christmas bonuses in September. Know that I love you all. This is not a good-bye. It's a pledge to always be friends," he concluded.

The room broke into applause and cheers as the staff opened the envelopes and found checks three times larger than any bonus they had ever received.

"And now, I'd like to invite Mrs. Claus up here for the final thing," Edwin said as Donna escorted Lee on to the stage. The curtains opened, and Jake Jacoby wheeled a large chest to the front of the stage.

Edwin introduced Lee as the attorney for the hotel. "Since this is an official part of the festivities, with a surprise gift for someone here, I think our attorney should officiate," he said. He handed Lee a key for the chest.

He instructed her to open the chest. When she tried, the key did not work.

"Since it is Christmas, and Christmas is a magic time, perhaps a few special words might open the chest," he said and whispered in her ear.

She looked at him, confused.

"Go ahead, just say those words. Someone is waiting for a big present," he said.

Lee said the words in a small voice. Nothing happened.

"You have to say them so everyone can hear them," he said. He held the microphone closer to her.

"I feel stupid, but will you be merry with me?" she said.

There was a small explosion and the chest opened.

"Now see who gets the gift," he said.

Lee looked into the trunk and froze.

"Yes, I'll gladly marry you, if you still agree," Edwin said.

He reached into the chest and brought out a diamond ring. She nodded yes, and put her left hand out to him as a tear ran down her cheek. He put the ring on her finger and kissed her. The room went wild, as red and green balloons fell from the ceiling.

"I thought you'd want to be in charge and do the proposing. It's a lawyer thing, you know," he said.

"So, you're going to tell the children I proposed to you?" she asked.

"Of course. I want them to know just how tough their mother is," he said. He escorted her off the stage, toward her parents and his mother. The congratulations kept coming until nine o'clock. The Hotel St. George had passed on to a new owner and a new life. So had Edwin.

One month later, Edwin and Lee were enjoying time together in North Georgia. They had been planning a Christmas wedding, fishing, hiking, and discussing the future. When Lee went shopping in the small stores on the town square or went to the spa, Edwin hung out at C.A. Mullin's auto repair shop. He loved talking with the locals and listening to C.A., who knew everything about every make of car. The big man was a walking computer on automobiles and their problems. Edwin had finally relaxed.

He and Lee were sitting on the porch of the bed-and-breakfast when his cell phone rang. When he answered it, he hesitated for a moment. He suddenly recognized the voice on the other end. He had heard it before and couldn't place it.

"You got some time to return to the city?"

"I've got the time, but I'm not sure we want to go back right now," Edwin answered.

"What if I said the St. George needed you?" the voice asked.

"Is there something wrong?" Edwin asked.

"There's something wrong, but good wrong, if you go back," the voice replied.

"Why are you always so mysterious?" Edwin asked.

"When you work for International Pipelines, it's part of the job," the voice said.

Edwin smiled. Ken Pierce was the last person he had met at International Pipelines, before going to South America. He was surprised he hadn't connected the voice before. It was also probably the electronically distorted voice of Carlo the Wolf he had heard so often.

"Anyway, the offshore group has been connected to some shady deals. The government seized all of their U.S. assets including the hotel and they need someone to manage it, and sell it again. This time, the price isn't as important. We thought you might be the right person to do that."

"You knew when you called me, and told me to take the offer, this would happen," Edwin said.

"I only admit I owed A.D. Christian a huge favor. I couldn't do it for him. I thought he'd be just as happy if I did it for you," Ken Pierce said. "You've got your money and you're rid of your brother. You want the job?"

The Hotel St. George was one of a very few hotels to be run without a manager on a long-term basis. Edwin set up an operating committee of the department heads. The chairperson rotated every month. The hotel was run by the people who had really run it all along. It did well. Edwin and Lee took their time finding the right buyer. The government didn't seem to care. The upgrades the buyers had begun and funded were bringing business back. Jake Jacoby was a master at renovation and could stretch a dollar better than anyone. Daphne was doing the promoting with her new company. She had turned Henry down when he asked her to organize his political campaign. Their mother Mimi had decided not to sell the family home. She wanted a fun place for the grandchildren to come visit. With Mrs. Martinez there, she had regained her self-confidence.

Slim Johnson was still chasing rogue limo drivers from the front door and enjoyed patrolling the parking decks. Wally used some of his money to start a foundation for the families of slain police officers. Jack was the director. Wally had decided he needed someone with sensitivity to run it. Captain LeRoy was the chairman. The two cops and the gay guy had bonded with a special purpose.

Marty took an extended vacation to spend time with his grandchildren in California. He visited Apistol and Baisch on his way out. When he got to California, he called Edwin and said it was fun, but he didn't know how he had lived through the trip. Mary Rodriguez ran the toughest committee meetings when it was her turn to chair the operating committee, but the hotel was cleaner than it had ever been. At the urging of Jack and Wally, Robert Mason had taken some public-speaking courses to improve his self-confidence. He was now out on the desk with the guests each day and they related to him. The chef and Andy Scott had leased space for an Italian meat market. Bubba's Tuscany Beef was a hit with the upscale crowd. Maurice Solomon made sure they got good mentions in print. Vinnie DeTesta and Bill Smith had a side bet on how much business they could steal from the new competition. The contest between the two was fierce.

Edwin and Lee spent most of their time in the Georgia Mountains waiting for a Christmas wedding. Jack sent an arrangement of Gerber daisies every two weeks. The note reminded them each time to keep looking for a bed-and-breakfast. It always ended with, "The hotel business gets in your blood."

It's check-out time. Hope you enjoyed your stay.
Travel well.

Follow Edwin, Lee and Jack as they open their Bed &
Breakfast and meet unexpected challenges, danger and the
legendary Black Dogs in the author's second book *Black
Dog Redemption*. It is a special tribute to our Military and
Law Enforcement for their sacrifices
and the dogs that make our lives richer.
Visit Amazon.com or createspace.com/3919515 for a
preview and purchase or meet a main character
George the dog at

www.dogonlife.com

66348687R00192

Made in the USA
Charleston, SC
17 January 2017